THE FOREVER MAN

ALLEN STROUD

Text Copyright © 2017 Allen Stroud
Cover Design 2017 Karl Eklund

First published by Luna Press Publishing, Edinburgh, 2017

The Forever Man ©2017. All rights reserved. No part of this publication may be reproduced, stored in a retrieval system, or transmitted in any form or by any means, electronic, mechanical, photocopy, recording or otherwise, without prior written permission of the copyright owners. Nor can it be circulated in any form of binding or cover other than that in which it is published and without similar condition including this condition being imposed on a subsequent purchaser.

www.lunapresspublishing.com

ISBN-13: 978-1-911143-26-0

Contents

Foreword	vi
Prologue	1
After Work	3
Distant Friends	10
The Terms of Engagement	19
Doing Your Research	25
Playing with Scrutiny	31
The Spider's Representative	37
Tea, Trees and Books	45
Other People's Moves	50
Good Intentions	56
The Spider and the Web	63
Crossing the Rubicon	71
The Pursuit of Knowledge	80
A Life Bargain	86
The Use of Rituals	89
Useful Resistance	96
Nest	101
The Other Side	106

Choice of Direction	114
Eternal Consequences	119
Something Stable	127
Hunters and Hunted	134
Testing Times	138
The Source of Knowledge	144
Making a Choice	152
Rite Work	165
Confrontations	178
Deliverance	188
No Place Called Home	197
Night Notes	206
Gifts	216
Leave	225
A Rescue	237
Solution	245
The Prisoner	254
Epilogue	262

To my sister Rachel,
who has always believed in this story.

Foreword

"The only way of finding the limits of the possible is by going beyond them into the impossible."

This is a famous quote from Arthur C. Clarke. It appears on the little trophy I won for my short story, Dancers, which will feature in a special commemorative anthology of short stories produced by Newcon Press and the Clarke Award to celebrate the one hundredth birthday of the late great master of science fiction. I was presented with the award as part of the ceremony that acknowledged Colson Whitehead's The Underground Railroad as the 2017 winner.

I'm very proud of my little award. However, I had no idea it would feature this quote. As it turns out, it's very apt for The Forever Man, both in the story and my process of writing it.

I started trying to write this story in 2006, a little while after I had completed my Master of Arts by Research degree in Creative Writing at the University of Bedfordshire. After the viva voce with Doctor Adam Roberts no less, it was clear to me that I needed a fresh story that was unburdened by all my formative attempts to be a novelist. My story needed to move away from the clichés I was stuck with and give my writing a chance to shine in a plot that would deliver something different and interesting. Of course, I can't claim this book is unique, but it was very different to what I was trying to do before then and, as such, marks a moment when I decided to experiment with different themes.

The Forever Man brings together some of my experiences and ideas I had about popular fantasy stories and the idea of us travelling to them. Some of its themes are wish fulfilments, while some are drawn from other genres; most particularly, crime fiction, which was (and is) something of a departure for me in my writing. This is perhaps part of the reason the book had such a long and difficult birth. When I started, and even when I finished the draft, I was a very different writer to the one I am now. However, there was enough of a good story hidden amongst the overwritten sentences for Luna Press to take a look at it and, thanks to some incredibly patient work by my editor, Robert S Malan, we have the much-improved version you hold in your hands today.

I hope you enjoy it and that it won't be quite as long before we're back visiting Durrington again, to tell another mysterious story.

Allen Stroud

Prologue – Forty Years Ago

As the sun sets, I hear the knock on my bedroom door. The same three taps, the same expression on my mother's face as she takes my hand, leads me down the stairs, out into the silent street.

When I was younger, I remember resisting; hiding under the bed, but it never did any good. My father would drag me out and carry me, arms pinned to my chest. I would shout and wail. I see curtains twitch and faces at the windows. I know they hear me, but no-one ever comes. *Monster*, they mouth soundlessly.

The church is dark when we get there. Father unlocks the door with a long key and we go inside. I sit on the stones where they point and mother takes up the chalk, drawing out the circle around me. When it is done she hands chalk to me. "You know what to do," she says and then walks away. Father follows her. They never look around.

I look around. The cloth is on the lectern, red triangles on black and the candles are lit. Who comes in before us to prepare everything? It is always empty when I am here.

When the shadows on the walls come alive, I know it is time. I take up the chalk and draw.

The symbols appear to me through instinct, an ingrained skill of muscle memory. I've done this so often the movements are part of who I am. I focus on the task and not the moving shapes. When I was little, I didn't know how to draw and instead, I would stare into the dark. I remember nothing of what I saw, only that I would awake covered in scratches, my own vomit and worse. My eyes would bleed for days after. I had been their plaything, their food and their sacrifice. I was lucky to be alive.

Now I concentrate on the chalk; the whorls and lines, each mark gradually unravelling the white rock in my hand. It disgorges itself to my intent, becoming smaller and smaller. Today there will be enough, but tomorrow? Who knows?

What happens when it runs out?

Out of the corner of my eye, I still see them move, watching and waiting for their chance. I know the circle holds them back. I feel their breath on the back of my neck. They whisper to me, begging, commanding, tempting. *Lick a finger, wipe away the line.* They promise me sweetness and sleep in exchange. *You are one of us*, they say. Many times, I've considered it, especially near the dawn when I'm tired, but I've never done as they ask.

As the hours pass, the circle fills. I can't read the writing, but its effect is clear. I am protected, safe from harm. Held at the edge of sacrifice, listening to dark whispers.

I wonder who could read the words and shapes around me. Do the shadows know? I finish in the grey light near sunrise and I know they will leave soon, defeated for another night by the chalk. I don't look up, but I sense the frustration. The threats come then, to hurt my family, but they are hollow curses from the fading dark and mean nothing. You can't care about people you don't love.

Dawn sun shines through stain glass windows and the shadows leave. I hear the key in the lock. Cautiously, mother comes in and takes a photograph of my work as she always does. The flash hurts my eyes a little. I stand and she kneels, washing away the chalk, erasing every trace of my presence in this place.

"Oh, Matty," she says to me. "You're such a good boy."

I take her hand and walk away. The street is quieter than before, as if something has been released or appeased. No-one watches us hurry through the fog, back to our house, to my room.

One day I will be too old for the shadows.

What kind of monster will I be then?

After Work

> *'...we reject all such merely probable knowledge and make it a rule to trust only what is completely known and incapable of being doubted. No doubt—'*

"We'll need to take a statement from you, Mr ...?"

Click.

The camera flash startled Andrew from his book. He glanced up and then around.

A young girl's body lay on the floor between the bookshelves of aisles 10 and 10a. He put the book down, struggling to take it in; not his usual trip to the local library.

"Excuse me, sir?"

"I'm sorry?" He turned towards the person speaking: a policewoman. She was staring at him, an earnest expression on her face.

"I said we'll need a statement from you." Her tone remained casual, but with a touch of anxiety; not a usual day for her either.

"Nothing to do with me. I've been sat here, reading." He nodded at the book beside him: *Rules for the Direction of the Mind* by René Descartes.

"According to the assistant, you were the only person up here." She seemed to weigh each word.

"But I was sat here reading when you came in," he replied. "I had no idea about any of this." He couldn't match her measured tone.

"I understand, Mr ...?"

"Doctor ... Andrew Pryde."

She smiled at that, a sweet expression made cute by her freckled face and dimples, but he caught a glimpse of her clenched teeth. "Well then, *Doctor* Pryde, I'm afraid we do need to take a full statement from you at the station." Clear blue eyes held him in a grip of expected compliance. "Wait here, please; my colleague will be with you shortly."

For a moment, he considered making a run for it. She was shorter than him and several stone lighter, despite the bulk of her reflective jacket and stab-vest, but the uniform kept him in check.

"Okay, I guess I—"

Too late; she'd turned away. He found himself staring at her back: shapeless yellow brilliance, topped by a tiny black hat, with tight brown curls peeking out on either side. The image drew the eye, but it couldn't hold his attention for long.

A young girl's body lay on the floor between the—

He stepped back as the policewoman and her colleague, an older man, busied themselves at the scene. A roll of plastic tape, a pair of scissors, and the alcove between 10 and 10a was sealed off. The gesture seemed hopelessly inadequate compared to the violence.

The girl's arms and legs were twisted, as if she were made of broken sticks. Strangely, she looked like she'd fallen from a great height. Her face remained obscured.

He felt detached, as if he wasn't in the room. Everything seemed unreal. Where did she come from? The first floor of Durrington Library contained reference books and dry academic works. It was usually deserted in the early evenings and his visits were a regular pastime. He couldn't recall hearing anything, even the small noises a person might make by being in the same room.

As he watched the police, he found himself edging closer. He wanted to see the girl's face, as if her expression would grant him understanding. There was something in her hand too: a book, half open, with a green cover.

The sound of a siren banished his wayward thoughts and brought with it guilt and apprehension. For a moment, he wondered if he could have been responsible for the girl's death without knowing it.

As the policewoman led him down the stairs, he took one last glance back and got a glimpse of a broken end of tape and a bare foot sticking out from between the shelves.

*

"Why don't you tell us from the beginning, what happened?"

On the table in front of him, the wheels of a cassette recorder turned hypnotically. Andrew found himself suppressing a smile that the police would use such old recorders.

"I, uh, well … if you mean in relation to the girl, I don't know."

He was sitting in a plain-walled interview room. After arriving at

Durrington police station, the desk sergeant had taken his personal effects and booked him in. He'd waited for an hour. They'd told him he was under arrest when they left the library, but he hadn't been charged.

Seated across from him was a crumpled man dressed in a crumpled suit. He'd introduced himself as Detective Sergeant Underhill, although that had been for the archaic machine that crouched between them. Behind him, the female officer from before leaned on the door. She'd taken off her luminous jacket and held her hat in her hands as she scraped at some unseen blemish on its rim.

"What d'you mean you don't know?" Detective Underhill's eyes seemed almost to disappear as he frowned.

"Well, as I said to your officers, I didn't see anything."

Underhill sighed. "Doctor Pryde, I need some indulgence from you please." Andrew recognised the same measured tone in the man's voice from earlier. "We can't piece together what you did or didn't see without an idea of what happened before the incident. So, if we go from the beginning, we'll get a picture of that."

"Okay," Andrew said. "Where do you want to start?"

"When did you get to the library?"

"About six-thirty, I guess." He shrugged. "I'm fairly regular on a Wednesday."

"Good." Underhill nodded. "Then what did you do?"

"I headed up to the reference and academia sections on the second floor."

"Not a fan of fiction?"

"Excuse me?"

"You didn't stop to browse downstairs first?"

"No, why, does that matter?" Andrew asked.

Underhill raised his eyebrows. "Not if you think I'm criticising your taste in books, Doctor. I'm trying to determine if anyone saw you in the library."

"Oh ... right." Andrew felt a warm flush spreading across his cheeks.

"Well, did they?"

"I don't know. I can't answer for them."

The policewoman at the door coughed. Underhill glanced at her. Their eyes met and she nodded to his unspoken request.

Underhill turned back to Andrew. "Anyone else around when you went in?"

"Um, I think so." Andrew tried to remember. "A few people in the aisles; a tall assistant stood at the desk."

"Mr Sanders."

"What?"

"His name is Luke Sanders. He remembers you."

"Oh, good." For some reason, the confirmation helped. "I don't think I spoke to him."

"No, he said you went straight upstairs."

"Right." Andrew gathered his thoughts, trying to examine the minutiae of what he remembered. "I went to the encyclopaedia stuff first and the geography section."

"Pick anything up?"

"No. I never do. I just like the big old books." He chuckled and immediately regretted it. "Sorry, I mean, no. I browsed for a little bit and went over to history and philosophy."

"Anyone come up the stairs?"

"No, no-one."

Underhill got up from the chair and walked across the room to stare at a patch of the blank concrete brickwork.

"Philosophy; that's your area?"

"What?"

"Philosophy; that's your interest, right? According to our records, you teach philosophy at the university?" The balding head turned towards Andrew again and narrowed eyes speared him to his seat.

"I teach history. I like reading philosophy, among other things," he said, swallowing.

"What were you reading?"

"*Rules for the Direction of the Mind*, by René Descartes."

"Good book? Useful?"

"It might help you, Detective," Andrew replied, "although I doubt it."

Underhill turned back to the wall. "And in all that time, you didn't see the girl or hear anything of what happened?"

"No, nothing until the officers arrived."

"You didn't look up?" Underhill stared at him again. "You must have been at least a half hour."

"I didn't have cause to," Andrew said. "I was reading, alone."

*

The next two hours became procedural hell. Andrew's fingerprints were taken, shoes removed, a swab from his mouth acquired for DNA records and they asked him to go over the story again, in more detail, with another plain-clothes officer.

In between interrogations, Andrew was left to reflect on his lot. *I'm innocent, can't you see that?* But of course, they couldn't; they had to follow the evidence.

The policewoman brought him some tea in a plastic cup; bitter, but hot. He drank it and carefully picked at the rim. Gradually, the cup disintegrated in his hands, a tiny act of rebellious destruction, creating a pile of shards on the table. After that, he started on the wall, digging at loose paint chips in a minor act of vandalism that revealed the dark grey concrete beneath.

They let him out briefly to use the toilet and he took a moment to splash water on himself. The man in the mirror was haggard and dishevelled. Tired blue eyes and receding light brown hair framed a weathered face that bore witness to a hard day.

Andrew gazed at his reflection. *Come on, Pryde, what happened? Some poor girl's dead and they think you killed her!* The exhaustive questioning made him begin to doubt his own judgment. Again, he tried to remember if he'd seen the girl before. The images of her body lying twisted on the floor between the aisles kept flashing into his mind, as if he was missing something ...

... There was no blood.

The sudden realisation nearly knocked him off his feet. His hands gripped the washbasin, knuckles whitened. *Why didn't I notice before?*

When he left the toilets, he found the female officer in the corridor. She'd put her hat back on and was standing outside the interview room door.

"I didn't catch your name earlier," Andrew said.

"PC Miriam Jones, Doctor Pryde," she said. "We'll be keeping you in here a bit longer, in case the detectives want to talk to you again."

"What happens then?"

"You take a seat in one of the cells until you can go home."

Andrew swallowed past a lump in his throat and changed the subject. "What book was she reading?"

"What?" PC Jones said, frowning.

"The book she was holding in her hand," Andrew persisted.

PC Jones bit her lip and hesitated. Finally, she replied, "It's called *Tree and Leaf*."

"Never heard of it."

"I hadn't either, but apparently it's by J. R. R. Tolkien."

Andrew went back into the room and sat down. A little while later, PC Jones returned and took him to the cells. As he went in, he found he was shaking, but he managed a half smile as she locked the door. Each thud of the locks made him want to run, but there was nowhere to go. The scraping sound of the metal viewing slot came last, consigning him to his dungeon.

Now what do I do? Andrew sat on the plastic-coated mattress of the thin bed. The springs squeaked in protest and he realised he was doing what countless people had done in this room before. He wondered how many of them had been as confused as he was.

So where's my phone call? In films and television, everyone had a phone call. *Who should I ring?* His mind went back to the interview. He couldn't shake the thought that in some way Underhill had asked the wrong questions.

Beyond the cell wall, a man began screaming. It was a muffled wailing sound, full of anger and frustration.

Somewhere in a little part of his heart, Andrew screamed too.

*

Yes, I can confirm it happened here this time!

Flicking back a greasy fringe from his pallid face, Ronald Gibbs peered at the computer screen as he typed his responses into a chat forum. The monitor was the only source of light in his cluttered bedroom. Next to his disheveled desk a CB radio wheezed as it scanned the airwaves, randomly announcing transmissions. "... Car twenty-eight, car twenty-eight, customer from the chip shop on Ainsley Street, pick up and drop at the Sabbeline Estate ..."

Comments appeared in response as the multi-coloured handles of each user scrolled up the screen. He scanned the messages, typing rapidly as he read.

Of course I'm going to check it out. You think I'd miss this kind of opportunity? Amazing! Right on my doorstep!

The questions came thick and fast, but Ronald knew which ones to ignore. Twenty-four years of age, he was an internet veteran and could separate the wheat from the chaff.

Yes, I'm sure. Listen, I've done my research. The evidence points to this being a perfect opportunity. Can't be a normal murder.

Ronald blew his nose with a ripped piece of tissue paper, squelched the contents into a ball and dropped it on the desk. Behind him, the radio continued to click and whirr. He yawned and rubbed his eyes before selecting a question that was important to answer.

No, this time the police have a witness. They think he killed her. He's a university teacher. Just the sort of person we need to make people understand the truth!

The sound of a buzzer made him jump. He extricated himself from his litter-strewn swivel chair, picked up a small rucksack and headed for the door, pausing only to retrieve an object that glittered in the half-light by the doorway.

Carefully, he tucked the long-handled flick-knife into the back pocket of his trousers.

Distant Friends

I awake to the sound of screaming from my childhood. The high-pitched cries of the damned that have circled around me my entire life, coalesce and metamorphose into something focused, urgent and demanding.

The shrill ring of my mobile phone, lying on the table beside my bed.

"Yes?"

"Sir, we've found a body and have a suspect. We'll need you to come in."

"What time is it?"

"Nearly three in the morning."

I sit up in bed. "What's so urgent that you ring me now?" I ask.

"Not urgent, sir; more unusual than anything else." The caller hesitates. "We can't work out how the victim ended up where she was. It's almost as if she just appeared out of nowhere."

I massage my temple with my free hand, thinking through what needs to be done. Details of the bedroom around me come into focus as my eyes adjust to the half-light. Familiar, safe, protected. A cocoon against the dangers of the world beyond. I will need to leave this place, but not yet.

"Whatever it is that's bothering you, you needn't bother me until office hours. So long as the crime scene is locked down, the suspect has been interviewed and forensics are doing their job, this puzzle can wait."

"Of course, sir."

"I'll see you when I get in." I end the call.

The phone screen remains bright, as if it knows I'm not done. I cycle through the address book and pick out a number intentionally left at the end, simply labelled '_z'. I dial it.

"Hello? Yes, it's happened again…"

*

"Yes, Mrs Pryde, he's being kept in overnight ... No, I don't know why he phoned me and not you." Linda Frakes checked a sigh as she attempted to keep up her best phone manner.

"Has he got counsel?" demanded the voice at the other end.

"No, I've not managed to arrange him a solicitor yet. It *is* ten o'clock at—"

"I'm aware of the time, thank you."

The evening was going downhill. Linda had been friends with Andrew Pryde for three years; they had dated for a few months, but the phone call had been a total surprise. They weren't close anymore and she hadn't expected to be talking to his mother again, let alone—

"I'll get him a solicitor," Mrs Pryde announced.

"Okay, if you have someone, that's fine. I'll—"

"No, I don't, but I can't ask you to help. We'll deal with this."

"Right, well, take care and I hope everything sorts itself out."

"Why wouldn't it? Andrew hasn't done anything!"

"No, I'm sure he hasn't."

"Exactly."

"Good. Bye."

Linda slammed the phone on its cradle. The electronic speaker chirped in protest and went still. She smoothed back her blonde hair and tried to compose herself. *Damn the woman.* She'd no idea why Andrew had phoned her, but she'd had to ring his parents.

She checked her makeup in the hallway mirror and dabbed her eyes with a neat corner of tissue.

"Who was that?" said a deep male voice from the lounge.

"Andrew's mother, darling," she replied. "I had to call her, given the circumstances."

His answer was terse. "Good job I don't get jealous."

Linda sighed; this evening's demands seemed to be without end. Her husband's curmudgeonly behaviour was designed to irritate, but she couldn't afford to get annoyed. "You're the only one for me, George!" she said in a light-hearted tone.

"Make sure it stays that way."

Linda thought about Andrew. She didn't believe for a minute he was capable of murder. *If he cared that much about anything, I might have stuck around.* For a moment, she entertained the idea of him as some sort of romantic lead, on the run and wrongly accused, but the gaunt, grim, passionate image just didn't seem to fit the dithering Doctor Pryde.

She picked up the receiver again and quickly dialled a six-digit number.

"Horace?"

"Linda, do you know what time it is?" a man murmured.

"Sorry to call you so late; I wouldn't usually, but I need a favour: a friend's in a bit of trouble."

The man sighed. "Fine, you want me to visit the station?"

"Would you? Thank you, it means so much."

"What's his name?"

"Who're you speaking to now?" George's voice rumbled out from the lounge again. Linda hesitated, but decided to ignore him.

"Andrew. Could you get to him in the morning, Horace?"

"Of course."

"Thank you. Perfect."

"What's he done?"

"I'll give you the details. It's quite complicated ..."

*

A taxicab pulled up around the side of Durrington Town Library. Ronald Gibbs, fresh from his stale bedroom and mind filled with internet conspiracy, burst out of the back seat and onto the pavement. The driver's window wound down and a hand extended from inside, palm up. Ronald fumbled in his trouser pockets and pulled out their contents.

"Here!" he said, breathlessly depositing a fistful of coins, chocolate wrappers and receipts into the expectant mitt, before running down the street towards the library entrance.

The repetitive flashing of blue light confirmed the presence of the police at the front of the building. He hurried back down the path to the other side. After a few moments, he located another way in and tried the handle.

Locked.

He pulled out the flick-knife and flipped out the blade, which flashed in the dim blue night. He inserted the tip into the lock and worked it carefully until he heard a click. He pocketed the knife and inched the door open before stepping through.

Inside, the library was pitch black. He waited a minute, hoping his eyes would adjust, but the gloom was so absolute it made little difference. The butterflies in his stomach threatened to run riot. He reached out for the wall to steady himself.

"Did you hear something?" said a male voice far away in the night.

"No, and I'm pretty sure you didn't either," said another man. "Good try though."

Ronald froze, desperately trying to keep his balance. He made out a dim light to his left and guessed the voices were coming from that direction. He paused for a good while, before moving to his right, reaching out with his hands to make sure he didn't bump into anything and get discovered. If the police caught him here, he would be arrested, but the opportunity to examine the crime scene was too good to pass up.

Ronald Gibbs loved mysteries about disappearing people. Over the last three years, he'd uncovered more than a dozen similar cases from all across the world. A body would show up in a very public place with no explanation. An investigation would be launched but no answers would be found. Each victim would be from the missing person's register. He collected information on every incident, filed and compared the circumstances. He had theories on what was happening, but nothing conclusive.

Tonight, at last, *he* would find answers.

He crept to the staircase and crouched beside it. The dim light was coming from the reception desk near the entrance. He saw two silhouetted figures, facing away from him. He considered heading up the stairs, but thought better of it; if either of them were to turn around ...

Instead, he made himself comfortable and decided to wait. He knew from the radio that the officers changed shifts regularly. Three years' worth of answers could keep for a few hours more.

*

"Wake up, Doctor Pryde. You have a visitor."

Andrew wasn't asleep. He hadn't slept all night. He opened his eyes and blinked in the early morning sunshine. He sat up on the plastic mattress just as the cell door swung back and an unfamiliar policeman entered.

"What's the time?" he asked, stretching the kinks out of his back.

"Seven-thirty. Your solicitor's here."

"What solicitor?" Andrew said. "I don't have a solicitor."

"Then someone must've got you one. Come on, we're letting you out."

Andrew hesitated. "I'm innocent, you know?" he said. "There's got to be someone else out there who has done this."

The policeman frowned. "Is there something more you want to tell us? If there is, I'll contact the DS and get another interview arranged."

"No, I was just saying you need to get after the real murderer."

"What makes you think we aren't?"

"Oh ... right."

Andrew followed the policeman back to the front desk. Standing beside it was a grey-haired man in a brown suit who turned around as they approached.

"Here you are, Mr Olson. He's all yours."

Andrew's hand disappeared in a warm handshake. A gap-toothed smile and horn-rimmed spectacles punctuated the jowly face of the hand-shaker. "Hello, Doctor Pryde. My name is Horace Olson. Mrs Frakes called me last night and I made my way here as soon as possible this morning."

Andrew nodded. "Right, so what happens next?" He glanced at the desk sergeant, who studiously ignored them both.

"Well, we get you out of here to start with," Horace replied in a breezy voice. "Detective Sergeant Underhill agreed to release you, pending further enquiries. We'll talk in more detail once we're in the car."

"You mean I can go home?"

"Yes, for now. The police would like to question you again, so you'll need to remain at your address and place of work; no sudden holidays or anything."

Andrew couldn't help but smile. The last twelve hours seemed unreal. The clatter of a plastic box brought him back. Wordlessly, the desk sergeant pushed forward his confiscated personal effects. He took back his shoes, watch, keys, wallet and the small amount of change left in the tray, taking a moment to return everything to its proper place. Horace held the door open and they walked out into the winter sunshine.

The air was cold and crisp. Andrew shivered.

"Mine's the silver Mercedes." Horace gestured towards the far end of the car park.

Andrew nodded and began to walk in that direction. A fraught and sleepless night had yielded no answers. How had the girl's body gotten there without him noticing?

In the car, the solicitor's easy smile disappeared and he leaned in close.

"I trust you understand the seriousness of all this, Doctor Pryde." It wasn't a question. Hazel eyes flecked with green bored into his skull, then flicked across his face and rumpled clothes. "You look awful."

"I feel pretty awful," Andrew admitted. "Anyone would, given the situation."

Horace frowned. "The police questioned you as a murder suspect, so they must think you were involved. I'm surprised they agreed to release you. They could've chosen to hold on to you for a bit."

"Why did they?"

"Well, the initial forensics came up clean. Your fingerprints weren't found on the body or around it."

"Does that mean they'll leave me alone?"

"No, I'm afraid not," Horace replied. "You were at the scene and the detailed tests, the DNA and so on, won't come back for a while. Besides, even if they did, you're still the nearest thing to a witness." He pulled his seatbelt across and started the car. The engine gunned into life with an expensive growl.

"Thank you," Andrew said. "You don't know how good it is to have someone on my side."

"The important thing was to get to you before the detective inspector took charge of the case this morning," Horace said as they pulled away. "He'd likely have kept you a bit longer."

"Sorry for getting you up."

"That's all right; at least I'll make an early start."

*

Twenty minutes later, Horace dropped him off outside his flat on the other side of town. It was a rented three-room space, converted from the upper part of a tall, three-storey house.

Andrew walked up the steps and fished out his keys. The sky had clouded and bright sunshine turned into a drab morning. As he fumbled with the lock, the urge to shut the world away became overpowering.

"Don't move," rasped a man's voice close to his ear. "Just open up and get inside!"

Stale breath filled Andrew's nostrils, making him gag. He felt the point of a knife pressed against the back of his jacket.

"Steady now, Doctor Pryde, we're all friends here," the voice whispered. "Get us inside and we'll talk everything through."

Andrew opened the front door of his small flat. It swung inwards and the man pushed him over the threshold.

"Quick, shut all the curtains!"

"No!"

Something in Andrew snapped. He stumbled forward into the lounge, ran into the kitchen and seized the first weapons he could find. When the man followed, Andrew turned to confront him with an unwashed wok and a carving knife.

"I don't know who you are," Andrew snarled, "but you picked the worst possible day to fuck with me!"

The man in front of him was slight, dressed in brown jeans and a battered parka coat. He had the hood pulled right up and zipped forwards to conceal his face, like a bad playground villain. In his hand, he was holding a knife of his own. "I mean it," he said, his voice a muffled threat from the furry depths. "Shut the curtains and sit down!"

"Who are you?" Andrew yelled back.

"Someone who can give you a few answers. But we can't be seen together, so please put down the fucking frying pan and shut the bloody curtains!"

"You first."

"What?"

"You put down your knife." Andrew struggled to keep his hands from shaking. For a moment, they both remained motionless; then the man flicked his wrist and the blade disappeared. "All right," he said, holding up his left hand, palm outwards. "All right, let's sit and talk about this." He backed into a large yellow chair next to the door.

Andrew nodded and, setting aside the wok, slowly drew the front curtains closed before sitting on the mismatching red sofa opposite.

He put the carving knife down on the seat beside him. "Okay, I'm listening."

The man unzipped the parka hood. Unkempt straggles of brown hair spooled out of the cocoon, followed by the sweaty unshaven face of an intense twenty-something whose appearance suggested he spent more time indoors than out.

"My name's Ronald Gibbs."

Andrew frowned and tried to recall the name. Was he a former student with a grudge? "That doesn't help."

Ronald nodded. "I understand; you academic types like your references. I'm a researcher, on Crowley, and other stuff like that."

"Mr Gibbs, but how does this—"

"Help? Doesn't in itself, but what I know will. First, I need to ask you some questions."

"I spent the night in a cell answering questions for the police," Andrew said. "They had the weight of the law behind them. What makes you think I want to answer yours?"

"Because it's in both of our interests for you to understand what's going on," Ronald replied.

"Why not explain it to me, or knock on the door, instead of threatening me with a knife?"

Ronald shook his head. "I had to be sure we got in fast and you are who you say you are."

"Who else could I be?"

"You wouldn't believe me if I told you."

Andrew sighed. "All right, question for question. I ask, you answer, and you ask, I answer."

"Fine." From somewhere, a scrap of paper and a pen appeared in Ronald's hands. "I'm ready."

For a moment, Andrew's mind went blank, but then a host of questions tumbled into his head. "Why are you here?" he demanded.

"To talk to you about the girl in the library."

"How do you know about that?"

Ronald wagged a finger. "Doctor Pryde, you can't break the rules of your own game." A smug smile spread across the young man's face. "Question for question, you said."

Andrew sighed. "Go on," he said.

"Thank you. What book was she reading?"

"What?"

"The book," Ronald repeated. "She had one in her hand; what was it?"

Andrew was incredulous. "How do you—"

"Not your turn."

Andrew remembered the policewoman's answer when he'd asked the exact same question. "*Tree and Leaf,* by J. R. R. Tolkien."

Ronald scribbled. "Excellent! A Tolkien connection!" He completed his note, then raised his head. "Now you."

"How did you find out about the girl?"

"I was listening to the police radio transmissions last night, then I went to the library after they'd taken you and the body away." Ronald leaned forward. "My go. What page was she on?"

Again, the question surprised him, but at least he had no choice with his answer. "I didn't see."

"Shame." Ronald made another note.

"Why are you interested in the book?"

"They always have one; it's part of what happens when they leave and always with them when they return. What were you reading?"

"*Rules for the Direction of the Mind* by René Descartes. Why am I important to you?"

"Because you're one of the only two people who've witnessed this happening. Why Descartes?"

"I'm not sure I follow you."

"You've got a Ph.D.," Ronald said. "You teach philosophy, research it, deal with it all the time; you can't expect me to believe you've never read Descartes?"

Andrew frowned. *Why did I choose that book?* He recalled taking it from the shelf; a battered copy he'd passed countless times. He had a hardback edition in his office at work and another in the bedroom. "I don't know why I picked it up," he realised aloud.

"We think it's subconscious, when they come back." Ronald's head was amongst his notes, his pen working furiously. "A refuge of the familiar, whilst it happens."

"Whilst *what* happens? Who is it that comes back?"

Ronald looked up, his expression grave. "When they cross over, Doctor Pryde, from another world."

The Terms of Engagement

Steel clashed on steel.

The light of the twin suns reflected off scoured metal in the bright spring morning. The thin sabre blade danced along the heavier broad sword to slice neatly into a deltoid muscle. Jennifer Samms winced and stepped back. She clutched the wound with her left hand and her fingers became wet with hot blood.

The man facing her smiled and withdrew, lowering his weapon. "I give you the option to quit."

Jennifer shook her head grimly in response and brandished her sword. The injury troubled her less than the fact it had cut a hole in her red t-shirt – her Boston Terriers shirt. For some reason, that was important, but she didn't know why.

Her opponent's smile vanished and he raised his sabre again, dropping into a duellist's crouch. Jennifer approximated the same; the man she faced was at least twenty years her senior, with thinning grey hair, a jutting beard and a harsh stony stare from eyes of the deepest blue. It was the face of a man accustomed to giving orders and having those orders obeyed; Michael Abbalyn was not someone to be crossed.

Jennifer knew she couldn't match him for skill. Her hope was that Abbalyn would tire as their fight wore on and youthful strength and stamina would win out. For now, the plan depended on her ability to survive, a proposition that remained in debate.

The sabre moved like quicksilver, flicking for her face before cutting low towards her ribs. She swung her sword in a crude response, like using a newspaper to swat a fly. Somehow, she managed to keep the blade out of her body, but she could do nothing to push Abbalyn off and was forced to back away. When Abbalyn did withdraw, Jennifer found herself gasping.

Shit.

Abbalyn's blade hummed through the air as he tested its weight, waiting for Jennifer to continue. The old man wasn't even breathing hard. "You called my wife a whore," he said coolly. "Take it back and this ends."

"No," Jennifer replied.

"As you wish." This time there would be no respite; Abbalyn came at her fast and high, his blade feinting at her eyes before going for her throat, but this time Jennifer didn't try to block. Instead, she grabbed the thin steel with her left hand. She felt a sharp pain as the edge sliced the flesh of her fingers to the bone, but she held on, wrenched the blade away from Abbalyn and head-butted him full in the face. There was an audible crack and the old man disappeared from view in a shower of blood. Jennifer threw the sabre away and wiped her eyes, trying to clear her vision. She found her opponent sat on the ground, blinking rapidly with a confused expression on his face. Never one to dwell on good fortune, she kicked him in the head, sending Abbalyn sprawling.

"Wait! He's had enough!"

Jennifer glanced around. They were in a field beside a rough road. Three other men stood nearby. The protest had come from one to the left, who had the decency to look concerned. The other two regarded everything with an air of professional disinterest. All three wore riding clothes and carried swords; not the light duelling weapon her opponent favoured, but heavy broadswords like hers. A carriage stood waiting for Abbalyn and his companions, with four extra horses tethered to it. Jennifer had no idea if anyone was inside, but there would be no-one else for miles.

She hesitated for a moment. The three men seemed reluctant to get involved. Whether that was because of their orders or own personal interest, she didn't care; she just didn't want them intervening.

The sound of movement brought her back to the task in hand. Abbalyn had regained his feet. Blood smeared his face and he swayed as if drunk, but the stony gaze remained fixed on Jennifer, eyes boring into her head as if trying to read the inside of her skull.

"Maybe he has had enough," she said, "but I haven't."

She stepped forward and grabbed the old man by his shirt before thrusting the heavy sword into his chest. Abbalyn gasped and coughed blood into her face, but Jennifer held on and twisted the weapon, feeling flesh and organs tear. Only when his blue eyes lost their focus did she let go, allowing the man to slide away and fall in a crumpled heap.

The sight of the corpse fascinated her; she wasn't sure why. In death, Abbalyn lost the last of his dangerous air, becoming small, old and vulnerable. A part of Jennifer's mind still expected him to get up, even though the wound was more than enough to kill him. She realised she was something of an expert on mortality, but couldn't remember why.

To her left she heard a sword being drawn. She glanced around: the man who had spoken stared at her grimly, weapon in hand.

"You have no honour," he hissed.

"Damn right I don't," she drawled. "That shit gets you dead real quick." She eyed the other two men and pointed at the carriage and horses. "I ain't got no quarrel with you. Take what you like and go. You won't see me again."

Jennifer walked to Abbalyn's body. She knelt and, with her left hand, grasped a thin gold chain around his neck. On the end was a long key; somehow, she knew there would be. She snapped the links and pocketed the jewellery before standing up, raising her sword again and glaring at the man, whose face had discoloured with rage. "If you have a problem with that, then you best do something about it."

In answer, he raised his sword and charged.

*

Amanda hurried across the courtyard. Midday was approaching and her husband hadn't yet returned, his lordly duties piling up in his absence.

Through her fretting came the familiar feeling of displacement. *I'm not supposed to be here*, she thought to herself for the thousandth time.

She approached Abbalyn Manor; the home she shared with him and her three children. One of the members of the household guard stood at his post, dressed in a tough leather jerkin, adorned with the crest of their house, the symbol of a white stag on green. She inclined her head to him and he saluted in response, before opening the oaken double doors.

"He is overdue, Gamm."

The guardsman nodded. "He must have been delayed."

"I will be upstairs. Please tell him when he arrives."

Once inside, she walked to the staircase, her riding boots ringing on the rich marble floor. She saw no sign of the other staff, but they would be watching and remain a quick word away.

She climbed swiftly, crossed the landing to her private room, and drew the door closed behind her. Alone, she permitted herself to relax.

The little green book was on a table in the same place, a permanent fixture since she'd come to live in the manor more than five years ago; dusted but not touched, as per her instructions. No-one was to touch it but her.

The sense of displacement grew stronger, as it always did when she was alone. She sat down in a chair in front of the table and loosened the pins from her hair. She forced herself to focus and stared into an ornate mirror. Almost ten years had passed since the sensation had last been this strong. She stared at her reflection, watching as the distortions tried to coalesce into something tangible on the edge of her vision, like the onset of a migraine. The image of her in the centre of the mirror bore witness to the time that had passed. Faint lines of age wearied her face; silver had begun a rebellion across her temple. She concentrated on that and willed the sensation to fade, at least for a while.

She still hoped her husband would be here in time.

As insurance, Amanda picked up a feathered quill from an inkpot on the desk and drew a thin sheet of vellum from the stack next to the table. She began to write:

Dearest,

I can't guess what delayed you, but I am afraid it is now too late. Goodbye, my love. I can only hope we will find a way to be together again one day – in whatever world that will accept us.

She folded the paper and placed it in the centre of the table, then replaced the quill in the inkpot and turned back to the mirror. Abruptly, the distortions around her reflection disappeared. Amanda frowned, stood up and glanced around the room. A man stood in the corner by the window. The last of the evening light from the two suns filtered in across the balcony, yet he'd chosen to position himself in the shadow of the thick velvet curtains. She wouldn't have noticed him at all, except for his eyes, which glittered in the gloom. They were yellow and glared out at her from a partially obscured face. Amanda didn't recognise him.

"How long have you been standing there?" Her voice projected a calm she didn't feel.

"Moments only," the man replied. "Although, such measurements are relative."

Amanda could sense an air of wrongness about him. "Are you here to take me back?" she asked.

The man laughed. "In a manner of speaking. Goodness! After all this time, is that all you managed to learn?"

Amanda wasn't sure what he meant. "Was that what I was supposed to do: learn about what happened to me?"

The man shrugged. "No. No rules. In fact, your ignorance makes my part easier – no preconceptions to deal with." He strode across the room towards her and she could make out more of his features: jet-black hair and a serious face that bore no evidence of his earlier humour. His clothes were simple and monochrome: a charcoal shirt and tight trousers, tucked into knee-high boots. The only other colour came from an angry red scar on his left cheek. A malevolence emanated from him; a threat she couldn't place. Something about his face didn't feel right. She backed a step towards the door and he halted.

"Please don't complicate matters," he said in a brusque tone. "We could do without difficulties, and time is short."

"I wanted to wait for my husband ... and the children."

The man shook his head. "I am afraid that isn't possible. They are still days away. This must happen now."

She acquiesced, burying her sadness beneath a veil of poise. "Very well. What must I do?"

He held out his hand. "You must accompany me onto the balcony. You may take one last look upon this place."

She took his hand, a light touch resting on his fingers, and strode forward. "Will it hurt?" she asked.

His eyes flinched from her gaze. "Perhaps," he admitted. "These things are never easy."

Amanda turned to face the light, moving out of the room and into the midday glow – *one last look*. The world seemed brilliant to her eyes, beneath the twin suns.

"I am ready," she said boldly.

"Good," he replied and let go of her hand.

A weight crashed into her from behind, causing her to lose her balance and pitch forward towards the rail. The wooden frames couldn't support her and, in a split-second, she smashed through them, plummeting the thirty-foot drop to the courtyard.

Doing Your Research

Andrew started laughing.

Ronald stopped writing and glared at him. The laughter choked and died on Andrew's lips. An uncomfortable silence followed, before the young man went back to scribbling.

They cross over, Doctor Pryde, from another world – a preposterous suggestion, but something in Ronald's eyes wouldn't let Andrew dismiss it out of hand. Ronald *believed*, that was plain; and how had he known about the book?

"So you're saying people, like this girl, came from another world?"

"Not quite. Her name was Amanda Baines. She disappeared from her bedroom in South London two years ago." Ronald pulled a second piece of paper from his pocket and glanced at the scrawl. "She was seventeen. The last person to see her was her mother."

"I don't believe this."

Ronald frowned. "No, you don't want to believe because your experience tells you otherwise."

Andrew stood up. "Would you like a drink?" he offered lamely.

Ronald shook his head. "Not now, and I'd prefer you didn't leave the room until we finish talking. Right now, you've half a thought to phone the police and report me as an intruder. If you get to the kitchen that idea could germinate."

Open-mouthed, Andrew sat straight back down. *Who is this man?* "I think you should explain all of this."

"Not quite yet. It's my turn in our game. Did you sleep in the prison cell last night?"

"No, I didn't," Andrew admitted. "I shut my eyes, but I couldn't—"

"You will tonight and, when you do, you'll dream. It's important you write down everything you remember." Ronald fished in his pockets again and held out a battered business card. "Get in touch with me as soon as you learn anything more. I can help you and you can help me."

Andrew took the card. Ronald put his pen and paper away and stood up. "You must be careful," he warned. "Even though they don't have anything on you, the police will be watching. We must make sure we aren't seen together, otherwise they'll start wondering about your new friendship."

"Hang on," Andrew said. "It's my turn now. I still have a question to ask."

Ronald stopped in his tracks and a slow smile spread across his face. "Very good; I hope you've saved the best till last."

"Why do you care what happened to Amanda Baines?"

For the first time, Ronald appeared surprised. He opened his mouth to answer, but reconsidered. "No, I can't tell you."

"You need me," Andrew reminded him.

"Games are one thing, Doctor Pryde. I don't trust you that much."

Andrew waved the card Ronald had given him. "Then you can forget about hearing from me if I dream."

Ronald's eyes narrowed. "You won't walk away from this, no matter how much you threaten to." With that, he moved towards the door. "I better go. Our chat is over. I do hope you'll take my advice. Please don't do anything stupid."

*

It took another twenty minutes for Andrew to calm down.

Ronald Gibbs had gone and the door remained ajar. He cast his eyes around the rented living room. Peeling wallpaper and mismatched furniture; a poor return on thirty-five years. He'd never been the settling type. His bric-a-brac life was comfortable, but not steady. He could walk out and not miss anything.

The phone rang, a piercing electronic squeal, shattering his new calm. He scrabbled for the handset and found it under the television cabinet.

"Hello?"

"Hello, Andrew? It's David Macker. Why aren't you at your 9am lecture?"

Andrew cursed. David Macker, his head of department at the University. "I'm sorry, David," he replied. "The last twelve hours have been pretty difficult. I forgot."

"Some sort of problem, Andrew? You are aware of the departmental procedure regarding absence, aren't you?" The voice implied he should be.

"Of course. I would have phoned, but the police only let me out an hour ago."

There was a sharp intake of breath on the other end of the phone. Macker didn't speak for ages. Andrew pictured his boss's horror.

Eventually Macker managed to answer. "Right ... do keep us informed." The line went dead.

Andrew tossed the receiver to the floor and sat back on the couch with a sigh. He reached down and removed his shoes, then swung his legs up onto the furniture's dilapidated arm, before closing his eyes. His mind ran over what Ronald had said: a pack of delusions and lies. He thought about reporting Gibbs as an intruder but, after a night in custody, he certainly didn't want to see Detective Sergeant Underhill again.

They cross over, Doctor Pryde, from another world. Ridiculous! Andrew pulled a cushion from the end of the sofa and stuffed it under his head. The closed curtains made the room cosy and he'd warmed up from earlier. Ronald had asked about the book in the girl's hand; the police hadn't thought it important. *I need to find that book.*

Vaguely, Andrew knew he was falling asleep.

*

A burning sensation filled his head, as if he was in hot water. *Where am I?* He opened his eyes.

Lights flashed all around. Beyond them, he could see people, a crowd, raucously shouting and screaming. He was moving, flipping, end over end, with no control over his body, strapped to something, spinning and turning of its own volition.

Fuck!

Gradually, the spinning eased. The lights picked out a figure standing some distance away, dressed in bright, striped trousers, a brilliant shirt and wearing a mask; a moulded clay façade, vaguely human in appearance, but with an exaggerated, leering expression. Yellow eyes fixed on him as the figure raised one arm and waved to the crowd.

Those eyes aren't human.

The arm dropped; something blazed across Andrew's vision and there was an audible *thunk.*

The crowd roared.

More eyes glittered out from the darkness, faces similarly masked and grotesque. They laughed and cheered as he struggled, pulling against the bindings that held him.

Thunk.

Thunk.

Sharp pain lanced through his hand and he screamed; the sound was lost amidst the cheers. The spectators luxuriated in his anguish, baying for more. The noise deafened him, wrapping him in a blinding assault.

Andrew screamed again and ...

*

... woke up, gasping.

He was lying on his stomach, his face pressed hard into the sofa cushions, his left arm numb, trapped beneath him at an awkward angle.

It was dark in the room; night time or early evening. He'd slept away the entire day.

His right arm dangled from the couch and felt wet and sticky. It was sore and he wasn't sure he should move it. He sat up, reaching out with his clumsy left hand to switch on a lamp. The room brightened with a warm glow; he blinked to adjust his eyes and glanced at his right hand.

Fuck!

The carving knife he'd threatened Ronald with was sticking straight through his palm. The serrated edge, covered with blood, had dripped onto the carpet and pooled in a clotting stain.

A muscle twitched in his index finger. He screamed, leapt up and ran for the kitchen. His arm hung limp, so he grabbed it by the wrist and thrust it into the sink, before turning the tap on full blast. The water in the basin turned red as it drained away.

Somehow, he made himself look down. The knife remained skewered in his hand, the handle an inch from his flesh, while the rest of the blade stuck out between the cords of his third and fourth fingers. He realised he would have to get it out or get to hospital. He considered phoning an ambulance, but Ronald said the police would be watching.

"Fuck, fuck, fuck!"

He took a deep breath and grasped the handle in his left hand. The world started to spin, reminding him of the dream. He leant against the kitchen counter and forced himself to examine the wound. The knife would do less harm on the way out, but the serrated teeth ...

Andrew clenched his jaw and focussed on a small mark on the window blinds, trying not to think about it.

Grimacing, he began to pull.

*

An hour later, he felt calm.

Once the knife was out, he washed the wounds and dressed them with a bandage. Then he washed the floor and, with his good hand, made himself a mug of hot tea. Paracetamol and Ibuprofen from the cupboard took the edge off the throbbing ache in his palm and fingers. The shock and loss of blood made everything a struggle and he was soon exhausted. The dark stain remained on the carpet. It would be impossible to remove; he didn't try.

Remembering what Ronald had said about dreams, Andrew found a pen and notebook from the bedroom, but he couldn't write anything, as his hand hurt too much. Instead, he picked up the battered card that the young man had left behind. The address, telephone number and email were faded, but still legible.

The police will be watching. He wondered if they were allowed to tap the phone of a murder suspect or monitor his emails? It was clear Ronald knew more about the case than he was letting on, but he wasn't prepared to share and, as long as Amanda's murder remained unsolved, a question would remain about Andrew's guilt. *I need to clear my name; I need to find out what really happened.*

Then he remembered the other thing Ronald had asked about – what the girl had been reading.

I need to find that book.

*

Tree and Leaf.

Andrew clicked on the search icon with his left hand and waited impatiently for the internet to provide him with a list of useless results.

Amongst them, he hoped he might find a golden nugget: the book he was looking for.

He vaguely remembered reading Tolkien when he was younger. *The Lord of the Rings* had been an alternative to homework during a half term break. Yet he couldn't remember *Tree and Leaf*.

A page of results included an illegal scanned copy of the text – *perfect*. He clicked on that result, suppressing the briefest flicker of academic guilt. *I'm sure students do it all the time.*

He scrolled through the title pages, pausing briefly at the contents to get a sense of what the book might be about. It appeared to be a set of essays. He wasn't quite sure what he was searching for, but the writing demanded something from him and he found himself flipping through the pages until one passage screamed at him to stop.

Words leapt out at him from the page ...*realm of fairy story... shoreless seas... stars uncounted...* He scrolled down, noting the mention of a *Traveller* and *the gates and keys*. The whole paragraph leapt out, casting an image straight into his mind. This was another world, teeming with possibility and purpose.

For some reason he was sure this was the page the girl had been reading.

The revelation horrified him. He leapt up from the chair, brushing his injured hand against the desk, reigniting the wound's throbbing fire. *How could I know that? It's impossible!* The page on the screen glared at him, as if promising violence. He was shaking and sweating profusely. *What does this mean?*

The mouse and keyboard had become a poisoned wasteland. Yet he knew he couldn't just run away from the monitor. He tapped a key and the printer whirred into action, dropping a neat copy into its tray. He picked up the A4 page and folded it neatly. Each crease muted the sensation that had called him to read the file, muffling it in white paper until he could drop it into the pocket of his trousers.

He turned the computer off at the mains, collected his jacket and walked out of the flat.

Playing with Scrutiny

It was raining. Andrew pulled his jacket collar up and made his way down the road. He fished in his pocket for Ronald's business card and read the address under a streetlamp.

Ronald Gibbs
16 Eleanor Avenue
Durrington
Wessex
(01781) 522141

Durrington was a small town, with Eleanor Avenue only ten minutes from his house. The street was deserted and unlikely to get much busier on a Thursday night.

He began walking in the direction of Gibbs' address, thrusting his hands in his pockets and striding out with a bravado that he didn't feel. As he walked, Andrew went over the facts of the situation again:

– Girl's body appears in library with a distinct lack of blood at the scene.

– Girl is identified as having been missing for two years, last spotted in South London.

– Witness *hears* and *sees* nothing.

He turned left off the main road and walked down a short pedestrianised lane. The buildings on each side leaned inwards, giving a sinister impression in the street-lit evening. The only conclusion he could draw was that Amanda Baines hadn't died in the library and had been moved there. The lack of blood supported that, but it did leave an obvious question.

Where did she come from?

The sound of breaking glass brought him back to the present. He stopped and looked around; the streets were deserted, perhaps owing as much to the weather as the midweek night, but someone was out there.

Ronald had said the police would be monitoring him, but Andrew wasn't sure it was them. The eerie silence was only disturbed by the patter of rain. The air felt tense, almost expectant.

He spotted a pair of yellowed eyes in the shadow of a doorway, ones he recognised from his dream. They blinked once and stared out into the night. Andrew flinched as the gaze raked over him – he could sense its malevolence. His injured hand began to throb and a wash of fear pinned him to the pavement. Something told him the mind behind that jaundiced stare was no stranger to death, or murder.

The eyes blinked again and were gone.

He remained motionless for several minutes, then walked across the side street to the spot.

Nothing.

Andrew's chest hurt. He realised he wasn't breathing. A lungful of air brought with it a bout of coughing and he collapsed, clutching his hands around his ribs. After a few moments, the spasm eased and he gingerly got back to his feet.

He resumed his walk, making his way down the side street and emerging into the orange neon glow at the other end. He crossed the market square and reached the rows of shops on the other side. Only when he was under the streetlights did he stop to look around once more.

Across the street, a black car was parked with its interior light on. The occupants stared in the opposite direction, an obvious ploy so as not to draw his attention. They had been watching him.

If he carried on to Ronald's house, the car would follow. If they were police and saw them together, they were bound to pick Gibbs up for questioning. Ronald had already told him he'd visited the murder scene; if the police had a reason to take his fingerprints, they would connect him with the crime.

But what if Ronald had murdered Amanda Baines? If that was the case, leading the police to him would be the right thing to do, but he couldn't be sure and he didn't want to put an innocent man in the frame.

Andrew walked on towards the bus depot. Lights blazed from the gleaming steel and concrete structure; several people waited at different stands. He felt like a moth, seduced by the light of a chandelier.

As he stepped out into the road, he heard another car approaching.

Headlights speared through the shadows and the vehicle raced towards him. He stopped, transfixed, then leapt back to the kerb to let it pass. Instead, there was a whistle of brakes and the car screeched to a stop.

The driver's window whirred and a familiar face emerged from the gloom. It was Linda Frakes.

"Goodness, Andrew, what are you doing out here?" she yelled in far too loud a voice. "You're soaked. Get in quick, before you catch a chill!"

Instinctively, Andrew obeyed, grateful to get out of the rain. He moved around to the passenger side, opened the door and got in.

"Where have you been?" Linda scolded. "I went around to the flat to check on you and I was on my way back home. It's pure chance I found you out here." Her tone implied she was trying to convince herself of that as much as him.

"I – uh – I'm not sure," Andrew replied. The car was dry and warm. He started to shiver as he realised how wet and cold he was.

"What is happening to you?" Linda was full of concern. "You need to get a hold of yourself. If you don't, you'll lose everything. You do get how serious all of this is?"

Andrew tried to offer a substantial answer, but couldn't stop his teeth chattering. Eventually he managed to say something. "Please, just drive."

"Where? Do you want me to take you home?"

"No. Away from here for a bit, so we can talk."

Linda sighed. "All right, but I do need some answers; you can't go on trying to cope with this on your own."

*

They drove in silence, Linda concentrating on the road. She took them out of town and up into the low hills to the north. Durrington golf course overlooked the gentle urban district below and Linda turned into a small public car park opposite its gates. The car bounced over the uneven stones as they pulled into a space. Andrew remembered there had been an archaeological dig here in the 1920s. They'd called the place 'Stonehenge' because of the broken rocks. Linda pulled on the handbrake, switched off the engine and turned on the interior light. Andrew turned his head to find her staring at him, an uncompromising expression on her face.

"All right, now tell me what's going on," she commanded.

"Just a minute," he replied, craning his neck around to check the rear window.

After a few moments, a pair of headlights flashed as another car sped past the park and into the distance. All of a sudden, talking became easier. "It wasn't me," he said in a rush, keen to establish his denial before explaining anything else. "I didn't kill her."

Linda smiled in the dim light. "You don't need to convince me. I spoke with Horace. He said he's never met a man less capable of murder."

Andrew smiled. "He was good to me."

"And so he should be; owes me enough favours."

They both fell silent.

"Come on, tell me what happened."

"I'm not sure," Andrew began. "I just glanced up from reading a book to find two policemen standing over a body."

"That's it?" The pitch of Linda's voice rose.

"Yes, pretty much. I don't know how she got there or what happened. Like I said, one minute I was reading, the next the police were there."

Linda frowned at this and thought for a moment. "Who called them?"

"What?"

"Well, if you didn't see anything and you were the only person there, who called the police?"

Andrew considered this, berating himself for not thinking of it before. "The librarian I guess; there's CCTV."

"If that's the case, it'll put you in the clear anyway. If you'd been near her, it would show that."

"Horace said the fingerprint results don't show anything either. On balance, they've probably decided I didn't do it."

Linda turned to glance out of the back window. "Then why are you worried about them following you?"

"Oh, they followed me all right," Andrew replied, "right into town. I guess because I'm still the only witness and my story doesn't make sense – I mean, how did I *not* notice?"

Linda turned in her seat to face him. "You're absolutely sure there was no-one else on that floor of the library?"

"Pretty sure," Andrew replied.

"And no-one came up after you?"

"No."

"Then it's beyond me."

They sat in silence again and Andrew went back over details in his mind until his unease coalesced into another question: "Why would anyone place an emergency call to the police if they didn't check how badly injured Amanda was? You've seen those little CCTV monitors. If someone was lying on the floor in a library, the first thing you'd do is go and find out how they are."

Linda glared at him. "How do you know the girl's name?"

"What?"

"You called her Amanda, but they didn't release her identity on the news. How do you know her name?"

Andrew realised he'd said too much. "Someone mentioned it to me," he mumbled.

"Who?"

"Someone at the police station, I guess ..." Even as he started speaking, Linda began to frown, so he switched to the truth. "Ah, no; a man was waiting for me after Horace dropped me off. We talked and he told me a load of stuff about the case."

"Damn you! It has to be him. Why else would he bother you about it?"

"I'm not sure," Andrew said, "but I think he knows more about what happened."

"Why didn't you phone the police?"

"I'm not about to put another innocent man in my shoes. I need to be sure he's guilty before I turn him in."

"Is that why you were out in the rain tonight?" Linda pressed. She was more thorough than either the police or Ronald had been. "Were you trying to find him?"

Andrew nodded. "I have his address. I wanted to go and talk to him again."

"You mean you were going to a stranger's house to talk about a murder that he may or may not have committed without telling anyone where you were going?"

A slow flush crept across Andrew's face. He wondered why Linda was interested, but he blamed himself for that. After all, he'd phoned her.

"I'm sorry," he said at last. "I just didn't have anyone I could tell."

"You always have someone to tell," Linda replied. Suddenly the car felt like a very small place.

"George will be wondering about you."

"You're right; I should get you home. You can't walk back from here in those wet clothes." Linda faced forwards in her seat again and turned the key in the ignition, bringing up the lights on the dashboard.

Andrew shook his head. "No, I don't want to go home. I need you to drop me on Eleanor Avenue."

"So you can meet this other murder suspect? I don't think so."

"Linda, please," Andrew said. "I must do this; I need to understand what's happening. You once told me to start living my life; I can't just sit by and let this all happen around me."

"I didn't mean to get involved in something like this!"

"I can't say I chose any of it, but I want the truth. The police aren't interested in clearing my name; they just want to find out who did it—"

"And quite right too!"

Andrew checked a sigh. "I'm sorry. Of course, the killer has to be caught, but no-one's fighting my corner. Unless I find an answer, there is always going to be a question about me in people's minds."

Linda fell silent for a minute and then turned to him again. "All right, I'll help; but you promise me something."

He had no choice. "Name it."

"I want you to be safe. You must make sure you tell me what you are up to; otherwise, if you're the next person to go missing, it'll all be for nothing." She pursed her lips. "You owe me that."

Andrew nodded. "Okay, I guess I can do that. I'll stay in touch."

"I want an email later tonight when you get home, so I know you got back all right."

"Fine."

As soon as she had Andrew's agreement, Linda's mood seemed to brighten. She started the engine and flicked on the headlights. "Right, let's go save your reputation."

Andrew sighed again. This wasn't going to be easy.

The Spider's Representative

Minutes later, Andrew found himself back on the pavement watching Linda's car drive away.

Eleanor Avenue was a small street and accounted for a fair percentage of the Durrington student accommodation list. The houses had seen better days, but a row of brightly lit living rooms proved most of them could still be called homes.

The rain hadn't eased. Andrew walked a little way down the road until he found number sixteen. A broken gate and a shabby front door confirmed his suspicions: Ronald was not a man who valued appearances. Andrew ignored the buzzer, assuming it would also be broken and rapped the letterbox instead.

In response, a bedroom light flicked on and the glow spilled out onto the dilapidated garden. Andrew heard noises inside the house and a shadow appeared behind the frosted glass. The door opened a crack and an urgent voice said, "Wasn't expecting you until tomorrow morning at the earliest. Were you followed?"

"For a while, but I managed to get rid of them," Andrew replied.

"How do you know that?"

"I saw the car drive past us."

"Who's *us*?" Ronald hissed.

"Me and a friend who gave me a lift."

"Did you tell your friend anything?"

Andrew sighed. "Look, if you make me stand on your doorstep all night it's going to attract more attention."

An uncertain silence followed, then the door opened just enough for Andrew to squeeze through. "Fine, come in," Ronald said.

Andrew did so and the door shut immediately behind him. A deft movement and it disappeared behind a heavy brown curtain. Ronald moved into the front room, where the windows were also drowned in long cloth.

Andrew peered around. Thirty-five years ago, sixteen Eleanor Avenue would have been a clean, modern house with fashionable furnishings and fresh wallpaper but, since then, the décor had been left to gather dust. The lounge looked its age, but it was warm; something he could appreciate after the rain.

"What did you tell your friend about me?" Ronald was in his face, knife in hand, eyes sparking with angry paranoia.

"Only that I was coming here," Andrew replied, starting to regret that choice. "And that you know things about the murder."

"Why the hell did you do that?"

"You threaten me and expect me to trust you? You might be the killer."

"Well, I'm not."

"How do I know that?"

"You wouldn't be here if you thought I'd murdered the girl." Ronald's eyes were inches from his, stale breath right under his nose. Andrew flinched and backed up to the door, his hands fumbling for the handle behind the curtain.

"I didn't come here to accuse you."

"So why did you come here?" Ronald demanded. "You fell asleep, didn't you?" He stepped back and his expression became smug, the self-satisfied arrogance of a boy proved right. "Ah ha! You did!"

"Yes, I did, but that's not why I'm here." He needed to get Ronald off-balance and take charge of the conversation. "I have something else for you."

Ronald ignored the bait. "And you'd like more answers to your questions, no doubt."

Andrew shrugged. "Well, that's up to you – you're the one who invited me in."

Ronald glanced down and noticed his bandages. "What did you do to your hand?"

Andrew concealed his arm behind his back. "Why do you want to know?"

Ronald smiled. "Because it's my turn, remember?"

"No, no – you asked me if I slept."

"That one didn't count."

Once again, Andrew swallowed an expletive. "This is childish. I'm here, aren't I? Doesn't that suggest I might be interested in listening to you?"

Ronald folded his arms. "If you want answers and are prepared to accept them, perhaps we can get a little further this time."

"Fine. I fell asleep after you left and cut myself."

"Anything to do with your dream?" Ronald pressed.

"Yes." Andrew was starting to regain his composure. "Something happened and I woke up cut."

"What did you dream?" Ronald's excitement was palpable; the rules had gone out of the window. "Did you write it down?"

Andrew held up his bandaged hand again. "Hardly."

Ronald grabbed a pencil from a dust-covered shelf. "Tell me about it. Be quick! The details tend to fade as your connection to the other world leaves you."

Andrew frowned. The boy was clearly obsessed with this mad theory. For a moment, he thought about refusing to answer, but he knew it wouldn't help. "Can I sit down first?" he asked.

"Of course!" Ronald suddenly discovered a sense of courtesy. He brushed at a seat on the sofa, sending a stale cloud of dust and crumbs into the air.

Andrew suppressed a wave of revulsion and sat down. "It's wet outside. Do you own a kettle?"

"Yes."

Andrew stared at him in silence until Ronald took the hint and made for the kitchen. He could tell Ronald didn't entertain very often, if at all. He took the brief respite as a chance to reassess his situation. When he glanced up again, Ronald had returned, carrying a mug that steamed with promise. Much of that evaporated when he announced, "It's black. There's no milk or sweetener."

Andrew accepted the tea. He stared at the dark liquid, aware that every moment he remained silent was another moment of frustration for his host.

"So, the dream?" Ronald prompted.

Andrew frowned as he struggled to put the fading images into words. "I was on a stage in front of a crowd, like a circus."

"Like a circus," Ronald echoed, leaning on a sideboard and using the pencil to scratch on a scrap of paper. "Try to stick to what you saw please, Doctor Pryde. We can draw conclusions later."

Andrew suppressed a chuckle. His official title had been given more of an airing in the last twenty-four hours than in the three years since he qualified. The lightening of the mood made recollection easier. "I was moving, strapped to something, turning and flipping around in the air, and a figure stood on the other side of the stage wearing a mask."

He glanced up. Ronald loomed above him, his expression ecstatic and the pencil making an indecipherable graphite trail across the paper.

As Andrew remembered the dream, the images were vivid and arresting. He wondered what Freud might make of his subconscious. "He was throwing knives at me," he thought aloud. According to Freud, penetration of any sort in dreams implied a specific sexual desire. Andrew couldn't imagine what being the target in a knife exhibition on another world might mean.

"And one hit you in the hand?"

"Yes, I guess so," Andrew replied. "I remember a sharp pain, but it was difficult to see. I was moving so fast, everything was blurred."

"Anything else you can recall?" Ronald pressed, his face almost feverish with excitement. "Even a little detail?"

"Just the eyes," Andrew said and shuddered. "Strange, inhuman yellow eyes."

"Why inhuman? "

"I'm not sure. A feeling I had." He thought of the eyes he had seen out on the street earlier, and shuddered.

Ronald nodded and wiped drool from his lips. "Absolutely fascinating!" He smiled, the expression childlike and enthusiastic. "I only hope there's enough time."

Time for what? Andrew frowned. The comment almost made him react, almost threw him off track, but he steeled himself against this new curiosity and put the instinctive question at the back of the queue. "My turn now," he said in a quiet voice.

"What?"

"It's my turn," Andrew repeated. "You have what you asked me for: the dream. Time for my answers."

Ronald appeared confused for a moment, but quickly recovered his poise. "I'm sorry, Doctor Pryde, but that'll have to wait—"

"No, it won't."

Ronald smiled again, wolfishly. "I'm afraid it will. You've told me everything, so I guess you'll just have to enjoy the tea."

"You're making a flawed assumption."

"Oh yes? And what makes you think that?"

Andrew reached into his coat and brought out the piece of paper from the printer and waved it under Ronald's nose. "I didn't tell you *everything*."

Ronald's face hardened. "What is that?" he demanded.

"I'm pretty sure it's the page Amanda Baines was reading."

Ronald made a grab for the sheets, but Andrew twitched them out of his grasp. "I did tell you at the start, no more freebies. Time to deliver, Mr Gibbs."

Ronald scowled. His hands curled into fists and his face turned a deep shade of red. "I warned you, Doctor Pryde, don't be stupid."

This time Andrew wasn't intimidated. "You can't threaten me. If I don't get home, my friend who dropped me off will phone the police."

Ronald paused, before replying through gritted teeth, "I guess I don't have a choice then."

"Well, you do – you can back out and not bother, or you can give a little to get what you want." Andrew tried to keep his tone reasonable. "After all, I may not think you killed the girl, but you're still a potential murder suspect."

"What do you mean?"

"Well, you said you broke into the library. Your fingerprints will be there. It wouldn't take much to implicate you."

"You wouldn't!"

"No, you're right." Andrew sighed. "I wouldn't, unless you continue to piss me off."

"I—I—"

Andrew held up his hand. "Please, stop trying to plot and scheme. This game of point-scoring gets us nowhere."

Ronald glared at him, but his shoulders slumped and his face sagged. "Okay, ask away."

"You can start by explaining how you got involved in all this business."

Ronald folded into a small wooden chair. He wilted under Andrew's gaze, flinched and stared at the floor.

"So, go on," Andrew prompted: "how did you find out about all this?"

"On the internet."

"I might have guessed. Your little web starts to unravel."

"It's not *my* web. I'm just a part of it." Ronald looked up, the fear that had shaken his voice now plain upon his face. "But you shouldn't just dismiss it ... you mustn't."

"So what do you do when you aren't inventing fairy stories? What do you do for a living?"

"It doesn't matter," Ronald retorted. "You're wasting your time and mine."

"I'll be the judge of that," Andrew said, but didn't pursue that question. It was plain Ronald still had answers that he needed, but antagonising him unnecessarily wouldn't help. "All right, I need a bit more about what happened in the library. You said you were listening to the police radio. Did they say anything about who made the emergency call?"

Ronald snorted. "That's easy; I did."

"What?"

"I made the emergency call."

Andrew was all but speechless. "But how did you—"

"Learn what was happening?" Ronald finished the sentence for him. "The Spider told me."

"Who?"

"The Spider – she's the one who runs the website and the chatroom; she told me it was going to happen. I received a detailed brief as to where the rift was to appear and an idea of who was going to return."

Andrew couldn't believe what he was hearing. "You're sick!" he spat. "I don't know how you're involved in this or what you want from me in your little game, but I've heard enough." He got to his feet and made for the door.

He was not quick enough. A hand grabbed his left wrist and yanked him back. There was a flash and he felt something sharp pressed against his throat.

"You're not in your little dream circus now, Doctor Pryde," Ronald rasped into his ear. Andrew instantly regretted pushing him so hard. "At this range, I won't miss." Andrew struggled, but his good arm was twisted behind his back. "Sit down. Ask your questions. I don't want to hurt you."

Ronald kept the knife against his skin, slowly edging Andrew back onto the sofa, before easing back into his own seat. He looked upset, his hands shaking.

"You're not going to kill me," Andrew said.

"No, I'm not," Ronald admitted. "I couldn't kill you and, as I told you before, I didn't kill that girl."

"Then why are you mixed up in all of this? What do you want from me?"

"As I said before, you're special. You were present at a rift, which means you were exposed to its magic." Ronald's eyes shone with the conviction of a true believer. "That's why you had that dream. Part of you is still caught between places. We're not sure how the dreams work yet but, when they happen, you're *there* as much as you're *here* now."

"But you said these things happen all the time."

"We think they do, but not usually with anyone around," Ronald explained. "That's why we can't waste this opportunity."

Andrew nodded. "Yes, you mentioned earlier that the connection would fade."

"It will," Ronald said, "but that's not everything."

"What do you mean?"

"Well, once they get a sense of you, they can see you in this world as well. Some of them can even follow you back."

Andrew felt cold, as though someone were stamping on his grave in hobnail boots. He remembered the eyes in the shadowy alcove on the street. "Why would they do that?" he managed to ask.

Ronald shrugged. "I'm not sure, but something came through; otherwise the girl, Amanda, wouldn't have appeared. From what you've told me of your dream, I can't imagine they're friendly."

"What am I supposed to do?" Andrew asked.

Ronald gave him a shrewd look. "You've seen them again?"

"Yes, on the way here." Quickly, Andrew told him about what he'd seen.

"They must be aware that you crossed over and travelled here."

It was too much to take in. Andrew found himself staring at the floor with his head in his hands. Beneath the bandages, his knife-wounds throbbed. "What do I do?" he repeated, his voice trembling.

"I'm sorry. I can't help with much more than the basics until she arrives."

"Who?"

"The Spider; the one I mentioned earlier."

"She's coming here?"

"Yes. She got on a flight the moment I confirmed it had all happened as she predicted. We had hoped you wouldn't find me until tomorrow, when I could take you to see her."

"And in the meantime?"

"In the meantime, drink your tea and I'll tell you what I can."

Tea, Trees and Books

The mug was empty.

Andrew wasn't sure exactly how long it took to drink the acrid brew, but he knew he'd made more effort than Ronald had in making it. *No-one seems to make a decent cup of tea these days*, he mused, but the bitter hot taste did help a little, making Ronald's truncated explanation easier to digest.

"Everything started for me about five years ago. I went to college, but didn't enjoy it. They gave me projects and coursework to do but I stumbled across this, which made more sense. When I started to piece together the clues and found other people who were doing the same, my studies became meaningless and a distraction. I dropped out and now I do this fulltime."

"How can you afford it?"

"You want my life story?" Ronald frowned. "I manage. I've a few interests to pay the bills and keep me; nothing that need concern you."

Andrew let the question drop. He cast his mind back to their earlier meeting. "You mentioned you started by researching Crowley. You meant Aleister Crowley, the nineteenth century occultist?"

"Yes, that's how I found the site and the others. I did a lot of research on Crowley. I think he experienced something like you did and that formed his interest in magic."

"How can you be sure?" Andrew asked. "Plenty of people examined his work. What makes you think your conclusions are right?"

"The clues are always in the writings, which is why the books are always important. We think he crossed over at least once in his life and he was trying to replicate the experience."

Andrew tried to recall what he knew of Aleister Crowley. "Most people thought him mad."

"Of course. But without any evidence, they *would* think that. To be fair, some of the believers are worse. I can understand your scepticism. Crowley wrote about and practiced magic from the late 1890s through to the 1940s. He was wrong in a lot of places but, from what I've found out since, he was on to something."

"And this is what you based your conclusions on?"

"No." Ronald folded his arms. "I said it's what got me interested in what The Spider had to say. I spoke with her and other people who were looking into these things."

"How do you think it works?"

Ronald stayed silent for a minute, composing his explanation. "You need to look at everything in a different way. Take this moment, this situation between us; think of that as the stem of a plant, or the trunk of a tree. Then take every possible thing that might happen whilst we're here. There are some obvious choices. You can choose to believe what I say or not. Either of these outcomes is probable, depending on a variety of things. You might choose to storm out and call the police." He paused and swallowed hard. "Or you might stay and come with me to see The Spider in the morning. These are obvious possibilities; large branches on the tree, you might say."

Andrew took a moment to digest all of this, then decided to return to the main topic. "So, what happened to Amanda Baines?"

"My best guess is she read the book and some part of the text, combined with her own beliefs, caused her to shift into another reality. Something happened to her and she died. The moment her mind stopped working, she couldn't remain in a reality that wasn't her own, so she ended up back here."

"But how did you know what would happen?"

"I didn't," Ronald reminded him. "The Spider did. She told me and asked me to make the call. You just happened to be in the right place. You can ask her how she found out."

Andrew nodded and both men lapsed into silence. The tension between them had seeped away, leaving only a choice of what to believe.

"Can I see the extract?" Ronald asked.

Andrew handed the paper to him and Ronald unfolded it. "Another one to add to the list."

"How many more are there?"

"Very few we can confirm, in the grand scheme of things, but lots, we suspect. Only a certain type of person is touched. Doesn't mean they travel like Amanda, but they've certainly had the same type of dreams as you and glimpsed another world, even though they may not realise it."

"But why this book?" Andrew asked. "Everyone's heard of Tolkien – why not *The Lord of the Rings*?"

Ronald shrugged. "No idea. Maybe it has passages too, but I expect it's because it's a more popular work, more contrived and more a part of the writer's conscious imagination, so it doesn't contain what's needed. Several well-known authors wrote about the things we discovered, but they don't tend to be from their popular works." He stood up and walked into the kitchen, before returning with another scrawled sheet of paper. "Here."

Andrew read carefully and again, words from the page stood out, calling to him intimately.

Great imposing structures ... temples ... a picture of Stonehenge ...

'Stonehenge'. *That was up by the—*

"It's an afterword from a really obscure book I've not been able to track down," Ronald explained, interrupting his thoughts. "The writer is describing the awakening of her imagination as a child. There's always a book though, as if the writers are glimpsing something real in their stories and it helps people make the journey."

Andrew frowned. "This 'Stonehenge' doesn't sound much like the place up by the golf course."

"But if you were from another world ..."

"Where did you find the extract?"

"Balled up in the hand of Jennifer Samms, a twenty-two-year-old law student found dead in a flat in Los Angeles a year ago. She'd been missing for the previous sixteen months and turned up covered in knife wounds. There were no witnesses."

Andrew was still doubtful. "I expect there are hundreds of similar cases."

"I agree." Ronald shrugged. "But she had been studying in Boston when she disappeared. She'd never been to Los Angeles in her life."

*

He roamed the streets at night, growing more accustomed to the new form. Four legs, clawed feet and a limited palette of colour in his vision, but that mattered little in the darkness.

He caught the stench of other creatures; dumb animals with little sense beyond their own self-preservation. They instinctively knew the danger of confronting him and stayed away as he searched, his mind gradually becoming attuned to the trail.

There were several transgressors to pursue. The one who had drawn him here remained unaware of the ramifications of his actions. At one point he'd found him, but the presence of others prevented him ending the man's life there and then; an intervention would have led to more attention than was permissible. When he pursued, the man had vanished.

Now he prowled and searched, acclimatising to this version of himself and this version of the world. Other, younger minds experimented on the verge of damaging the boundaries and, beyond them all, a strange scent, old and familiar in some way, but faint and difficult to determine.

He wandered the gutters and alleyways, staying in the shadows, despite the late hour. A light illuminated a window or two in the brickwork dwellings of the ignorant. He sensed others shrouded in the gloom, huddled against the world they couldn't see, and their activities: the rutting, the reading, the talking, and more. Few ventured into the night, remaining inside, secure in their fear of the unseen.

One room was dark, the two minds within unconscious, but exploring. There were hundreds like them in each place like this that he visited but, under the old laws, he wouldn't have been permitted to intervene.

But those laws and those who enforced them were long forgotten to anyone.

Except him.

He climbed metal stairs to a wooden door. The lock proved no boundary to his mind. The threshold was more difficult, but the accommodation hadn't been occupied long. The male of two lived here; the female visited occasionally, yet had some kind of implied ownership. Both claims remained tentative at best and offered little resistance. He was able to push his way into the hall and make his way up to the first floor.

The man and woman lay naked and entwined in bed, their thoughts roaming free of their bodies and the room. For a moment, he worried they would sense him. His presence in their world was an anomaly brought about by a violation of the boundary, but they too were innocent and ignorant of their power.

He inched closer, his wet snout close to naked female flesh. In another place, such a sight might have aroused him, but not here and not like this. The instincts of his form didn't respond to the sight in that way. Instead, his soul salivated over what he sensed of them.

A forbidden tryst between two stifled spirits, one contained by an unloving marriage, the other by the burdens of caring for siblings; only together in this place could they forget their shackles. Only here amidst rumpled sheets, in the aftermath of their physical union, would their minds run free.

He loomed over them, jaws wet with drool. They would be missed, but they wouldn't be found. They were not his prey, yet they would sate his hunger, for the time being.

He lunged forward, jaws closing around the woman's throat. His fangs gripped flesh and cartilage. He tore out her larynx, severing the jugular vein and exposing her windpipe. Her eyes flew open as she thrashed and drowned in her own blood.

He moved quickly to the man, who was facing away and beginning to stir as the woman's death throes kicked in. Jaws clamped into a human neck, strangling any attempted scream. He locked eyes with the man; saw the fading panic and realisation; watched the light leave them, until they were glassy marbles in the half-light.

When it was over, he leapt down from atop the mattress, his fur matted with blood and gore. He padded to the end of the bed and took the woman's foot in his mouth, dragging her body onto the floor with a crash that no-one else would hear in the otherwise empty house. He stared into her vacant face. Saliva dripped from his mouth, mingling with her blood. The feast would be fresh, if he could find a way into her skull before the boundary drew him back.

Other People's Moves

It was past ten o'clock at night before Linda Frakes finally returned home.

As she drove into her cul-de-sac, she noticed the lights in the front room of the house were off. George had gone to bed.

She parked the car, climbed out and picked up three bags of shopping from the boot. She let herself in and carried them through into the kitchen at the back of the house, flipping the light switches as she went.

"Where have you been?" George was standing at the bottom of the stairs, dressed in his blue striped pyjamas, with greying hair flared wildly around his head. Not the most flattering look, as the elasticated waist had long since surrendered to his advancing years. The shirt and trousers no longer met at his belly.

"Sorry, darling," Linda said in her best contrite tone. "The supermarket queue was massive. You'd think there was a famine!"

"I've an early start," he growled.

"I know. I'll put this stuff away and be right up."

He turned away, lumbering back up to bed. Linda moved into the kitchen. It took five minutes to empty the bags into the relevant cupboards and a further five to clean up the remains of George's evening meal. She flicked on the kettle and headed into the lounge.

She found her laptop and set a send/receive for new messages, but there was nothing from Andrew. Something must have gone wrong.

Faintly, she could hear George turning in bed; he would never settle without her. She felt guilty about deceiving him, but it was for the best. He was unlikely to understand, particularly as she didn't understand herself.

But she knew what had to be done.

She shut the computer, tucked it back into the corner and went out into the hall, picked up the telephone receiver and dialled 999.

"Hello? Yes, can I have the police please?"

*

"So, what are you going to do now?"

Andrew glanced up at Ronald. The young man seemed genuinely concerned, although who for was unclear. "I'm not sure," he replied.

Ronald yawned and tapped his wristwatch. "It's getting late." He pointed at the sofa. "You can stay here if you want to."

The prospect of spending the night on a crumb-strewn couch wasn't appealing, but Andrew lacked alternatives. "What if I sleep?"

"You'll dream again," Ronald told him. "Might not be the same dream, but you're sensitive now and, when you sleep, you'll travel more often than not. Well ... at least that's what we *think* happens."

Andrew traced his fingers over the bandages on his right hand. "Not the best time to be alone."

"You need to be careful, either way. The police will be outside your house. We can head out to meet The Spider in the morning. I'll get you a blanket." He left the room and clomped upstairs.

Andrew stood and looked around. Battered paperbacks lined the far wall next to a dated television set. Neither would offer much of a diversion. He shivered; despite the central heating, his trousers were still damp. He contemplated leaving while Ronald was upstairs, but he would face more risk, not to mention rain, if he did.

A moment later, Ronald returned, carrying a woollen blanket and two stained cushions. "Trust me, best that you stay. The inner circle agrees."

"Who?" Andrew asked.

"The other researchers from the website." Ronald gabbled the words. "You're the talk of the chatroom. Everyone wants to be here."

Andrew sighed. "I'm not even sure I believe all of this."

"What do you mean?"

"I mean, I guess this explanation of yours hangs together, but it's still pretty farfetched."

"Then what *do* you believe?"

Andrew hesitated for a moment. "I'm not sure yet, but I do want to find out who killed Amanda and clear my name. If what you say is true, then that's not possible. I mean, who's going to accept all this?"

Ronald's expression became pained. "I'm afraid that's difficult; the whole process doesn't sit well in people's subconscious. It sort of gets edited out.

That's why you didn't remember seeing anything when actually you did; a sure sign to me that you'd been in an event."

"You mean they wouldn't believe me even if I could show them the proof?"

"Well, they'll be convinced when we submit our research," he enthused. "That's what got me involved. After all, no-one believed Copernicus when he said the Earth revolved around the sun. If we can get enough evidence and put it to the United Nations—"

"Hold on," Andrew interrupted. "You actually believe that will work?"

Ronald frowned. "They *must* listen. It could be the greatest discovery since ... well ... anything!"

Andrew took the blanket and cushions from him and sat down. "I'm not in this for your pseudo-science. I told you: I want to clear my name. If I can't do that, I at least want be certain what happened to that poor girl and that I didn't have anything to do with it."

"I'm sorry to disappoint you, but there's no way you could prove that," Ronald said.

"Don't confuse the limitations of your knowledge with the impossible," Andrew warned. "You're asking me to accept a lot of things that two days ago I believed impossible. The least you can do is give my views as much respect."

Ronald shrugged. "The only way you could is to pass over," he replied. "You'd need to work out how and find out where she went."

"Then that's what I want to do."

*

"The DI's back."

Detective Sergeant Mike Underhill glanced up from his computer screen. "Thanks, Emily," he said to the smiling Detective Constable, who had poked her blonde head around the door. Some people had too much energy this late at night.

He stretched in his chair, taking a moment to rub at the sore muscles in his neck. It had been a long day, a nine o'clock start that ran into late evening, including three hours on surveillance. He glanced at the screen once again, noticing the time: just gone ten-thirty; a thirteen-hour shift. Not something he would do all the time.

"Are we keeping you awake, Michael?"

Mike stiffened instinctively, stood and turned around. At five-foot-three inches, dressed in a faded brown suit, sporting a pair of thick black spectacles and a thin mop of blonde hair, Detective Inspector Matthew Davies was anything but physically imposing. However, he still exuded a faint air of corporate menace.

"No, sir," Mike replied.

"Good. We wouldn't want that." Davies frowned. "So, you going to explain why you let Pryde out this morning?"

Mike flinched. "We didn't have anything more on him. Forensics were clean and the solicitor was pushy."

"So where are we at?"

"Waiting on the DNA."

"You'll tell me if there's anything new?"

"Of course."

Chastened, he sat back down. The DNA results weren't due for another two days. With nothing to go on, he was beginning to wish he'd found an excuse to keep Pryde there so he could properly grill him.

Where am I going to find anything new?

He turned to the computer and opened up the digitised copy of the CCTV footage from the library. The camera had been set to record a date-stamped monochrome snapshot every second. It didn't specifically cover aisles 10 and 10a, where Amanda Baines had been found, but it did show the staircase. He scrolled through the images, watching as Andrew Pryde walked up the stairs and headed for the reference section. He clicked forwards a little more, poring over each frame. The grey pixels were blurred and indistinct, revealing nothing out of the ordinary. *He was the only one up there*, he mused. *It had to be him.*

He realised what he was missing. *How did Amanda Baines get into the building?*

He went back over the footage again, searching through the earlier files, before Pryde had arrived, but there was no sign of her on the stairs. Eventually he gave up, updated his notes, tucked the sheets back into the envelope and made his way over to DI Davies' office. He knocked once, waited for the muffled reply and walked in.

The Detective Inspector's office was a clue into his mind. Faded furnishings and décor styled twenty years ago, to arrive here when others had no use for them, reminded Mike of how the department was run. Old procedures and processes were stuck to wherever possible.

Mike always had an odd feeling walking in here, as if he were passing through customs or border control to a previous decade.

Davies was reading a printed report. Aside from that, there was a bible and a pen on the desk. He peered over his glasses at Mike. "What is it?"

"Nothing on CCTV with the girl arriving. Body just seems to appear next to Pryde."

"That's odd; must be a glitch on the tape."

"Yes, but it shows Pryde coming in, so he didn't arrive with her."

"Any idea why she didn't have any shoes?"

"No."

Davies sighed. "Pick Pryde up again in the morning."

"Sir?"

"We'll need to re-interview him as a witness." Davies' eyes were back on the papers he'd been reading. "Gives me a chance to go at him."

Mike bit his lip. "We're not sure where Pryde is. He gave us the slip when he met up with Mrs Frakes this evening."

"Shouldn't have let him out then, should you?" Davies looked up and fixed him with a stare.

"Probably not."

"Fine. Get a uniform to check the house first thing, then call on her," Davies ordered. "Go home; there's nothing more to be done here tonight."

Mike nodded. "Right."

"Where did he meet the woman?" Davies asked.

"Near the bus station. They drove out of town somewhere."

The DI considered this. "Maybe we can use that," he decided. "Get her in as well – but later in the afternoon, tomorrow. Tell Emily to sort it out."

"Anything else, sir?" Mike tried to keep the edge from his voice.

"No. That'll do for now. Go home and get some rest." Davies waved his hand dismissively. "If anything else comes up, I've other people I can rely on."

Mike felt his face colour and swallowed an angry response. "Yes, sir," he replied. Home was a third floor flat with few distractions; all he could afford to rent after the divorce and, after that conversation, rest was the last thing on his mind.

Good Intentions

This time, Andrew was aware he'd fallen asleep.

"It's not going to work."

"Of course it will, if you let it. Live a bit, you chicken-shit!"

He was floating in between places. It felt strange, as though he was not quite anywhere, yet the words were real; he could hear them clearly.

"You must keep your hands on the board!"

"Whatever. Where's the beer?"

He could tell they were children, young boys of no more than thirteen or fourteen, with unfamiliar voices that cracked around the edges, betraying their lack of maturity.

"And you can't just push it around; that's pretty obvious!"

"Oh come on, this is boring."

"Give it a chance. You have to concentrate! Ask a question and wait till we get an answer."

There were at least three people somewhere below him. Everything was grey and indistinct, like a thick fog, but with no hint of shadow or shape.

"Is there anyone there?"

"Shit, Tim, that's so lame. What's next? Take me to your leader?"

Andrew recalled some of his other dreams. He dreamed of flying quite a lot, but not hovering over people or listening to their conversations. Usually, he would visit places he recognised, but in this … there was nothing in the grey soup.

"It's not moving. We must be doing it wrong."

"We need to focus, like it says in the manual."

He wondered if they were talking to him or someone else. He tried to recall if he knew any teenagers. They seemed to have no idea he was there.

"You sure it's not broken?"

"How do you mean?"

"Well the board's all old and stuff. Could be broken."

"Worked the other day. You gotta be patient."

He thought about trying to speak to them and opened his mouth but no words emerged. He had no sense of the rest of himself; no arms or legs present. He was aware that nothing had actually happened to them; they just weren't there. The realisation should have made him panic, but he remained calm.

"Try something else."

"Like what?"

The change in their tone indicated they were about to give up and Andrew felt a wash of desperation. If they were talking to him, he had to make contact. Somehow, he needed to reply.

"I don't know; something simpler."

"Yes or no are pretty simple. We're not getting anything."

He took a deep breath, concentrated on his body and began to shout.

*

"Bloody hell, shut up!"

Hands grabbed his shoulders and Andrew's eyes snapped open. He was lying on his back on Ronald Gibbs' couch in the living room. Ronald was leaning over him, shaking him roughly.

"All right," Andrew managed to cough. "All right, I'm awake!"

He sat up as Ronald stepped back. The morning sun streamed in through the faded blue curtains, revealing the dust in the air.

"I thought you were going to howl all morning. Another dream?"

"Yes."

"Connected?"

"I don't know."

Ronald shrugged. "Okay, but we've got more immediate problems. You better take a look out the window."

Andrew got up and peered outside. Parked on the street opposite was the same black car from the previous night.

"They're police. I've seen those unmarked cars before," Ronald explained. "BMWs. They always use them. They arrived about an hour ago and they aren't being subtle."

Andrew remembered what Linda had said. *I want an email later tonight when you get home, so I know you're safe.* Linda would have phoned the police.

"They worked out I'm here," Andrew realised.

"No shit," Ronald spat. "You told me you weren't followed!"

"I wasn't," Andrew replied. "But I told my friend I'd contact her."

"So now we're going to get busted. Brilliant!"

Ronald stormed out of the room and ran upstairs. Bangs and crashes echoed above. Andrew went into the hallway and shouted up after him, "What are you doing?"

"There's restricted information up here. I must make sure our research isn't compromised!" Ronald came running down the stairs with a backpack over his shoulder. "Right, let's go."

"Where?"

"The house backs onto a footpath that leads into the next street. We can go through the back door and over the fence."

"Then what?"

"We walk for a bit and get an early bus. It's not far." He picked up his parka from the chair and walked into the kitchen. "Come on."

Andrew followed him into the back and out of the door into the garden. Much like the front and the lounge, the grounds had known better days. The grime-caked patio and litter-strewn flower-beds were damp with early morning dew.

"Won't the police think of this?"

Ronald turned around. "Perhaps. You brought them; got a better idea?"

"Not really."

"Then we make a run for it."

Ronald hopped across the grass to the crumbling larch lap fence that ran along the back of the plot. He broke into a trot and leapt up at the thin planks, scrabbling for a handhold. There was a muffled crash as he hit the fence and bounced off, landing in a cursing heap among the weeds.

Andrew glanced around; there was a moss-covered rockery near the opposite corner of the wooden panels. He picked his way over the stones and climbed from there onto the top of the corner post, before leaping down on the other side.

Muffled expletives came from the garden before Ronald appeared, pulling himself over the post in the same way. Andrew stepped back as he jumped down.

"Thanks. I guess I got a bit carried away."

"Where to now?"

"This way," Ronald replied, gesturing to their right down the narrow footpath. "Runs all the way along the back of the houses. Come on."

"Oi! You!"

A policeman appeared to their left, running towards them. Ronald grabbed Andrew by one shoulder and took off down the street. Panic fuelled Andrew's legs and filled his lungs. He overtook Ronald as they got to the end of the path.

"Where now?"

"There!"

Ronald was pointing frantically to the road. A double decker bus was moving away from the stop just ahead. Andrew sped up, managed to grab the pole and swing up onto the step.

"Two singles into town please," he gasped.

Ronald was only a few steps behind and pulled himself aboard. Andrew dropped a handful of change into the tray and tore off the tickets as the driver shut the doors and the bus drove away. He glanced out of the window and saw the policeman run out of the alleyway, talking into his radio.

"They'll pull us over," he warned Ronald.

Ronald nodded. The vehicle turned left around a corner, out of sight and away from Eleanor Avenue. A few hundred yards further, Ronald pressed the buzzer. The driver pulled over and glared at them.

"Forgot something," Andrew said, smiling apologetically as they got off. "Thank you."

*

"So, Mrs Frakes, when did you last see Doctor Pryde?"

Linda glanced up at the uniformed female police officer, who was sitting in her living room, pen and notebook in hand. She had clear blue eyes, freckled cheeks and had introduced herself as PC Jones. On the other side of the room, George stood in the doorway, glowering. He was dressed and waiting to go to work.

"At about 8pm last night," Linda confessed.

"I rang you a couple of hours later, when I got in. He was supposed to contact me once he got back."

"And according to your emergency call, you dropped him off on

Eleanor Avenue?"

"Yes, that's right." Linda could feel George's eyes boring into her. "He was going to meet a strange man who told him things about the murder at the library."

"That's what he told you?"

"Yes."

PC Jones made a note. "Did he tell you anything else?"

"He mentioned the girl's name: Amanda."

"We didn't release that information."

"I know. He said the man mentioned it."

George gave a snort and, as Linda glanced up, he disappeared into the kitchen, returning with his jacket. "Well, you don't need to talk to me," he said, "and I'm late for work."

"I'll see you later," Linda called out.

"If you're lucky ..." George growled.

Once he was gone, a weight lifted from Linda's chest. "Do you need to ask me anything else?"

PC Jones frowned over her notepad. "Hmmm ... I don't think so."

"I had hoped this would be anonymous."

"Mrs Frakes, you did give your name. If we didn't trace and investigate our emergency calls, people might think we weren't taking them seriously," PC Jones explained in a disapproving tone. "As the officer told you last night, we don't usually follow up on a missing person case until twenty-four hours have passed, but you mentioned a current murder witness, a man we're anxious to keep an eye on. I'm sorry for the inconvenience but you waived your right to anonymity when you made that decision."

Linda bristled. "I shouldn't have bothered."

"If you hadn't, it could have been a lot worse. We wouldn't want you labelled as an accomplice."

An accomplice? Linda's whole body went cold. She clasped her hands together to stop them from shaking.

"We may contact you again," PC Jones continued. She reached into a breast pocket and produced a business card. "We'd prefer it if you ring the station direct if you need to tell us anything else. The CID number is on the back."

Linda accepted the card with a trembling hand. "Thank you."

"In the meantime, might be best if you left the matter to us, just to be on the safe side. Much as you say you know Doctor Pryde well, in the circumstances, we wouldn't want you getting yourself into trouble." She cast a meaningful look in the direction of the door, where George had been standing.

Linda nodded and stood up. "Well, if there's nothing else?"

"No, nothing else," the police officer said with a smile. "I'll leave you to it. I can find my way out."

A moment later she was gone, leaving Linda alone amidst the wreckage of the last two days. George would come around. His brooding resentment would last a while, but it would thaw. However, if he found out she was doing anything more, he would surely be packing his bags. She cursed her own stupidity in making the phone call.

Andrew was still missing.

She rang work and told them she was sick. The lie was less complicated than the truth. It was partially true after all. If she went in, she felt certain she would lose her temper with someone. She made another cup of tea and sat down to brood. George would return in the late afternoon and she knew the police would be watching her.

Damn!

*

"It's down here."

Andrew followed Ronald down the street. It was eight-thirty on a Friday morning, and Durrington was starting to get busy. Quick, sharp strides took them out of the bustling shopping precinct and into the quieter suburbs. Eventually, Ronald picked a driveway and opened the little white wooden gate into a plucked garden. It was the kind of terraced house you might find at a seaside town. The only clue to their location was a hand-written sign in the window.

ROOMS VACANT
REASONABLE RATES.
APPLY WITHIN.

"Her real name is Ana Arachnovic – she's flown in from Hungary," Ronald explained hurriedly. "She doesn't do fools, or foolish opinions."

"She's from Eastern Europe?" Andrew asked.

Ronald gave him an odd look. "Make no assumptions," he warned, before pressing the electronic doorbell on the wall. A reassuring chime echoed from within. After a moment or two, the door opened on a chain and the half-concealed face of an elderly woman peered out at them.

"Yes?"

"Aunt Jane, it's me, Ronald. I brought a friend. We're here to meet Ana."

Andrew felt disconcerted as the woman's rheumy gaze settled on him. He tried to smile, but his lips could only tighten in a grimace. His bandaged hand began to throb again and he clasped it tightly behind his back.

"He's tired," Jane remarked.

"Yes, we had quite a morning," Ronald replied. "Can we come in?"

The chain rattled as she undid the bolt. "Come in, come in. Is Ana expecting you?"

The door opened wide and Ronald hurried into the hall. Andrew followed suit, the warmth of the indoors immediately starting to thaw his bones.

"Yes, I am," said a cultured voice from somewhere above. Andrew saw a gleaming white staircase and glanced up to see the matching balustrade on the landing. Standing behind it was a middle-aged woman. She wore a long dress that reached the floor, almost concealing her bare feet underneath; yet none of these things were her most striking feature. What drew his eyes and caused him to stare was her hair. It was a stark, vibrant white, almost luminescent in the early morning sunlight.

"I'll leave you all to talk," Jane said. "Breakfast will be in a half hour, Miss Ana."

"I'll be there," she replied and smiled. The expression melted the last of the cold morning from Andrew's heart. "Come upstairs, both of you. We have a lot to discuss."

The Spider and the Web

Andrew's hand hurt. Despite the burning list of questions he'd been storing up, the throbbing sensation nagged at him, growing worse as he walked up the stairs and into the hotel room.

"So, this is your witness, Ronald?" Ana asked in a soft, musical voice.

"Yes ma'am, this is Doctor Pryde."

The woman's gaze was like a strange caress, unsettling Andrew further. He was giddy as he approached her; an odd sense of dislocation gripped him.

"You feel it too?" Her lips thinned into a smile. "That confirms to me you are who Ronald believes you to be."

"What do you mean?"

"That you were exposed to an event. A privilege, I assure you."

"I don't understand."

"Your body is reacting to being in the proximity of other displaced dimensional matter. I'm afraid the effect is irreversible, although in time you may learn to control the symptoms." She moved past them and closed the door. Her dress shimmered around her as she walked. "Make yourselves comfortable," she added. "We will be talking for a little while."

"Aunt Jane will be expecting you for breakfast," Ronald pointed out.

"Your aunt likely forgot the time the moment we left the room," Ana remarked in a measured tone, which made the comment sound a little cruel. "I will not be dictated to, no matter how kindly."

Ronald fell silent, but Andrew was grateful for the interruption; it gave him a moment to gather his thoughts. He selected a stiff-backed wooden chair near a small dressing table on the other side of the room, as far away from the woman as he dared, without making it obvious, and sat down.

"Ronald calls you The Spider."

"Yes, the name they gave me," Ana answered. "Those that chose to listen since I came here."

"I see," Andrew said. "How many of them are there?"

"I don't know, but they listen and that's the important thing." She glanced at Ronald and smiled again. "Some of them even start to investigate for themselves."

"I'm still trying to make sense of all of this," Andrew said.

"No doubt you are," Ana replied, "and that is the fundamental mistake you people make."

"What do you mean?"

"You are a product of your society. I used to believe the religious ones were bad – minds like iron bars, deaf to any word or deed that made them question their precious God – but no, you secular people are worse. Your souls are made of bricks, walling an emptiness you long to fill, refusing to accept anything that does not conform to your rules." The woman's gaze never left him as she spoke.

Andrew frowned. "I don't understand."

"Of course you don't." She smiled once more, but this time without humour. "Horrible, isn't it?"

An awkward silence fell between them all, broken only by the sound of Ronald blowing his nose into a tissue. Andrew glanced at him and the young man appeared embarrassed.

Andrew's attention returned to Ana. "Then what do you want me for?"

"I don't want you for anything," Ana replied. "Ronald suggested we might meet."

"But I thought you had theories; an inner circle, a website, all the rest?"

"He has questions, ma'am," Ronald explained. "I thought you might be able to help him."

"Indeed. To answer your questions, yes, I do have these things, but they are just tools; a means to seek the truth. There is no need for theories and supposition, or persuasion."

"But I thought you wanted something from me."

Ana shook her head. "No, I have everything I need from you, thank you very much. By visiting, you confirmed what I travelled here to find out."

"What is that?"

"As I said before, though, perhaps I need to clarify: a rift occurred here. I can smell it on you, just as you can sense something about me." The beatific smile returned and Andrew felt like a child being told an important truth for the first time. She sat down on a wooden chair, facing him and ignoring Ronald. The pain in Andrew's hand intensified and he clenched his teeth. He found himself staring into her eyes; only then did he realise her irises were completely black.

"You're not from Hungary."

"Not originally, no, but then, some people always retain a little of where they were born."

Ronald was staring at him too. Neither he, nor Ana, were making this easy. They wouldn't say the unspoken answer and, once uttered, he knew he would be crossing a line; a personal Rubicon he instinctively baulked at. "You can't expect me to—"

"No, you're right." Ana's eyes bored into his skull. "I don't expect. Actually, I expect you to deny and prevaricate from the conclusion your own senses have led you to. It isn't your fault; it's in everything around you."

"I told him about editing," Ronald muttered, seemingly unhappy at being left out.

"Good, then you understand something."

"Doesn't mean I accept it," Andrew said.

"Of course you don't. As I said, we're not trying to persuade you. At least, I'm not," Ana said. "But Ronald has some idea you may prove more useful."

"I've heard his plan."

"Indeed. Well, I can assure you, much as I admire him, his plan is not my plan."

"What is your plan then?"

"I am here to visit your rift. I want to open it up again."

"You mean it's still there?"

"Yes, they remain for some time, which means we may yet make use of it."

"What for?"

"You know that answer," she replied with a laugh. The sound was like the chiming of bells. "But again, you're afraid saying it will countenance or imply some strange acceptance of my views." She stood up and grew stern. "No, Andrew Pryde, I am not here to cajole you. You make your choices as you wish. The time and effort it would take to free your mind from the sludge of secularity, rationality and dogma is not time I choose to spend. After all, I have a fine breakfast awaiting me." She headed towards the door and the throbbing in his hand lessened the further she got from him.

"Wait, I ..." Andrew started, struggling to gather his thoughts. She paused at the doorway.

"Yes?"

"Why do you want to open up the rift?"

It was a desperate question, designed to keep her in the room while he puzzled about how he could gain something from their meeting, but her eyes narrowed.

"Why do you ask?"

"Because you must have a reason."

"Indeed I do."

"What is it?"

"I already said, I intend to make use of it," she hedged.

"Define that use," Andrew pressed. "What will you do?"

Ana smiled at him again. "I will find out where it leads."

*

Outside, the crowd roared.

Jennifer Samms clenched her fists around wooden bars. She squinted into the sunlight and made out three figures standing in the arena. She knew she had to kill them. Her life depended on it.

The cage containing her was made of strong timber poles, lashed together with thin woven ropes. It was barely big enough for her to sit in without her head scraping the roof. The shirt she wore was little more than rags; cuts and nicks from splinters covered her bare skin. They were insignificant wounds; far higher in status were her scars: long welts and slashes covering her chest and arms, including one across the deltoid muscle on her right arm; clear marks of her rank in this place. She remembered that day: swords in a clearing under a tree and a victory in a duel she'd expected to lose. She remembered all of her fights, but it was becoming harder to recall anything else.

Jennifer felt disoriented as the Gaoler approached. Yellow eyes peered in between the bars, accompanied by a scarred face twisted with a bloodthirsty grin.

"Almost time, little one."

Jennifer spat at him. She hated the Gaoler. She'd always hated him, though she wasn't sure why. She couldn't remember how they'd met, but those eyes stayed in her mind, haunting her at night, prowling her dreams as well as shackling her daylight hours.

The cage door jerked open. Jennifer leapt into the sunlight, snarling. She dropped into a crouch, toes digging into the sand to find purchase. Ahead of her, the silhouettes she'd glimpsed from within her confinement became more substantial as she grew accustomed to the light.

The nearest moved toward her: a lizard-like face with malevolent red eyes that gleamed from under a torn cowl. Scaled hands curled into claws and green skin undulated as the figure adopted a similar posture less than a metre away, legs braced with a powerful tail-balanced stance. The lizard displayed its teeth; rows of razor sharp incisors glistened and a forked tongue flicked out as it sized Jennifer up. The sight was alien and alluring, her opponent so exotic and wondrous it was easy to forget only one of them would survive. Jennifer was giving away at least fifty pounds in bodyweight.

At these points, the old memories always kicked in to help. She remembered Nickerson Field and her football coach at the Terriers shouting in her face as she crouched in the front row. *'Tackle, Samms, tackle! Take him out!'* The textbook was clear: you had to attack or dig in if you were to have any chance against a heavier opponent.

Damn, I want to go home, she thought.

Jennifer leapt forwards. The creature hissed and rose to meet her. She crashed into it, hoping to find some weakness in its balance, but the sinewy legs and thick tail refused to give. No-one had said anything about lizard men in the gridiron training manual. Scaled arms locked around her as the reptilian creature supported their combined weight and Jennifer found herself inches away from its face. It was all she could do to keep the teeth from her flesh.

Finally, the extra burden told and the lizard man threw her off, casting her into the air in a prodigious show of strength that drew a roar of approval from the onlookers.

Jennifer hit the sand hard, painfully hard. The stone beneath her announced its presence on her battered body. The impact knocked the breath from her and something in her chest cracked. The noise of the crowd reverberated in her head, bringing with it a sense of fear.

She looked around desperately. People were yelling, unintelligible alien words that she couldn't understand, but the general meaning was clear – *Get up! Fight!* They didn't care who or what she was, only that she entertained. She'd learned that lesson long ago.

She scrabbled around and managed to get her feet underneath her before the lizard closed. She grabbed a handful of sand and threw it into the creature's face, aiming for the lidless red eyes. It took another step backwards, allowing her to regain her feet.

Jennifer glanced around. Off to the side, another two figures, the ones she'd glimpsed before, were locked in their own private duel. One was covered in fur and snarled as it swiped at an opponent clad in steel plate, who stalked forward, swinging a large, single-bladed axe.

Jennifer backed away toward the edge of the arena. The onlookers heckled her, but she stuck to her plan. The walls were decorated with rusting weapons that had been used in previous tournaments and were nailed to wooden boards. With an effort that drew more pain from her injured chest, she grasped the handle of a broken sword and wrenched it from the barrier.

The creature charged and she swung the weapon wildly, forcing it back. It didn't blink, and charged again. This time a scaled hand closed around Jennifer's wrist and the side of her face exploded with pain. She sagged backwards and glanced up to see another clawed hand curled into a fist. The sword fell from her fingers, the world tilted and her head snapped back from the force of a second blow.

Vaguely, she was aware she'd lost her balance and was slumped against the arena wall. She watched with a sense of detachment as the creature walked casually around her to retrieve the rusted sword from the ground. The blade was notched and pitted, but it glittered in the sunlight. The lizard-like face drew close to her, so close it filled her blurring vision and the inhuman eyes stared into her own. Jennifer glared, defiant yet powerless to resist. *Go on then – do it! What are you waiting for?*

The tip of the metal brushed her ribcage, then pushed against her skin. It was a battered, imprecise instrument and her adversary was in no hurry. She felt the hot pain of the blade pressing into her flesh, inconsequential at first in comparison to her other injuries, but she knew it would bring the only release she could look forward to now.

She focused on the red eyes, pouring her soul into the lidless orbs just as the iron pressed into her chest and claimed her heart.

*

At just before 9am, Mike Underhill got out of his car in Durrington Police station car park. He still felt tired; a heavy head reminded him of the long hours of the night before and refused to budge, despite the paracetamol and coffee.

He made his way to the CID office. As he got to his desk, he found a piece of A4 paper stuck to the front of his computer. It had three words scrawled on it in marker pen: *Bring in Pryde!*

He sighed as he plucked the note from the screen. The tape left a slight smear on the screen.

"Something wrong, sir?" said a woman's voice. He turned to see one of the uniformed female constables standing behind him.

"Not really," he replied, a little firmer than he'd intended. He tried again. "Can I help?"

"DI Davies told me to wait for you," the constable explained. "I'm Miriam Jones. I was the one who brought in Doctor Pryde and sat in with you for the interview?"

"Yes, I know who you are," Mike said. "Hello Miriam, what can I help you with?"

"Well, the DI said I should talk to you. I went round to see Linda Frakes this morning."

"Right." He took out a pen and put the piece of paper down on the table. "Anything I should know?"

"Well, we found out she dropped him off on Eleanor Avenue last night, so Davies sent two of your people out to find him."

"When did all this happen?"

"Around ten or eleven last night," Miriam replied.

Mike cursed silently and balled the paper into his fist. "Right. Did Mrs Frakes say anything useful?"

"She mentioned Pryde had met a man at his flat who told him Amanda's name. That's why he was going to Eleanor Avenue, to meet him again."

"Any idea who the man is?"

"No, I don't think she knew."

He glanced around, looking for Emily. "Have you seen DC Jacobs?"

"No. I think she was one of the people Davies sent out to Eleanor Avenue."

"Fine." Mike made a quick decision. "Looks like we'll be working together again. I need you to get a list of all the people who live on Eleanor Avenue. We'll need to go through them. Find out who Pryde went to see."

"But I'm on shift."

"I'll talk to your sergeant," he reassured her. "I'll do the odd numbers; you can do the even ones."

Miriam frowned. "I only agreed to pass on a message. You're not going to make me popular."

Mike shrugged. "Welcome to detective work, Constable. At least you won't need your stab vest. It's all *very* glamorous around here."

Crossing the Rubicon

Andrew could smell bacon. His stomach growled, reminding him he'd hardly eaten in the last two days.

"Do you think we could go down and join them?" he asked.

Ronald shook his head. "Aunt Jane would get confused; she doesn't like anything to be out of the ordinary."

Given their situation, the irony of that remark was palpable. Andrew picked at the bandage around his right hand. As soon as Ana left the room, the pain subsided into a muffled throb – enough to remind him that she was still in the house.

"I'm starving," he said at last. "Sorry, but I can't wait here for her to finish eating." He got up and opened the door.

"All right." Ronald sighed. "There's a café down the road."

They headed down the stairs. With each step, Andrew felt sure the entire visit had been a mistake. When they reached the hallway, he made a decision. "I think I'm going to go."

"What do you mean?"

"I'm going to head home. I'll leave you and Ana to your plans. I don't want to be involved."

"Wait a minute." Ronald grabbed him by the shoulder. "You are involved. You can't just walk away."

"I can and I will." Andrew's temper started to flare. "Your theories, your website and your mystic woman reveal isn't enough to keep me here."

"You can't say you still don't believe?" Ronald protested. "After everything that's happened to you?"

"Honestly, I don't know." Andrew clenched his fists. "Something strange is going on, but these ambiguous words and mysteries aren't enough. This is my *life*, for fuck's sake."

Ronald let go of him and stepped back. "Hold on, let me tell them where we're going. Then we'll go sit in the café, get some food and talk."

"I'm done talking. All I get from you is more crap!"

"It's not crap," Ronald hissed.

"Look, the only reason I'm listening is because I need to find out about the girl," Andrew said. "Who killed her?"

"I don't know."

"Then what use is all this? I need to clear my name!"

"Breakfast and a short talk," Ronald repeated. "I'll pay – I owe you for the bus ticket."

Andrew hesitated. He was angry, but the rational part of his mind knew that twenty minutes and a meal wouldn't make his situation any worse. "All right," he agreed reluctantly.

Ronald smiled. "Good. Wait just a second." He disappeared into the back of the house, re-emerging a few moments later carrying a thin black file. "Okay, let's go. Ana will meet us after."

"If I'm still here."

"Yes, if you're still here."

*

Ronald took him down the street a little way until they came to the Albany café, an innocuous building on the corner of the road they had walked up earlier. The front windows remained fogged with the promise of hot food. The scent made Andrew's stomach growl again as they entered. Ronald chose a table and went to the counter to order.

Two platefuls of Full English later, Ronald started the conversation again. "You can't leave."

"Why not?"

"Because you're involved now," Ronald repeated. "We need your help."

"I told you I'm not interested in your plan to approach the scientific community."

"No, but you did say you want the truth about Amanda. This is your chance."

"How?"

"Well, if we find out what's through the rift, we can learn what happened to her."

Andrew thought about this. "Your friend Ana doesn't want me around."

"No," Ronald corrected, "she said she had no *use* for you. There's a difference."

Andrew picked at the remains of a desiccated sausage with his fork. "It's asking a lot of me. I still don't believe all this."

"Ana's not asking you to," Ronald replied.

"No, but *you* are."

Ronald's expression became pained. "Well, I want your endorsement of my research. I think I deserve it, the amount of work I put in, I—"

Andrew held up his hand. "Two days ago, I wasn't part of any of this. I think I need a little time to adjust and maybe wait until the police back off."

"You may not get that time," Ronald said.

"What?"

Ronald pulled his wallet out of his coat and placed it on the table. "You said you'd seen something in the street last night that was the same as the thing in your dream. Eventually, whatever it is will catch up with you."

"So what do I do?"

"Well, I'd stay near Ana until I could figure out what it was."

"How will that help?" Andrew asked.

Ronald opened up the black folder that he'd brought with him. From what Andrew could see from his side of the table, it contained battered notes. "In here is a record of every book extract that we found relating to a similar case to Amanda's. More than twenty of them. I'm sure there are hundreds more."

"So?"

Ronald flipped through the pages and selected another torn slip of paper. "Read this."

Andrew took the proffered scrap. It was different to the other extracts. Instead of a circled paragraph, it was a section of dialogue. "C.S. Lewis," Ronald said. "I read the book, like I do with all of them. It's the only one Ana ever showed any interest in beyond the key extract."

The passage was a conversation between two characters. Andrew went over the words and felt the same sensation as before, when he'd read *Tree and Leaf*. Phrases leapt out ...*a place that isn't in any of the worlds ... this wood ... and ... once you've found the place you can get to them all ...*

"*The Lion, the Witch and the Wardrobe?*"

"No, it's from the prequel, *The Magician's Nephew,*" Ronald said. "The rest of the chapter discusses 'The Wood Between Worlds'. The latter part is a fantasy retelling of Genesis. What's even more interesting is that this copy was found half burned. None of the Christian allegory stuff survived."

"I don't understand the significance," Andrew said.

"You remember what she said earlier, about religious people? *Minds like iron bars*. It's fixed faith and fixed ideals; people who aren't open to possibilities and impossibilities. Well, the theory is there are no impossibilities."

Andrew shook his head and sat back. "Like I said before, it's too much to take in."

Ronald banged his fist on the table. "Throughout history, magic's been used as a label for things that people can't understand or explain. Why can't there be things that don't fit into the boxes we feel comfortable with?"

"Because it's too much to ask," Andrew replied.

"But that's because you're trapped, thinking the way you do." Ronald's arguments were relentless and his voice was gradually becoming louder, drawing the attention of the other customers. "I'm not asking you to deny that two plus two equals four, just to accept that it could equal five and six as well!"

Andrew winced and glanced around meaningfully. Ronald caught the hint, sighed and opened up his wallet. A sheaf of newspaper cuttings fell out.

"What are you doing?" Andrew asked.

"You asked me yesterday how I live; this is it." Ronald pawed through the scraps and selected one. Andrew saw they were vouchers, dozens and dozens of them, carefully stored in bunches. "When I was fifteen, they were building a shopping centre next to my school. One of the lorries ran over my foot. My dad worked in litigation; he sued the company and won me damages. Since then I got used to finding different ways to buy things." He held up the cutting he'd chosen; it was a voucher from the local newspaper, the Durrington Gazette. The words '**Free Breakfast at the Albany Café**' were printed on it in bold back type.

"I collect hundreds of these," he explained. "I found out where the paperboys dump their undelivered copies."

Andrew was stunned. "How long have you been living like this?"

"Pretty much my whole life. Sorry, I didn't bring one for you. Besides, you have to buy a breakfast to get the free one."

"So you weren't offering to pay?"

"No, I just said that to get you here."

Andrew stared at him. Ronald held his eye without flinching, plainly comfortable with his voucher-led life. Andrew sighed. "Okay, what was the point you were trying to make about the extract?"

The rabid expression reappeared on Ronald's face. "Lewis talks about a place between places, like a corridor or a tunnel with intersections. That's where Ana wants to go."

"Why?"

"You guessed she wasn't from Hungary. You do the maths. According to her story, she fell through a rift into this world when she was a child. She's trying to go back to where she came from. If she just steps into another passageway, she could end up anywhere; literally anywhere. I guess travelling to some sort of intersection improves her chances of finding a way home."

Despite not accepting the story, Andrew realised he was becoming more and more interested in the explanation. "How will she get through?"

"That's the bit she doesn't talk about," Ronald replied. "She's been working on how to open and manipulate the rifts for years, but as to how she does it, I don't know. That's why I want to be present."

Andrew considered his options. "I've been pretty much absent from my life for the last two days."

"You realise what will happen if you go back to your house? The police will pick you up straight away."

"Yep."

"Then what are you going to do about it?"

"I'm not sure. I mean, there isn't much more I can tell them. They already know everything."

"They don't know about me."

"No," Andrew admitted, "they don't."

"Good. Keep it that way," Ronald said in a low voice.

"I've no intention of enlightening them. After all, you didn't kill the girl."

"What made you decide that?"

"Because, if you had, why the hell would you be talking to me?

Much better just to stay away."

Ronald smiled. "Finally, that's out of the way!" He sat forward and beckoned Andrew closer. "Ana will want to go to the library tonight, after they close. She needs me to get her in. We'll be there around midnight. You can either head back with me to Aunt Jane's now, or meet us."

"I'm still not convinced."

"You said you wanted to find out what happened to Amanda Baines. You may never find out, but if you don't come, you've no chance at all."

*

It was half past eleven before Mike saw Miriam again. She approached his desk, clutching a sheaf of papers. He noticed a spring in her step and smiled. Perhaps working with CID was better than the uniform shift after all? He remembered his own days on the beat. Back then, anything was better than the uniform shift.

"I found those addresses for you."

"Great," Mike said. "Here's mine as well. Let's cross-reference and we can work out a list of suspects."

She placed the papers on the desk, pulled up a spare chair, and sat down next to him. He caught the faint scent of her perfume. "So, where do we start?"

"Well, I think we can rule out most of the student names, unless they link to Pryde at the university."

"Okay." Miriam picked up a pen and started making notes. "It'll leave us with about ten."

"About the same for me. We can count out the women too, since Mrs Frakes said it was a man who gave Amanda's name to Pryde."

"I'm down to six now."

"Right, I have four. Let's dig up everything we can on these." He handed her his list.

"Thanks." Miriam stood up. "I'll check if they have files and get back to you." Mike watched her as she walked towards the doors and almost collided with a tired DC Emily Jacobs coming the other way.

He found himself smiling again as he recalled Emily's ambitious enthusiasm the previous evening. "Early morning or late night?" he asked, by way of a greeting.

Emily scowled in response. "Fucking Pryde never showed. We didn't get the house number and Davies didn't want us to do a house-to-house because he thought it would flush him."

"Guess he gave you the slip."

"Uniform chased two people down an alleyway. Kids, we think, but might've been him. Still, it doesn't matter now."

"Why?"

"Because Davies pulled us off it. He's got uniform waiting at the bloke's house."

"Maybe you should have waited," Mike remarked.

She looked at him. "If we had, we might have missed him."

"You missed him anyway and the forensics ruled him out."

"DNA isn't back yet."

Mike shrugged. "Only a matter of time. We need him in for re-interview. The conspiracy theory stuff about the other man can wait."

"What do you want me to do about it?" she said. He could tell she was angry now.

"Not a lot. The DI will want a report though. When you talk to him, tell him I'm heading out to interview the librarian again." He got up from the chair and picked up his jacket. "Shouldn't take long. I'll update on the rest when I get back."

"And in the meantime?"

"I'm sure you'll find plenty to do. If not, just ask the DI. I'll bet he has lots of errands that need tidying up."

*

After Ronald left, Andrew stayed at the café for a couple of hours.

To start with, he was still hungry. Two orders later, the pangs were blunted sufficiently for him to think about something else. He sat stirring another cup of tea, mulling over his options.

He went through all the things he needed to do. The important ones were easy to identify. Work would want an update on his situation, but that could be done with an email. Linda was a different matter. She would want to speak to him. Both would require him to return to his flat.

He took up the chipped cup and swallowed half of its contents before heading to the counter to settle the bill.

Once he was outside, he set off at a brisk pace towards the town centre. The air had warmed during the morning and his clothes were dry from the café, but the lack of a shower, shave or clean underwear for two days was beginning to bother him.

He passed the Saxons supermarket and took a right into a short alleyway. The streets of Durrington were much busier now and he picked his way through them, mindful to avoid any possible police presence. The diversions down alleyways took their toll. It was nearly an hour before he had made his way back across town.

As he turned into Dene Street, a hundred yards from home, he saw the police car parked across the road. The officers had chosen a good position, far enough back so that he wouldn't see them until he came around the corner, but he was expecting them and planned his response accordingly. He'd had enough of being treated like a murderer.

A policeman got out of the car. It was the tall one who'd been at the crime scene in the library. Andrew forced himself to stay calm and continued to walk towards his flat.

"Doctor Pryde?" Andrew knew there was no intended question behind the words. "Detective Inspector Davies sent me out to find you. We'd like another chat with you down at the station."

Andrew halted as the policeman blocked his path. "Are you arresting me?"

"No, sir; just a few more questions, to clear up—"

"In that case, I'm not coming. I've been out all night. I'm not going anywhere until I've had a shower and a shave."

The quiet determination of the answer confused the officer, whose stab vest and baton made him look more prepared for some form of physical, rather than verbal, resistance. "Look, I don't want any trouble—"

"Neither do I."

"—but I do need you to accompany me—"

"Then you can wait, can't you?"

The officer's mouth snapped shut and he stepped off the pavement. The small victory sent a jolt of exultation through Andrew. He headed up the steps to the front door, pulling his keys out of his pocket as he did so. Only once he was inside and had closed the door did he allow himself to relax.

He headed straight to the bathroom and set to work on his list of priorities. First, he unwrapped his right hand. The wounds had scabbed over, but removing the bandage broke them open.

He washed the injuries carefully, wincing at the touch of the water. His hand was still clumsy and awkward, but he managed to use his electric razor without incident. A further fifteen minutes standing under a hot shower and he began to feel better. Somehow, the cleaning process washed away his doubts and hesitations along with the dust and grime of the last two days. It stripped away the questions and answers, boiling everything down into a clean and clear choice. By the time he completed all of his bathroom rituals, he felt purged and restored.

He knew what he had to do.

When are you going to start living life? It was the question Linda had asked him when they broke up. The end of the relationship had hurt, but he'd never forgotten what she had said: *You're such a good observer.*

The problem was he'd let her question define him. He flitted from experience to experience, never taking a risk or committing emotionally, relying only on what he could touch or see.

Now Ronald was asking him to make a commitment without security, to accept the improbable and find his own truth amongst it.

In some ways, if he had a reason or obligation, it would be easy, but Ana had told him she didn't want him for anything. The only person who did want him at the library was Ronald – *and I don't even like him.* Yet, in other ways, he found this very fact empowering. If he went, he wouldn't be going for anyone but himself. *I'd be doing it for me.*

By the time he was dressed, he'd made a decision.

There was a perfunctory knock at the door. He crossed the room and opened it to find the policeman standing on the doorstep. "Sir, I'm afraid we can't wait any longer. I—"

"That's all right," Andrew cut him off. "I'm ready now."

The Pursuit of Knowledge

"Okay, let's go."

Miriam glanced up from her computer in surprise to find Detective Sergeant Underhill standing behind her.

"Where?" she asked.

"I cleared it with the duty sergeant; you're with me for the afternoon."

She followed him out of the office. They went straight to the car park, where he held the passenger door of his car open for her.

"Thanks, sir."

"Call me Mike."

"Where are we going?" Miriam asked, once they were on the road.

"The library. I need you for some follow ups on the Baines' case. I want to question the librarian again. Your report said he's a nervous type. He knows you, so having you with me should settle him down."

Miriam wondered if he was flirting with her, but discounted that. DS Mike Underhill's reputation as a 'cold fish' preceded him in the department, and he was old enough to be her father.

They pulled up outside the building on the double yellows and climbed out the car.

"You'll get a ticket," she warned.

Mike laughed. "The warden'll recognise my car. Besides, we won't be long."

Together, they pushed through the glass doors. Miriam made a quick inquiry with the woman on the desk, who said that Luke, the assistant they were looking for, was on lunch. Another assistant led them up to the staff room, where they found him sat at a breakfast bar, eating soggy noodles from a cardboard box.

"Mr Sanders?"

"Yes?"

Miriam could tell he wasn't pleased. She could appreciate why: lunch was the only time she relaxed at work, so he was probably the same. Plus, she already knew, he tended to get anxious, which wouldn't make things any easier.

"Sorry to bother you again. I'm PC Miriam Jones. We met before."

"I remember."

"This is Detective Sergeant Underhill. We have a few more questions, if you don't mind?"

Underhill wasn't helping. The minute they walked into the room, his affable smile had disappeared and his eyes had narrowed into beady pinpricks. "Let's go over this again," he said, not waiting for the librarian to answer. "You saw Pryde come in and head upstairs?"

"Yes, that's right," Luke replied, sounding a little apprehensive.

"You watched him go up to the second floor just like he always did and you thought no more about it."

"Yes, Detective."

Miriam felt bruised by Underhill's tone; all the warmth from before had evaporated, the same as when he'd interviewed Andrew Pryde; all business, no distractions.

"What about the girl? Did you see her come in?"

"No, I didn't."

"So, in all the time you were stood at the desk, no-one else went up the stairs?"

Luke hesitated before answering. "I couldn't be absolutely sure. I mean, I can't see the whole staircase from the front. It might be possible for someone to go up from the first floor without my noticing."

Underhill's eyes bored deeper into the librarian's skull. "That's not what you said in your statement."

"I've been thinking about nothing else," Luke gabbled. "I remember I said I was sure, but I've gone over it again and again in my head. I might be wrong."

"You might be *wrong*?" Underhill echoed tersely.

"All right, Luke, I'm sure you were right the first time," Miriam interrupted and gave him another reassuring smile. "We understand these things can play on your mind long after you've said them."

Luke nodded. "I checked the monitors at the desk as well, so I'm pretty sure no-one else went up there."

"Right." Underhill scowled and turned to leave, his disappointment palpable.

"Wait," Miriam said. "Tell me about the book."

Luke looked puzzled. "What book?"

"The book that was in the girl's hand when we found her."

By the door, Underhill sucked in his breath through his teeth. Luke ignored him and stared at Miriam. "I'm sorry, I don't know anything."

She frowned, confused. "This is a library; the girl had a book. Did she loan it out or was she returning it?"

"What was the title?"

"*Tree and Leaf,* by Tolkien."

Luke shrugged. "Well it's not from here then. I've read all the Tolkien here."

"You're sure?" Underhill asked from the doorway.

"Yep."

"Then where did the book come from?"

"No idea."

"Fine," Underhill said and sighed, clearly frustrated.

Miriam gathered from this that the interview was over. "We'll find our own way out," she said.

It didn't take long to make their way out of the building. As they returned to the car, Underhill's phone rang. He plucked it from his pocket and stared at it for a moment before answering. "Hello?" His face tightened. Whatever had been said was clear and brief.

"What's going on?" she asked, when he put the phone away.

"We need to head straight back. They've picked up Pryde."

*

"Come upstairs, Ronald."

"Yes, ma'am."

As Ronald followed Ana Arachnovic to her room, the entire situation seemed so surreal to him. She was 'The Spider' – mistress of the mysterious, and visitor from another world. He couldn't help but be nervous. To him, she was a vision: white hair and porcelain skin, resplendent in a silken silver dress. Everything about her reinforced his impression of her as both alien and a source of mystical knowledge.

She walked back into the little room and gestured for him to sit on the chair Andrew had vacated a few hours earlier, then seated herself facing him, a curious expression on her features. "Tell me what you believe of magic, Ronald."

The question confused him. "That'll take a while I—"

"I need to learn what you believe and what you do not," she said, "so I can make proper use of you this night."

Ronald hesitated. He didn't want to disappoint her. He assumed the question was a test. "Well, we have many theories," he hedged.

"But what do *you* accept as truth?" she pressed.

"It would depend on what you are trying to attempt, ma'am."

She laughed. "Come now, Ronald, you are aware of my intentions. We will go to the library this evening and I will reopen the rift. After this, I will pass through it, to another place."

Her words inflamed him. Listening to her talk stirred his blood; the months of dedicated effort now all worthwhile. "Theoretically, it could work," he replied, conscious of the tremble in his voice. "Crowley claimed the *Book of Abramelin* was central to any act of *transmortation*. We know that séance rituals tap into the same power. Pryde proved that last night, so a variation on those, imbuing them with more significance by using artefacts, such as the books, would aid us."

"What about blood?"

"What do you mean?"

Ana smiled. "For some time, you correctly identified that each of the events involved a quotation from a text, but there's also something else: a death."

"A sacrifice?"

"Yes."

The fire she had ignited in him vanished and he went cold all over. "I – I'm sorry, but I can't—"

"Why not?" Her smile became sinister and he began to have second thoughts.

"I won't kill anyone."

"I understand," she replied, still smiling at him. "But do you think it is necessary?"

"I'm not sure," he said. "Most documented rituals from any society involve some form of extreme behaviour, whether it be violence, sex or something else."

She laughed at this and the tension between them eased. "Ronald, I am a little old for you."

He was disappointed, but the ice around his heart thawed. "That wasn't what I meant."

"Indeed."

Embarrassed, he concentrated on the subject at hand. "Our advantage is that the rite will be performed in the vicinity of a previous event, so the passageway should be easier to create."

"Go on."

"What I mean is, the kind of power that a human sacrifice would generate might not be necessary."

"Are you sure of that?" she pressed.

"Yes. After all, we're only recreating something that has already been done, so we should need less effort."

Ana seemed satisfied by this answer. She stood and glided towards the window.

"What do you know about Durrington?" she asked him, staring at the street below.

Ronald frowned, confused by this change of topic. "I've lived here all my life. I know it very well."

"Do you? How old is this town?"

He shrugged. "I never thought about it."

She turned back to face him. All traces of the smile had disappeared from her lips. "Durrington is one of the oldest settlements in the entire country. Men and women have lived and died here for thousands of years."

"Really?"

"Yes, really. I do not say such things for my own pleasure. In the earliest times they built henges, stone pillars with lintels, monuments to their ancestors, shaped like doorways into the past. The ancient people named this place Caer. It was the largest settlement in the land. Later, they chose to venerate their dead and celebrate the passage of the sun here. This town has been built and rebuilt upon itself for millennia. The divergent beliefs of countless generations lie under this ground."

Ronald was intrigued, but not sure what she was getting at. "Then it must have significance."

"Of course! Great significance!" Ana sounded angry now and he winced. "Don't you get it? This isn't just about thinking in a different way, or ancient devices and rituals; everything is tied into the most powerful collective force of all."

He felt ashamed, but asked the obvious question. "What's that?"

"Belief."

*

George Frakes stared coldly through the window that looked into his own living room.

He was waiting in his car, across the street from the house. It was half past two in the afternoon. Linda sat in the front room. Even from a distance, he could see her agitation. She would settle into one task or another, watching television, working on her laptop, or something else, then get up and abandon everything. He prided himself on being able to read Linda's emotions, even if he knew she didn't love him.

He had the radio on at a low volume. The noise barely rose above a background murmur, but then a women's voice broke into song: *"... Listen as the wind blows, from across the great divide ..."* He didn't recognise the tune, but it drew his attention. She had a pure soaring tone and the words were haunting. *"... Voices trapped in yearning. Memories trapped in time ..."*

Linda didn't feel the same way; he'd always understood that. When they'd started the relationship, she'd confessed that she was 'rebounding' from someone else, yet he'd accepted it. At forty, he was happy to find someone who shared some of his interests and values, or at least professed to. After all, relationships that began in middle age were bound to come with baggage. However, they couldn't work with three people involved.

She got up again, and this time left the room and disappeared into the hallway. He guessed she might try to make another phone call while he was out, but there was not much she could do beyond that, unless she'd been lying again and knew where Pryde was.

Linda went back into the lounge. She was carrying a duster, which made him chuckle. She hated housework, but the cleaner would never get anything done to the standard she wanted, so she always cleaned before they arrived in the mornings. Now she pawed at invisible cobwebs in the nooks and crannies of the French windows.

He opened the glove compartment in the car and took out his revolver. It was a low-calibre handgun. Earlier in the morning, he'd retrieved it from a locked box in the attic before heading in to work. He opened the cylinder and loaded three cartridges into the six-barrelled chamber, then placed the weapon on the dashboard, before sitting back in his chair to decide what to do.

85

A Life Bargain

"Second Interview with Doctor Andrew Pryde commencing at 2.45pm. Officers in attendance: DI Davies and DC Jacobs. Please note the witness is no longer under caution."

"So what did you want to ask me?" Andrew said.

Davies didn't answer straight away. Instead, he stared down at the desk, gathering his thoughts. He pressed his thick-rimmed glasses against his forehead and glanced up.

"There's a few things to tidy up; firstly, your whereabouts last night?"

"I was home until mid-evening and then I went out."

"Where to?"

"Just for a walk."

"Okay." Davies frowned. "Doctor Pryde, we tend to take it as read that men such as yourself, who are suspected of a crime, will comprehend the foolishness of getting themselves further embroiled in what is already a complicated situation."

"I understand."

"If you do, you'd be better off telling me where you really went."

Andrew decided to stop fencing. "You followed me?"

"We kept you under surveillance."

"Well, then you know where I was."

Davies took over again. "You were in town near the bus station. Linda Frakes picked you up from there. You drove off and, sometime later, she dropped you on Eleanor Avenue."

"Yes, she did."

"What you need to tell us is who you went to meet and why."

Andrew tensed. He'd known since the early morning they would ask that. "This isn't important," he said. "It won't help you find the murderer."

"I'm sorry, Doctor, but your friend Mrs Frakes said you were going to see a man who had given you information about the case."

Damn. Andrew dearly wished that he'd emailed Linda that night. He leaned back in the chair and scratched his forehead as he tried to think of what to say.

"Doctor Pryde, protecting someone who is involved in a murder is illegal," Davies warned. "Please don't make trouble for yourself."

Andrew sighed. "You need to understand my point of view. The last time you questioned me, I was treated like a criminal. I've only begun to realise how all this will affect my life."

"Any individual under suspicion of a crime is innocent until proven otherwise in a court of law."

"That's not how people think. You're asking me to help myself by putting someone else in the same situation," Andrew explained.

"If he's guilty and you don't tell us his name, you'll have been culpable in letting him get away."

"But, what if he's not guilty?"

"We come back to what I said to you earlier, Doctor." Davies didn't blink as he said this. "You must leave the investigating to us."

It was an impasse, but Andrew could tell he was going to lose. He couldn't get to the library to meet Ronald without giving them a name. "I know he's not guilty," he repeated.

"Then tell us who he is and I'm sure he'll be fine."

For a moment, Andrew considered doing just that. The opportunity to unburden his conscience was tempting, but they would never believe him. From listening to everything they said, he guessed, contrary to popular belief, the principle of Ockham's Razor wasn't a cornerstone of police investigative training. "I don't think he will," he managed to reply at last.

Davies frowned. "Why?"

"Well, because you hear stories of wrongful arrest and conviction all the time," Andrew said, stalling.

Davies snorted. "If that was reasonable grounds to withhold information, there wouldn't be any law in this country. Come on, Pryde, tell us who you went to meet."

Andrew glanced at the tape recorder. The wheels turned and turned. Whatever he said, the machine would play a part in condemning him.

"We can detain you overnight if necessary; another night in cell number six, if you like?"

The idea wasn't a pleasant one. "I'm not giving you a name," Andrew replied, ignoring the threat.

"Okay." Davies pulled a folded piece of paper from his pocket. "I have a list of four people: these are all residents of Eleanor Avenue who you might have visited. As soon as I leave here, uniformed officers will knock on every door on that street and these individuals will each be brought in. We'll go through every record we have on them. Tax returns, computer hard drives, benefit claims, everything." He placed a piece of paper on the table, and spun it around for Andrew to read. "Point to one," he urged. "The sooner you do, the easier it will be. We'll find him anyway, but if you don't help us, it'll be harder on everybody."

Andrew scanned the list; Ronald's name was the fourth one down. He picked it up and pretended to study it, tracing his finger along each of the entries and glanced up at the two policemen; both were watching him. He realised he was out of time and excuses. He slapped the paper down and tapped the name, 'GIBBS, Ronald'.

Davies smiled. "Mrs Frakes mentioned that he told you the victim's name."

Andrew nodded. There was no point in denying it. "He said he'd been listening in on the police radio."

"That's a felony in itself," Davies said and stood up, tapping Jacobs on the shoulder to follow him. "Thank you, Doctor, you can go."

"He didn't do it," he blurted out.

Davies gave him a pitying look. "If so, I'm sure we'll find that out."

Andrew swallowed, trying to get some moisture into his mouth. He felt like Judas and could almost see the thirty pieces of silver appearing on the table.

The Use of Rituals

Durrington Library closed at ten o'clock. Ronald had to be ready by then.

By the time he got back to Eleanor Avenue it was early afternoon. He saw the unmarked police car had disappeared, but there was a marked one a street away.

Taking no chances, he climbed back over his fence and into the garden. Once inside the house, he gathered everything he needed into two plastic bags before climbing the rockery and jumping back out onto the footpath.

He made his way back into town, found a coffee shop across the road from the library and settled down to wait. Four hours and six vouchers later, the staff were becoming soured by his presence. He could understand why; an unkempt man in a faded parka, carrying two bulging bags, was not a great selling point for a comfortable establishment aimed at a middle-class clientele.

However, the caffeine-fuelled hours were productive. He went over his notes again, poring over every detail of the extracted quotations in his folder and writing down incantations in a frenetic, almost unintelligible scrawl. More and more, he turned to his old research on Crowley. The ideas of the occultist offered his best chance of success.

Real magic. How can I be sure this will work?

He wondered why Ana had asked him to do this. She was more than capable of managing without him, but she talked about his opinion as if it meant something, as if he was integral to her plans. The thought excited him more than anything; he felt alive – more than alive – catalysed into action. When he thought about the other chatroom users, he knew how jealous they would be. The very possibility that the ritual might work and open a portal to another world was making him daydream like a young boy again. Except, this time, there was a chance it could be real.

So, he wrote down everything he thought of, drawing pictures and referencing the books he'd brought with him, in case he needed more information later. When the staff finally asked him to leave, he took his papers and bags out into the street and squatted down on the pavement around the corner, drawing even more disgusted looks, but he was past caring what anyone thought. He wanted to use the time productively and to stay in sight of the library.

The sun went down around seven and the floor-length windows of the building's reception lit up with an inviting glow. Outside, under the light of a streetlamp, Ronald continued his work. The dim neon made it difficult to read, but he wasn't about to stop, feverishly scribbling down ideas, his pencil a living thing in his hand. Gradually, everything took shape. He structured his writing, drawing on themes from all of the evidence he knew and believed. He thought about Pryde's dream and the séance; the eyes in the night, the book extracts, theories, Thelema … everything.

He remembered what Ana had said about a sacrifice. She'd been strangely insistent and that worried him. All of the documented examples involved death and each individual had been found dead on their return. He still hoped blood empowerment wouldn't be necessary.

At ten-thirty, he glanced up. A taxicab pulled up outside of the library, containing Ana. He stood up, shivering with excitement, and collected up his notes and plastic bags. He crossed the road and walked around the cab.

The back door of the taxi opened and she floated out of the passenger seat. She wore a long dark cloak, concealing robes beneath, with hints of silver sparking in the electric light. She glanced meaningfully at Ronald and he dug a hand into his pocket, pulling out a handful of coins, which he counted out before giving them to the driver.

"Thank you," Ana said. She smiled at him. "Do you have everything you need?"

"Yes, ma'am, I'm ready."

They waited until the cab drove away, then made their way down the road to the side entrance that Ronald had located two nights ago. However, a Friday night in Durrington carried its own problems. The streets were quiet, but not empty, and Ronald took pains to make sure they weren't seen. He ushered Ana onto the pathway in front of the door and glanced around before following her. At the door, he took out his knife. The lock hadn't been checked since his last visit and quickly gave way. They were inside.

The door swung shut behind them and, once again, the darkness was all-consuming, but this time Ronald was prepared. He dropped the plastic bags and pulled out a torch. The tiny halogen lamp was bright enough to make out the shelves. "It's this way," he said and picked up the bags again, before moving down the aisle towards the foyer.

They reached the stairs and went up to the second floor. Ronald led her to the reference section. Police tape still sealed off the corner, preventing them from entering the gap between aisles 10 and 10a.

"This is the place," he said.

"You know what you have to do?"

Ronald nodded, handed her the torch, knelt down and emptied the carrier bags onto the floor, to find a box of matches and tea-lights. With trembling, excited hands, he struck a match and began lighting them each in turn. When he'd lit a dozen, he arranged them in the space, creating two rows, one along each line of the bookshelves.

"We will need to cross their barrier," Ana instructed. "The tape must be removed."

"Why?"

"Because it is a barrier of intention, a forbiddance that carries the weight of the minds who constructed it," she replied. "You must break the barrier, to symbolise the nature of our purpose."

"Can't we just go under it?"

"That will not remove its intent."

"But they'll know someone's been here."

"It will not matter. Not after the ritual is complete."

Ronald was out of arguments. He took the knife out again and broke the police seal. He returned to the candles, creating a soft glow all along the lines of books, illuminating where the girl had been.

Amanda Baines.

Andrew had called him a 'heartless bastard' and, looking back on their conversation, he realised the doctor had been right at the time. Now though, he pitied her. Amanda had been a sacrifice for someone else's magic.

He began to remove the books from the shelves, stacking them in two neat piles, arranged so they wouldn't topple. When he was finished, he went back to his bags. He picked out the C.S. Lewis quotation and placed it on the top of the pile to his left. Next, he took the Tolkien quote that Andrew had given him and put it on the right.

As he worked, he was aware that Ana had moved away. He glanced around and saw her shed her cloak and stand on the other side of the staircase, her white robes aglow in the candlelight.

"Are you ready?" she asked.

Ronald found his mouth was dry when he tried to answer. He swallowed hard. "Almost. Just a few small details."

"Explain your ideas to me."

"The flames light our passage; they are a guide, just as we have always used fire, since ancient times. They illuminate the way to the gate, the place where the portal should appear. The piled books are a store of potential knowledge, making the frame of our doorway, like the standing stones you mentioned in the Caer."

"And the lintel?" she asked.

Ronald turned to one of the metal shelves he'd emptied and grasped it with both hands. He took a deep breath and lifted it off the supporting brackets. There was a scraping sound and he strained to keep a hold of the panel as he stepped back, removing it from its place. He adjusted his grip and raised the object above his head, bringing it in line with the books. He was just tall enough to hold the shelf above the stacks and inched forward until they were underneath each end. Carefully, he lowered it, gradually withdrawing his support and resting them on top of the two piles. When he was confident that it would balance, he let go and moved away. He expected the whole structure to topple over. By rights, it should have. It didn't, though.

Ronald began to smile. It was a ridiculous construction, but he'd built it with passion and purpose. It had taken nearly an hour and he was bathed in sweat, yet, in some way, he felt special. This labour anointed and suffused him with conviction in what he was attempting. It made him believe.

"The weakest points are the corners, the joins between the lintel and pillar," he explained. "That's why I put the extracts there: the strongest focus of magic, to bind the arch in place."

"I see." He turned towards her voice. She picked up his knife from where it lay discarded on the floor and idly stroked the edge of the blade. "What happens next?" she asked.

*

It was dark outside by the time Andrew was allowed to leave. His promise to Ronald was broken, but he clung to the things he'd been able to withhold. The police would return to Eleanor Avenue and try to arrest him, but Andrew knew it was unlikely Ronald would be there. By now, he would be back at the library.

DI Davies grudgingly agreed to get someone to drop Andrew at his flat. It was not where he wanted to be, but it would be better than arousing any further suspicion.

He sat in reception, conscious of the duty sergeant pretending not to be keeping an eye on him. Two uniformed officers emerged from the corridor at the back. Andrew froze as he recognised them as the same two who had spoken to him at the murder scene. It seemed a lifetime ago. He remembered the name of the woman: PC Miriam Jones.

"Are you here to take me home?" he asked.

"I'm sorry, Doctor Pryde, but something's come up," she said. "I'm afraid you'll have to make your own way."

"That's a bit inconvenient."

The older male officer shrugged. "We've a call to respond to: gunshots at the Sabbeline estate. Babysitting you is no longer a priority."

Andrew frowned. Sabbeline? Linda lived there. Whatever was going on would keep her mind elsewhere for the rest of the evening. "Fine," he said, "I'll sort myself out."

After they had gone, he waited a few more minutes before leaving. It had grown colder and a brisk easterly wind whipped across the car park as he made his way back onto the streets. He turned left towards town and quickened his pace, anxious now to put the police station far behind him as fast as possible.

Andrew knew he would have little chance of persuading Ronald not to take part in Ana's attempt to reopen the rift, but he had to try, and the more time they had to talk, the better the odds.

He found himself breaking into a run along the pavement, all effort to conceal his purpose abandoned. He was past caring. He rounded a corner, into a short alleyway that ran between two shops just the other side of the street from the library. It was barely wider than the width of his shoulders. He stopped and peered into the shadows. Two familiar yellow points of light stared back. They grew larger even as he recognised them, moving towards him from their obscurity in the pitch black. Once again, his hand began to ache and he felt the same sense of dislocation and wrongness as the last time he had encountered those eyes. The difference now was that he was certain they were staring at him.

"*Well now, you are a pretty find on such an intricate chase.*"

He was surprised to find that he understood the words, even though they hadn't been spoken aloud. Somehow, meaning had passed to him without any sound or gesture. *What is that thing?*

"*I am what you see and more,*" came the reply. "*I seek you, among others, my appointed task and my chosen hunger.*"

The creature was close enough now that he could make out other details of its appearance. Sharp teeth shone behind black lips and the coarse hair that sprung from its back cast a vivid, beastly shadow in the soft neon streetlight. The eyes held him in their thrall again, black pupils shining with malevolence; a destructive glare, one that spoke of hatred and a thirst to destroy life – his life, in particular.

Andrew stepped back, determined to flee, but there was no escaping that stare. His legs refused to obey and the pain in his hand had become a fire that was enveloping his whole arm.

"*Such a pretty thing, wounded as well, and by my arts, no less. No wonder I can smell you!*" The words oozed with a hunger that terrified him. He was powerless as each eye sucked him into a deepening abyss. The distance between them narrowed and the lips curled into a sneer that exposed the rows of glistening white canines in all their glory, wet with the promise of violence.

Something struck him over the back of the head, the world tipped over and the pavement rose up to slap him in the face. Drunken laughter echoed in the night and a face drew down beside his, leering at him. "Where's your money?" the man said.

Hands fumbled over Andrew's body, before settling on one of the pockets of his jeans. He tried to struggle and grab at the man's wrist, but he had no strength left and couldn't stop him as he pulled out the leather wallet. Then the hands were gone and he heard the man running away.

Andrew rolled over, wincing at the pain in his head. The ground wouldn't stay still long enough to stand up. He dragged himself over to the side of the street and used the wall to pull himself up. There was no sign of the creature, yet he was sure it hadn't been a dream.

He remembered Ronald and sprang back into action. He lurched into a run, putting as much distance as possible between himself and the alleyway.

Useful Resistance

"What the hell is happening to this town?" Davies said.

Mike Underhill kept quiet, but inside he was wondering the same thing.

They stood in a garage on the end of Dene Street. A few hours ago, it would have been a neat storeroom, full of stacked cardboard boxes against the walls, with an open space in the centre. The Anderson family were in the middle of moving house and had packed up in preparation. Now it was a scene of carnage. Blood was smeared across torn containers, with ripped packaging and clothes strewn all over the place. Mike had seen many crime scenes, but he'd never seen anything like this. It looked like a wild animal had fought its way out. The garage door was dented and clawed. Whatever had attacked the boxes had then slashed its way through the sheet metal to escape.

Mike took refuge in his notes. "According to the wife, there were three children in here; her boy Steven invited some friends over to play board games."

"What time did she last check in on them?"

"About six o'clock, before she went shopping."

Davies was all business. They'd managed to catch up on the Baines case before they left to follow up the anonymous call. Mike guessed finding Ronald Gibbs could wait while three kids were missing.

"Suspected kidnapping then," Davies said. "As if we didn't have enough to deal with."

"There's a trail of blood that leads to the other end of the road," Mike added. "It's still fresh."

"Where does it lead?"

"Back into town."

*

It was nearing eleven o'clock by the time Andrew arrived back at the street across from the library. The floor-length windows of the reception were dark. The building had long since closed, yet a soft glow emanating from the second floor told him someone was up there.

The urgent energy that had powered his lumbering run had lasted no more than a hundred yards. Now he felt sick and dizzy. His head still throbbed from the mugging, but fear and guilt pushed him on.

Andrew wasn't sure how to get in. Ronald had mentioned a hidden entrance of some sort, but hadn't said where. He loitered, trying to recall if there was another door. The distant hubbub from the pubs and nightclubs in town beat a steady rhythm to accompany the throbbing in his head. He realised that, while they might keep the yellow eyes at bay, they also meant people and people meant potential witnesses.

Finally, he grew impatient and walked around the side of the building. He scoured the hedges and bushes along the path, searching for a doorway and hoping he wouldn't see the creature again. Eventually, he found a fire escape at one side. It was open. He guessed that Ronald must have opened it.

When he reached the door, Andrew hesitated. He thought of Pandora and the box she'd opened; curiosity and the cat. *Inquisitive people rarely get a happy ending.*

He took a deep breath and went into the library.

*

Ronald took hold of Ana's hands. They knelt together in front of the archway he'd constructed. The lines of candles bathed them in a warm glow. He was exultant as he stared at her, shimmering like a silver angel in the flickering light. She was holding his knife and its blade cast flashes out into the darkness.

By contrast, his sweaty parka coat felt like an unwanted second skin, but it was too late to do anything about it; the ritual demanded all of his attention.

"Focus on the doorway," he instructed, more accustomed to his role now. "According to Thelemic law, we must open the rift and then do what we will."

Her eyes gripped his; her concentration far outstripped his own. "Do we require any words?" she asked.

"It shouldn't matter; everything is in place; no invocation is necessary."

He fought to clear his mind, submerging his worries and concerns beneath a focused, meditative calm. Her eyes provided an anchor and guide, reflecting the light of the candles like a beacon amidst the dampened confusion in his head. He pictured the arch and tried to imagine an invisible door inside. Mindful of the séance Andrew had told him about, he reached out with his senses, trying to identify any kind of presence in the room. For a moment, he caught a hint of something; a vague dissonance that seemed to hang in the air.

"Ronald, are you up there?"

He glanced around, his focus broken. Andrew appeared at the top of the stairs, looking bruised and beaten.

"You revealed where we were going?" Ana said to Ronald. The irritation in her voice was plain.

Andrew climbed the last few steps towards them, his expression shocked. "Not difficult to work out where you'd go, Ana. What's all this?"

"It is necessary," Ana replied, "for opening the rift." She was angry, more so than at any time before.

Ronald let go of her hands, stood and turned to Andrew. "Please, join us," he said. "Perhaps you can help—"

He felt a hot, sharp pain in his back, an itching sting that became instantly strong and insistent, followed quickly by another. He gasped and the world spun. He fell to his knees. By the stairs, Andrew screamed.

Ana ignored him and loomed over Ronald, her hair and eyes shining in the candlelight. The blade of the flick-knife in her hand was stained red with blood. "You shouldn't have invited him," she said. "I wanted to spare you this, but you were not strong enough."

*

The sight of Ronald slumped on his knees galvanised Andrew into action, but he was too far away and could only watch as Ana stabbed Ronald again, burying the blade in his back.

Andrew leapt forward, closing the distance between them in several long strides, and crashed into her, sending her flying into the empty bookshelves.

He turned back to Ronald. A childlike expression of hurt gripped the man's face. Andrew caught him as he fell backwards, the knife still lodged in his body. He was alive, barely. His breath came in shallow gasps, causing his chest to shudder with each horrible effort.

"It must happen like this." Ana had regained her feet and stood over them, her white eyes cold and uncompromising. "I hoped he would manage without it, but he couldn't let go of his doubts. This was the only way."

She was no longer looking at them. Instead, her attention was fixed on the space between the two piles of books and the metal shelf that spanned them. The structure remained intact, but a spilled candle had rolled against the volumes at the base of one column and flames were beginning to feast on the pressed paper.

"You see, he lied to me," Ana intoned. "He said he believed."

"But why kill him?" Andrew cried out.

"Because it was the only way to make this happen."

The strange sense of dislocation gripped Andrew again. He could sense a gathering of power in the room, a magic wet with possibility. His eyes were dragged back to the piled books, which had been placed exactly where Amanda Baines' body had been found. Suddenly, the missing pieces of his memory fell into place. He recalled now, seeing her arrive, materialising out of nowhere in her fatal repose, the air tensing and then, impossibly, she was there. The sensation accompanying her arrival had washed over him like an invisible storm, forcing his mind to flee from it and shut it all out. In a daze, he'd turned and picked up the first book he recognised: *Rules for the Direction of the Mind*. The clue had been in the title. Even under extreme duress, his subconscious had been trying to give him clues and warn him.

About *this*.

The space between the aisles expanded and contracted in a way that defied conventional explanation and then there was *something* there; something writhing and twisting. Ronald's creation thrilled with potential; an eerie breeze stirred the hairs on the back of Andrew's hand. The archway became the doorway it was intended to be: a portal to another world.

"The sacrifice was necessary," Ana shouted, sounding triumphant in the building tempest. "Blood and life are the most powerful catalysts of magic. The same is true in countless worlds. It has always been this way!"

"You tricked him."

"I allowed him his chance to be special – unique, in fact. Is that not everyone's dream?"

"And for that he should pay with his life?"

"It is necessary."

She moved towards him, her gaze still fixed on the portal, the whites of her eyes aflame with an inner power. She seemed ethereal now, clearly intent on passing through the portal. A part of Andrew wanted to let her go. The sense of wrongness that emanated from her was stronger than ever, and his right arm had become a mass of throbbing agony. The only way to find relief from it would be for her to leave.

Yet, he knew he couldn't let that to happen. If he did, the police would arrive and arrest him for two murders: Ronald's and Amanda's. He needed answers, and justice.

He pulled himself up, cradling Ronald's heavy body. He knew he wouldn't be able to hold him for long. Blood soaked through the right sleeve of his jacket. "Step back," he said in a trembling voice.

Ana's eyes refocused on him, as though he'd become significant. "You would do well not to hinder me," she warned.

"Fuck you;" he spat in reply. "I don't take orders from murderers."

She hesitated and he took the opportunity to edge back towards the arch, making sure he was blocking her path.

"You will not stop me." Her voice was calm. "I have waited for this longer than you have lived."

"Well, you'll wait a bit longer." He took another step backwards.

Her eyes blazed in the dim light and her white hair whipped around her in the gathering wind. She raised a hand in a hooking gesture. Something invisible clutched at Andrew's heart. The strength in his arms and legs evaporated and he almost dropped Ronald.

Ana was closer to him now, glaring with murderous intent. Somewhere in the depths of those eyes, he saw something familiar: a naked hunger, reminding him of the yellow-eyed creature.

He stumbled, but somehow stayed on his feet. The newfound sense of purpose he had discovered that afternoon held him up. He gritted his teeth and made the only choice he had left.

Bending his knees, he threw himself backwards through the portal.

Nest

"With respect, sir, this is pointless."

"I'll be the judge of that, Sergeant."

Mike Underhill checked a sigh. It was well past midnight and he and Detective Inspector Davies were back in the car, driving along housing estate streets at ten miles per hour, trying to follow a trail of bloodstains. Every few yards, they'd stop, Davies would get out and check the road and pavement, then get back in and tell Mike which way to go.

"We should leave this to Uniform," Mike said.

"They're already stretched tonight," Davies replied. "Seems we have a random crime wave going on, so you and I get this gig."

Mike nodded and carried on up the deserted street. "They can't have got too far, taking three kids on foot."

"Indeed. Makes you wonder why anyone would try."

Further on, the houses became intermittent and overgrown. Mike could see a dead end up ahead. He glanced at Davies, who shook his head and pointed. Mike looked again.

There was a dog in the road, staring at them. Actually, it wasn't a dog really; it couldn't be, because it was the size of a small horse. It didn't move; its eyes glinted in the headlights as it stared them down. Mike sensed it was looking right at him, inside the car.

"I … err …"

"Pull up just in front of it," Davies said.

Mike eased the car forward and stopped a couple of metres away. The dog-creature looked like the kind of beast you read about in the local news reports with fuzzy pictures, claiming to have found a 'beast of the moor'. It remained stock still as they approached, the light revealing its black-haired body and large white canines.

"What do you want me to …" Mike's sentence trailed away as Davies ignored him and opened the car door. "Wait, are you crazy?"

"Stay here," he answered, as he got out. He closed the door behind him.

Mike sat dumbfounded, staring as Davies approached the creature. He knelt in front of it, his lips moving, but Mike couldn't hear what he was saying.

After a few minutes, Davies stood up, walked back to the car and got in. "Drive," he said.

"What about the kids?"

"It's being handled. Get me back to the station and yourself home. You've done enough tonight."

Mike stared at the dog as it turned away from the car and moved towards the bushes at the end of the road. "Sir, you can't expect me to—"

"Actually, I can. Keep your mouth shut about this and you'll get an explanation. Keep whining and you won't. Understand?"

Mike shrugged, put the car in reverse and eased them away from the end of the road. "Right you are, sir. Back to the station it is."

*

"You need a hand?"

"I doubt it, Dave. He's a got a reputation for being a bit of a mouse."

It was one-fifteen in the morning. The police car pulled up on the Durrington roadside in front of a set of terraced houses and PC Miriam Jones got out. The driver, PC Dave Harker, did the same, locking the car but leaving the roof light on. Blue lights illuminated the roadside. "Best we do it by the book," he said. "Doubt we'll be long."

Miriam shrugged. *By the book* meant looking out for each other, but Harker, with twenty years of experience in uniform, had overprotective tendencies. "Just leave the talking to me then," she said.

Harker smoothed his greying hair as he put on his hat. "Of course. You're the one working with CID."

They walked up to the little white gate. Miriam unlatched it and went in, with Harker a pace behind her.

When she got to the door, she pressed the electronic bell on the wall and heard it chime in the darkness. Jane Gibbs lived here, a landlady in her mid-sixties who took in the occasional boarder. Miriam felt a bit bad calling on her this late at night, but orders were orders and if her nephew Ronald Gibbs was hiding out …

The door opened on a chain and the half-concealed face of an elderly woman peered out. "Yes?"

"Mrs Gibbs? I'm Police Constable Miriam Jones. This is Police Constable David Harker. Can we come in?"

"It's very late."

"Mrs Gibbs, it's about your nephew, Ronald."

"Is he in trouble?"

"It'd be better if we talked about this inside."

The old woman disappeared and Miriam heard the sound of the bolt being drawn back. She also heard shouting from the street.

"Kids," Harker spat. "Hold on, this won't take a moment."

Miriam nodded. "Okay, go, meet us inside."

"Will do."

The door swung open and Miriam stepped into the hallway. "Mrs Gibbs?" she called.

"Call me Jane." The old woman's voice came from some distance away, in another room.

Miriam frowned and fumbled on the wall for a light switch. Finding nothing, she made her way further into the house, unclipping the flashlight from her belt as she did so. "Have you got a problem with the power, Jane?"

There was no reply.

Miriam waited for a minute in the quiet so she could listen, but she couldn't hear anything ahead or from outside. She switched on her flashlight and pointed it in front of her, in the direction she thought Jane had gone. Past the staircase, the door to the kitchen stood ajar. Miriam made her way towards it.

"Jane?"

She pushed the door open. The torch beam splashed off the floor and walls, illuminating shapes and shadows. There were thick black vines wrapped around the cupboards and shelves, erupting through the tiles and windows.

"What on earth …"

Miriam's gaze fell upon the kitchen table. Jane was sitting there, in her nightie. Thin black strands ran from her bare arms and legs, the old flesh a mess of puncture wounds and puckered scars.

The old woman smiled. "Come in, dear, and sit down." She pointed to a vacant chair, which was covered in black tendrils. "I'm sure we can explain some things to you."

Miriam backed away and something touched her shoulder from behind. She turned as a mass of darkness erupted from the wall, grabbing at her arms and legs and pinning them to her sides. The torch clattered to the floor and she screamed until thick, sinuous flesh invaded her nose and throat.

*

"I'm so sorry, Mrs Frakes."

Linda barely heard the plainclothes police officer's words. He was a short man with thin blonde hair and thick black glasses. She vaguely recalled that he'd introduced himself as 'Davies' before he'd mumbled his apology.

"I'm afraid we'll need to take you to the station," he continued.

Numbly, she glanced at her watch: three in the morning. Less than four hours since she'd heard the gunshots and run out to find the body. She looked at the bloodstains on her hands. George had been slumped over the wheel, his balding head covered in blood from a bullet wound. She thought about how it had reminded her of an egg, broken from the impact of the bullet. "Surely that can wait until the morning," she heard herself reply.

"Yes, it can," the man replied carefully. "Do you have any idea why he would do this?"

The question barely penetrated the fog in her mind, but she recognised its importance. She glanced around her lounge. She couldn't remember how she'd got back into the house. Everything was just as she'd left it, a peaceful, serene oasis built to mirror the careful, comfortable life she'd made for herself with him. With George.

"No, I don't know," she managed to reply in a voice that faltered. She cursed herself for this weakness – it wasn't like her. "He was harmless. He never hated anyone."

"What about your relationship with Doctor Pryde?"

She thought about this vaguely. George had never liked Andrew. "They didn't get on, if that's what you mean."

"Enough of a reason to do something desperate?"

"No. George wouldn't hurt anybody." Maybe that had been the problem.

Davies fell silent – something that Linda welcomed – but she could sense he wasn't finished with her. She wished he was.

"And you've not seen Doctor Pryde recently?"

"Not since the day before yesterday," she admitted, "before I spoke to your colleagues."

The police officer nodded sagely, as though what she said was a vital piece of information. "It's just that we've had someone break into the library again. Any idea if he might have done that?"

"No, I don't know anything about it."

Again, they lapsed into silence. The man's discomfort was palpable.

"I can get someone to stay with you—"

"No, that won't be necessary."

"Then I'll send a car to collect you later in the day, late morning. In the meantime, I would try to get some sleep, if you can."

"Thank you. I'll try."

He left the room quietly, disappearing into the mists beyond her thoughts. The quiet that followed was soporific and, despite everything, she felt her eyelids droop. Suddenly, the leather couch seemed very inviting and she curled up in a foetal position. Sleep that had been impossible only moments before now seemed the most natural thing. She recalled the police officer's question: *Why would George have done this?* She thought. *Perhaps he didn't and it's all just a bad dream.*

The Other Side

The first thing Andrew became aware of was the grass.

He was lying on his side in a carefully trimmed field and he was damp. The thin green shoots gave off an earthy smell, as if he'd awoken in the early morning dew. The air had a crispness to it, a freshness that banished any thought of rest and demanded attention.

He sat up and opened his eyes to find himself surrounded by standing stones.

Each was at least eight-foot tall, arranged in pairs and bridged by another stone lintel of almost equivalent size; the whole thing was oddly familiar. He glanced around. Similar monuments covered the land as far as he could see, obscured only by a mist that hung over everything like a blanket.

Another figure lay a few feet away; someone he recognised, but he couldn't remember. A faded blue parka with wisps of fur peeking out from an assortment of tears and nicks; each one like a battle scar. The vague sense of recognition Andrew felt was as foggy as the rest of the world around him. He struggled to focus on the sensation so it would provide him with a name: *Ronald Gibbs*.

Suddenly, everything came back in a rush, dragging him to his feet and across the ground to his companion. Ronald was still breathing, despite the knife sticking out of his back. Shallow gasps shook his huddled frame, some instinct making him fight for oxygen around the object lodged in his body. Pulling it out would free the wound to bleed. The alternative was to do nothing and watch as his lungs filled, drowning him.

Andrew looked around frantically, powerless to help. Not for the first time, he wished he was a medic, instead of a glorified theoretician, draped in the self-gratification of academia.

He grabbed the knife handle with his bandaged right hand, his own wound throbbing as he clenched his fingers. He placed his other hand on Ronald's back and braced himself so he could pull the weapon out in one swift motion.

"Seems like you're havin' a tough day."

Andrew turned, surprised. Solemn grey eyes stared into his from a craggy face framed by a waist-length grey beard. The man seemed kindly and concerned.

"Who are you?" Andrew asked.

"Someone who can help." The stranger's gaze dropped to Ronald's prone form. "Move away, son; be better all-round if I do this." Andrew stepped back and the stranger knelt and took the handle in his gnarled hands. "The rules are a little different here," he said and glanced at Andrew's bandage. "I'll examine that in a moment as well."

The man had an accent: Australian or American, or something else. Andrew couldn't place it. The old man bowed his head. A vague tingling sensation ran through Andrew, scratching at the inside of his skull. The blade slid out easily, the wound didn't bleed. Ronald shuddered and coughed in a lungful of air.

"Well done, lad. Go steady now," the old man said. "There's no rush around here just yet."

Ronald spat bright red blood into the grass and pulled himself up into a sitting position. He looked confused. His betrayed facial expression from the library was slow to fade. "What happened?" he managed to croak.

"I'm not sure," Andrew said, glancing at the old man. "I think he saved you."

The stranger grunted. "Just nudged you a bit, that's all. I don't get many visitors at the best of times. Can't let the few I do die on me."

"What do you mean by 'nudged'?" Andrew asked.

"You don't know where you are?"

"No."

"Well that makes things tricky. I guess you don't understand how you're doing that either?" He gestured at the stone arch nearest to them.

Andrew noticed a distortion in the air between the pillars, like a heat haze, only more pronounced. "I have no idea what that is," he said.

The old man rubbed at his whiskers. "We all start somewhere. For you, may as well be here with me." He gave Andrew a kind smile. "Give me your hand."

Andrew found his bandaged fingers held in a weathered grasp and the old man staring at him intently. Slowly, he unwrapped the gauze.

"Wounds like this don't actually heal," he explained; "they just don't matter in this place."

Warmth spread through Andrew's hand and up his arm. The sensation grew stronger until, on the verge of being painful, it vanished. His hand was whole, with no trace of a cut on either side.

"How did you—"

"Do that?" The old man chuckled. "Most of the work was done by you, not me." He leaned back on the grass. "Time's not infinite, but we've got a little bit, so no point in getting things wrong. Make yourselves comfortable; I'll start at the beginning. You'll get a chance to make sense of everything in the way you want."

Andrew sat down. At the mention of an explanation being offered, Ronald swung himself around to face them both and started patting his pockets for a notepad and pencil.

"My name's Gideon Smith." The old man held out his hand and shook each of theirs in turn. "Or at least it was, the last time."

"What last time?" Ronald asked.

"The last time I went anywhere. All gets a bit technical, I'm afraid, so if you don't mind, I'll ask you a few questions and join some of the dots for you – it's the best way."

In response, a flicker of annoyance crossed Ronald's face, but he managed to master himself. "Okay."

The old man glanced at Andrew. "All right with you?"

"Of course."

Gideon favoured him with another smile. "Great. Makes things easier. Let's start with what's here. What do you see?"

"Stone pillars with lintels placed on top of them. Don't you?"

"What I see isn't relevant at this stage." He turned to Andrew. "You get that too?"

"Yes."

"We were trying to get to the Wood Between Worlds," Ronald added.

"Hasn't been called that in a while." Gideon laughed. "Most people call this place the Caer. Essentially, it's the same, but it isn't truly a woodland."

"What do you mean?" Andrew asked.

"Well, what you perceive is an expression of this place's function; what your mind translates its function into. For some people it's a corridor; others, a forest. For you, it's stone archways."

"Why do we both see it, though?"

"Because the Caer is a bit more flexible than anywhere else. It tends to reset to whoever has the strongest mental definition. One of you is dreaming up stones and grass strong enough to ensure we all get what you decided. Like everything, the rules exist because we believe they should. They can change wherever you go, but the principle remains constant."

"So, who's doing this?" Ronald asked.

"Not you, that's for sure. Your mind's having a hard enough time coping with the physical trauma."

Andrew frowned. "Why would I see things like this? The only idea I have about where we are comes from a book describing it as a wood."

"I'm afraid, deep down, only you know the answer," Gideon replied. "But we shouldn't dwell. What we need to get to is how everything works."

"Okay."

"Right now, you're between places; a sort of purgatory, if you want to give it a religious definition. Then again, I guess neither of you are particularly religious, or you wouldn't be here."

"Why do you say that?" Andrew asked.

"Because people with that kind of belief have a crystal-clear idea of how their world works and that doesn't include magic portals for you to come and go as you please." The old man laughed again. "Don't get me wrong; I'm not against faith, but it can be restrictive to believe too hard in anything. It's dangerous or just plain dull," he continued, chuckling to himself, before lapsing into a thoughtful silence.

"You were talking about here," Ronald prompted.

"Oh yes. A few rules exist beyond your control. You must remember that this place is sort of timeless or stretched between moments; but again, your definition of it makes time pass. Beyond here, events continue, just as before." Gideon pointed at the nearest arch around them. "Other than that, you can go wherever you want. You'll find each of these will take you to a new place. Some will be similar to yours, while others will be different. They tend to be more alike the further away you go from where you came from."

"Counterintuitive," Ronald said, "but that fits with what we were told."

Gideon's eyes narrowed. "Who did you speak to?"

"Someone we'd rather forget," Andrew replied. "We left her on the other side. She called herself 'The Spider'."

A flash of recognition crossed Gideon's face. "Yes, you'd do well to be rid of her," he said in a low voice. "Now, I understand that …" he cocked his head towards the portal, "… you're holding it shut."

Andrew frowned. "What do you mean?"

"You're keeping the way closed and stopping her from following you. It won't last, of course. The minute you leave here, it'll open or close, when the reality of your world reasserts itself."

"Do you know her?" Ronald asked.

"I know many travellers," Gideon answered. "She's one I would avoid. Her real name is Arachne. I knew her back when she fell through a hole for the first time, just like you two."

"We didn't fall through," Ronald said. "I invoked it with a ritual – with magic."

Gideon laughed again. "Like I said, belief governs the rules. This particular door appeared a little while back. All you did was open it back up; not through any prescribed method, but because you believed it would happen. That was enough to make it work." He tapped the side of his head with his index finger. "It's all up here."

Andrew recalled what Ana had said just before they had passed through. *Blood and life are the most powerful catalysts of magic. The same is true in countless worlds. It has always been this way.*

"What about sacrifice?" he asked.

Gideon stared at him and nodded. "So that's what happened. The knife was her handiwork?"

"Yes," Andrew confirmed.

"Always something primal: murder, execution, suicide; anything that sheds blood. They say, in the last moments of life, a person's mind is totally free. She did that to harness this power and break the barrier." Gideon peered at Ronald. "Your death opened the portal."

Ronald looked elated, then hurt, as he absorbed Gideon's words. "You mean I died?"

"I'm not sure, but the effect is the same. Your friend here saved you by stepping through but, if you go back, you'll still be wounded. What healed you is the knowledge that you aren't in the real world. It's like a dream state that way. In fact, the two have a lot in common."

"We understand a bit about dreams," Andrew said.

"Do you?" Gideon sighed. "Dangerous things they are, and more dangerous once you learn about them. It's the same with all things; the only real way to be safe is to stay ignorant. That's no option for both of you anymore. Now you're out, you'll want to keep moving."

"So, what do I do?" Ronald asked, sounding worried. Andrew couldn't help feeling sorry for him.

"You can do whatever you like," Gideon replied, "but I wouldn't go back through a portal to your world, or another one that's too familiar, otherwise you could really be dead."

"I can't go home?"

"I wouldn't."

"How do I know which doors lead to somewhere familiar?"

Gideon made a face. "I'm sorry, but there's no exact way of knowing other than what I said before. The strength of your subconscious isn't a measurable thing and the only advice I can give is that, the further away from here you go, the more similar a place you'll end up."

Ronald got to his feet and walked away from Andrew, leaving him with the old man. "What about my hand?" he asked.

"It should be fine." There was no trace left of his earlier good mood. "It may open up again in a similar place, but it will heal naturally. Did she stab you as well?"

"No. I fell on a carving knife while I was asleep."

"Were you dreaming?"

"Yes."

"Then you didn't just *fall* on a carving knife." The old man tried to stretch feebly. He appeared to have aged since the start of the conversation. "What was the dream?"

Andrew shrugged. "Something strange involving some kind of circus and a man with yellow eyes."

"Candleswick."

"Who?"

"The yellow-eyed man; his name's Candleswick. He's an enforcer; part of the natural order, trying to keep all these realities separate. He hunts those who get free or start experimenting with spirits and the like. To him, people like you are infections that need to be cut out. The more disturbance you make, the more likely he'll find you. You don't want that." After a moment or two of wincing, Gideon tottered over to another archway, next to the one they'd arrived through, and slumped against the stone pillar.

"Are you all right?" Andrew asked.

"I'm sorry." Gideon's voice was little more than a whisper now. "It appears our time is over."

"What's wrong with you?" Ronald had returned, and took hold of the stranger's arm.

"Nothing. Remember, it's all about perception and belief." Gideon jabbed a finger in Andrew's direction. "Your friend is getting tired from holding the portal closed. He thinks time has passed. That makes it more difficult for me to reach you. You need to go before your friend Ana finds you."

Andrew glanced around in panic. "Where?"

"Doesn't matter. Pick an archway and walk through it!" Gideon slipped to his knees against the stone, his face haggard and his breath wheezing. "From this side, you don't have to do anything fancy; just get under the lintel."

"But we're trying to find what happened to someone: a girl called Amanda," Andrew said. "She turned up dead in our world two days ago. I need to know who killed her."

Gideon's breath was as shallow as Ronald's had been before, and his eyes were glazed. "She didn't come through here. She must have travelled directly." He raised a feeble arm and pointed at an arch a few yards away. "That one was last active a little while ago. Might be the right one."

"How can we be sure?" Ronald demanded.

"You can't. You just have to hope." Gideon's eyes were now closed. Within seconds, he had slumped to the ground, unconscious.

Andrew checked the old man's wrist and found a ragged pulse. He was barely breathing and his lips were a faint shade of blue. He turned to Ronald. "We need to go."

"But I could die!"

"Would you rather face Ana when she gets here?" Andrew demanded. "We don't know what the fuck we're doing, but she does. She's already tried to kill you once."

"She got what she wanted: the portal's open."

"And you think she wants witnesses to all this?"

Ronald sighed. "Fine. Let's go."

They walked away from the old man and Andrew touched Ronald on the shoulder. "For what it's worth, I'll do my best to make sure you're all right. Any sign of trouble and I'll get us straight back."

"How?"

"I'll find a way." He gritted his teeth and, together, they stepped under the arch.

Choice of Direction

Record of the after-time – Entry three hundred and seventy-three since the burning.

The times grow older; the candle becomes dim. Doubtless, in your present, you read these entries, looking back for some sign or clue to aid you, as we delve through the ancient records, copying and re-copying rotting parchment so we might preserve what knowledge we have.

Upon this day, it is seventy-seven cycles after the coming of the Lady Harbinger. The old tellers still speak of her arrival, stepping into the centre of our elder's council and appearing in front of them as a beacon of arcane power, although no-one still lives who can remember the time she remained amongst us.

In that time, no sacred chamber existed; it was she who ordered its construction to permit her travel onwards. Her presence offered hope and, in the earliest of writings since her time, we find elation at the possible end of our plight.

Some believe she may return, as she claimed she would, to guide us from here, delivering us from the slow evil; yet these words are hollow, as they echo in the colder halls of the Arcane. In the tunnels below where the people dwell, such promises are long forgotten and few choose to place their faith in a hope of the past, succumbing instead to the despair at our present life in this endless darkness. No doubt, you are all too familiar with this.

The census records seven deaths among the tunnel folk. Five succumbed to age or malnourishment, but a further two were murdered in a riot in the lower catacombs. These places have become lawless of late and the militia refuse to patrol beyond the rock pools. There is little we can do but tighten our grip upon those we can reach, preserving as many as we can. In time, if this continues, the Arcane predict the runes in those will fail there and the catacombs will fall away into the abyss. It might be, in your time, they are already lost and forgotten.

We have recorded one birth among our people: a babe who was tested and found to be gifted – a faint cause for celebration at her naming ceremony. She will not want for a vocation.

The memories of the old world grow dimmer still. The stories of the fields and forests that once surrounded our glorious city, the jewel of the realm, are long since gone. They remain only upon our precious store of parchment, which dwindles still further. We must find a solution soon, else there will be no place for you to continue our tradition.

The record shall state with these announcements, the population of our city stands at four thousand seven hundred and forty-six ...'

*

This time, Andrew was prepared for the transfer.

He took a deep breath and gritted his teeth, determined to witness the process. As soon as he passed underneath the lintel, warmth spread through him and his eyes lost focus. He blinked repeatedly, trying to clear his vision, but the world became ever darker. When he opened his mouth and tried to call out to Ronald, the words stuck in his throat. Instead, the darkness pulled him into its depths, making him small and insignificant in the gathering void.

He was alone. He felt weightless, as if he were outside his body, staring into a storm of black that revealed nothing of itself; but he judged it to be endless. Endless and ... *alive.*

He fell into its jaws, further and further into a bottomless eddy that drank his consciousness into its emptiness. For a moment, he wanted to let go, succumbing to the promise of oblivion. It seemed easier than attempting to struggle onwards through the dense expanse, but then some instinct responded and he steadied himself. He was falling faster now and, though he couldn't see, he knew whatever lay below was racing towards him at impossible speed.

At that point, Andrew's mind shut down. The heady experience resonated with snatches of memory from the library, when Amanda had appeared, but this was a far more potent brew; an addictive rush, threatening to claim his life or his sanity. The threat of madness bubbled up and he welcomed catatonia, placing trust in his brain's natural defences as it shut down, rather than face something it couldn't rationalise or comprehend.

The faint sound of whistling wind brought Andrew back to his senses. Then he remembered to breathe; the air had a stale edge to it and he began to cough, doubling over on a cold stone floor. He opened his eyes to darkness, yet the echoing sounds reassured him that he was kneeling in a confined space.

"Where are we?" Ronald's voice echoed around the room. "It's so dark."

"I don't think there's a light switch," Andrew spluttered.

As though in answer, a flame sprang into life some distance away. A moment later, another appeared to the right of the first, then a third a similar distance away from that. Andrew watched in fascination as they were gradually surrounded by lights that revealed the room.

Sixteen torches illuminated the space: it was a large stone chamber, hewn from the rock. Ronald and Andrew found themselves crouched on a raised dais in its centre, underneath an arch. The light came from flaming wooden brands in brackets, set into the walls.

"I'm not sure what I expected," Andrew confessed, "but it wasn't this." He ran his hand over the pillars. Their surface was pitted and scarred, unlike the structures they had seen before in the place the old man, Gideon, had called the Caer. The entire structure was covered in sculpted indentations that reminded him of hieroglyphic symbols or runes. "Do you know what these are?"

Ronald climbed to his feet and joined him, peering intently at the stones. "They might be Norse or Celtic."

"Can you read them?"

"I wish."

They lapsed into awed silence as they examined the room. Andrew was fascinated by the ornate symbols, which were not limited to the arch, but ran across areas of the floor and the walls. The torch brackets were also decorated and the metal frames etched with still more elegant icons.

"Is there any chance we can save her?" Andrew asked.

"Who?"

"Amanda. You said her beliefs caused her to shift into another reality; might she still be alive out here somewhere?"

Ronald frowned. "I'm sorry; I don't think so."

"Why not?"

"Ana said, once you pass through, your choices don't count anymore," Ronald explained. "You don't diverge in the same way. You just remain a singular possibility. If we were able to find her at all, it would be in a time before she travelled and she wouldn't need saving."

"Are you sure she's right about that?"

Ronald shrugged. "No idea, but I can't think why she would lie about it."

"Does that mean we can't change anything?"

"I don't think so. Multiplications of reality depend on other people; the ones who stay in their own worlds."

This frustrating explanation only served to worsen Andrew's mood and raise more questions, although he guessed he was running up to the limit of Ronald's knowledge.

A rumbling interrupted their conversation and Andrew turned to see a new light appear between two of the torches. A crack in the stone wall widened and the rock slid apart to reveal a dimly lit passageway beyond. There was a hubbub of voices and a crowd of people gathered around the entrance.

"What do we do now?" Ronald asked.

"Let's see what they have to say."

An awed hush descended as the people caught sight of them. "Harrowers!" intoned a strident voice. "You are long-sought and most welcome!"

A dark-robed, hooded figure walked towards them, carrying a long staff that glowed blue at its tip. A hand drew back the hood; a woman in late middle age, with long brown hair, gazed at them. Her face was set in a severe expression, but Andrew sensed an effusiveness about her. As she drew close, she dropped to her knees and bowed her head in homage.

The chamber lapsed into expectant silence as the gathered people waited for a response. Andrew glanced at Ronald, who shook his head, indicating he expected him to take the lead.

Andrew stepped forward towards the kneeling woman. The greeting, coupled with the runes they had discovered, indicated these people were much more aware of the portals than anyone back home in Durrington. The genuflection, however, implied worship, which discomforted him. He certainly didn't want to be an idol, especially as he had no idea what the implications might be.

Not knowing the appropriate verbal response to her greeting, he elected to address the issue of status. He knelt in front of her and reached out, taking her hands in his own. She stared straight into his eyes, her elation and hope encapsulated in one word – '*Saviour*' – which she mouthed as he raised her to her feet.

"We have waited for you a long time," she said, projecting her voice so that the gathered people could hear. Her accent softened the harsher sounds of each syllable slightly, yet it was plain that English was her native tongue. "It has been seventy-seven years since the visit of the Lady Harbinger, who promised your return."

Her passionate conviction was impossible to refute and Andrew found he couldn't bring himself to deny the responsibility it placed upon his shoulders. He gave her his best smile. "What do you want from us?"

"We beg your aid. We were told to remain ready. My heart rejoices that it has come in my lifetime."

"How can we help you?" Ronald pressed.

The question drew a look of confusion that brightened into a smile. "The emissaries are wise to test us," she answered, her voice soft. "As chosen Arcane, I shall not fail your challenge, for the sake of my people."

She stepped up onto the dais and faced the people in the hall. "Travellers, we ask that you deliver us, as ordained. We ask that you end the suffering of our people and take us to another world!"

As the people began to shout and cheer, panic ran up Andrew's spine. He felt the muscles of his jaw go slack as his mind blanched at the unknown implications behind what the woman was suggesting.

By contrast, Ronald managed to keep himself together. "How many of you are there?" he asked.

"You test me again." She smiled again. "As of this morning's census, four thousand, seven hundred and forty-six."

"And you want us to take all of you out of here?"

"No-one must be left behind. It is in the prophecy."

Ronald, the woman and the crowd in the stone hallway all stared at Andrew, awaiting his response.

"We are very tired," Andrew managed at last. "Is there somewhere to rest?"

"Of course," the woman replied. "Follow me."

Eternal Consequences

The woman led Ronald and Andrew away from the circular chamber into a set of living quarters, like a small cloister. Every passageway was a mixture of stone blocks and hewn rock, lit by candles and torches. Not once in the journey did Andrew see daylight.

The place in which they found themselves now reminded him of his night in Durrington police station, but instead of whitewashed concrete, this room appeared to be carved out of the bare rock. The walls were smooth and decorated in places with etched runes. The furnishings were no more than basic: two low stone beds, a glowing torch on a bracket and a large, plain hourglass.

Andrew and Ronald sat on the beds as the robed woman lingered by the door.

"My name is Gwuina," she said. "I am the Speaker Arcane."

"What does that mean?" Ronald asked.

"It means I speak as the voice of the Council, the order that governs Corbenic."

"That's what this place is called?"

"Yes, it is the name our ancestors gave to our city. This is but a fragment of what once existed."

"What happened to it?"

"It was destroyed in a terrible war between wizards. We have lived in all that remains, waiting for a traveller to arrive and redeem us."

Ronald coughed and cleared his throat. "Forgive me for asking, but how does this all work? I mean, if this is a fragment of a world, what's holding it all together?"

Gwuina gestured to the walls. Andrew looked and saw more of the runes like the ones in the chamber. In here, they were small, and faintly etched into the rock. "The Arcanes maintain the warding, until the deliverance arrives. Those who are worthy will be saved."

"You mean you expect us to save you?"

Gwuina nodded. "We have strived to be worthy of you. These people need your aid; you must—"

"Please!" Andrew realised he was shouting. He held up a hand apologetically and lowered his tone. "Please. This is a lot to take in. We have travelled a long way and we are very tired."

Gwuina gazed at him and frowned. She seemed about to say something more, but thought better of it and smiled instead. "I shall leave you to rest a while," she said, opening the door and stepping outside into the passage. "I will send for the Keeper. He will be able to answer your questions."

"Thank you," Andrew said.

The door closed and keys rattled in the lock.

*

After Gwuina had gone, Andrew sat back and thought over their situation. However impossible it all seemed to be, the Arcane's words made sense, and it was clear she believed what she was saying. They had come through a portal into a dying fragment of a world, where thousands of people needed their help to escape. *We barely know how to do this for ourselves*, Andrew thought. *Let alone for five thousand people.*

On a low stone shelf near the door, there was an hourglass. The sand ran from the top chamber to the bottom, but there were no markers to indicate hours, minutes or seconds. Andrew wished he knew what time it was, but his watch had stopped at 11.30pm, about when they'd left the library. He had no idea if time ran the same in Corbenic.

He glanced across at his companion. Ronald sat on the other pallet beds, picking his nose, his face slack and pale. It was a methodical action, each time using the little finger of his trembling left hand, examining the drying phlegm under his fingernail, before rolling it into a ball and wiping it on the floor, then repeating the gesture. Andrew was struck by just how frightened he seemed. Ever since the portal in the library had appeared, Ronald hadn't been himself.

Eventually, Ronald returned his gaze. "What are we going to do?" he asked.

"We're going to ask questions and think very carefully about our decision."

Ronald snorted. "They want us to transport five thousand people out of here. Sooner or later, we're going to need to tell them we can't."

"Why can't we?"

"Because we don't know how!"

Andrew knelt down in front of him. "That ritual you did nearly worked, you know."

"That means nothing. This is a totally different world."

"Yes, one where they practice a form of magic and all believe that we can take them out of here."

"Do you realise what you're suggesting?" Ronald protested. "Even if we do accept what that crazy old man told us, two people travelling between realities is one thing. Thousands is a whole different scale!"

"I'm not saying we should or that we can, but we need to understand these people. You heard how Gwuina spoke: it's like a religion to them."

"All the more reason to stay out of it. If we try to be these 'emissaries', we'll only screw up."

"What other choice is there?" Andrew snapped. Ronald's sullen intransigence worried him. It was a complete reversal of how he'd been before. He needed to snap him out of his sulky negativity. He grabbed the collar of Ronald's parka and pulled him toward him roughly, until their faces almost touched. "Yesterday, this was everything you ever dreamed of. What happened to that passionate little nerd who wanted to learn about real magic?"

Ronald stared at him. "He died back in the library."

There was a crushed look in the young man's eyes; Andrew let go of his collar.

They were interrupted by a soft knock at the door. Ronald glanced in its direction.

Andrew stood up. "Just promise me you won't say anything to them," he said.

Ronald sighed. "All right. We'll keep quiet for now, but this discussion's not over."

"You're damned right it isn't."

The door opened. An older man, dressed in identical robes to Gwuina's, stood outside, his hood down. He had a chiselled face, long grey hair and clear blue eyes. "Greetings, emissaries," he said in the same softly-accented English. "My name is Arta. I am the Keeper Arcane."

Andrew nodded in response. "How can we help you, Arta?"

"It is I who wish to help you. The Speaker said you had questions. As Keeper, my responsibility is to preserve the stored knowledge of our people."

"So, you are here to bring answers?" Ronald asked.

"I am here to face your tests of our lore and understanding, as the Harbinger ordained."

"Who was this 'Harbinger'?" Andrew asked.

Arta smiled. "The first traveller to visit us. She appeared unsought in the middle of the room that you also arrived in, seventy-seven cycles ago. At that time, it was our council chamber. It was she who decreed that it should be rebuilt with the arch in its centre to best assist your arrival."

"So that entire room was built for us?"

"It was built for the emissaries – the travellers who will deliver our people."

Andrew decided not to pursue this line of questioning any further. "What about your symbols? What do they do?"

"The runes protect the people and the Arcanes protect the runes," Arta replied.

Andrew frowned. "How do they do that?"

"Ah, now I understand your question." Arta's smile widened. "According to our records, the Harbinger was also most interested in our runes." He moved back to the door and opened it. "It might be best if you saw for yourselves."

Arta guided them back into the narrow stone corridors, but this time headed in a different direction. Andrew's hands and legs shook as they walked. The passageways were claustrophobic. They were rounded at the ceiling and seemed shaped to fit the people who moved within them. Each wall was decorated with similar runic script and punctuated at intervals with torch brackets like the ones he'd first seen, but the etched symbols were less concentrated here than in the arrival chamber. At every intersection, Arta took the left-hand tunnel and gradually the corridor inclined.

As Arta led them, he continued to explain more about his people's history: "We have told you that we are all that remains of a larger civilisation, but we have not yet shown you what this means."

"Are we going to the roof?" Ronald asked.

"Essentially, yes," Arta replied. "I am taking you to the top of this tower, as it is the best place to get a clear idea of our plight."

The passage finished in a dead end. On the right was a tight spiral staircase. Arta went straight up and Ronald followed close behind. Andrew glanced around. His eyes were growing used to the gloom of the tunnels, but revealed no more detail as to how they had been constructed. Apart from the symbols, the walls were smooth, with no trace of brickwork or any other craft.

Andrew headed up the steps after the others. The stairs were cramped and rotated in a clockwise direction. He quickly lost count of how many there were in the darkness and became disoriented as he climbed, leaning heavily on the wall as he shuffled upwards. So much rock all around felt oppressive, like a great weight closing in on him. Something within him screamed and he was reminded of an eerie, echoing cry he'd heard back in the police cells: a muffled wailing full of anger and frustration.

"We're almost there."

The air grew colder, but didn't feel any fresher. Andrew glanced up. A soft glow emanated from above and he realised he was looking up at darkened sky. The walls of the staircase gave way to a flat summit of the same smooth texture. He grasped the edge as he made his way up the last few steps to look around. A circle of lights illuminated the top of the spiral stairs, yet everywhere else remained cloaked in darkness.

"We're here," Arta announced.

"I can't see much," Andrew said.

"Forgive me. Give me a moment."

The Arcane moved away into the darkness. Then an illumination flared a few feet away and he appeared once more under its glow. A small glowing ball, no bigger than a fist, hovered above him. Arta took hold of it, reducing the light. "Making such things takes a certain amount of concentration and power," he explained. "Its use is something of a waste of resources, but it will illustrate the point far better than any explanation I might give you." He turned to Andrew. "Keep watching the light."

Without further preamble, he drew back his hand and threw the globe into the darkness. The spark pulsed on its passage into the gloom. Like a miniature sun, it brightened, casting incandescence in all directions.

They could see now that they were standing at the top of a watchtower, high above the ruined battlements of a castle, or a citadel of some sort. Far below lay the broken buildings of a forgotten medieval age. The tower was a corner turret of a much larger defence, but it had no matching siblings. Instead, the entire structure sat on a cliff, as though the sea had eroded its perimeter and consumed three quarters of the bastion. Beyond the walls were clouds: a blanket of gossamer white that besieged the stone defences like a soporific invader.

"It's beautiful," Ronald remarked.

"Yes, beautiful without meaning. Beautiful to the ignorant," Arta replied. "What you see is the desolation of our world."

The two men lapsed into silence, Ronald plainly insulted and Arta melancholy. The city below was a battered remnant of its former glory, but the sight didn't explain the constrained lives of the people he'd seen.

"Are we on an island?" Ronald asked.

"In a sense – the last island."

"Will the mist clear so we can see the waters?"

"That is no mist; there is no water beneath those clouds. It is the *veyl* that shrouds us. Once, in ancient times, it was invoked to hide our kingdom from its enemies, but the spell became too powerful to control. Now all we can do is resist its depredation. Below us is nothing. The cloud is merely a product of how we perceive it. This little kingdom fights an enemy it can't defeat: oblivion."

"So, there is no way out of here?"

"Not unless you save us. The only choice we have is to die in the darkness or cast ourselves from here into the clouds."

Andrew hadn't stopped watching the globe. Far below them, glimmers of light flashed in the gloom. He sensed something there, confirming Arta's words; a living, hungry presence, kept in check by a fading strength. There was little conscious thought behind it, only instinct, like a nerve. "And this is what your runes are for," he reasoned. "This is what they protect you against?"

"Now you understand."

The circle of lights around the stairs flared and the Keeper Arcane turned back towards them. "We must go; it is unsafe to stay here for too long."

Andrew followed him, with Ronald sulking behind. They began to climb down once more, their progress slower as they took greater care with the descent.

It was a tense and silent journey to begin with. Andrew sensed that neither Ronald or Arta would initiate further conversation. He considered leaving them to a frosty impasse but, in the end, his curiosity won out. "Have there been any other visits to this place?"

"Since the Harbinger, no," Arta replied. "Before this? We can't be sure. The arrival chamber hadn't been constructed, so there was no method to control such visits."

"That's why you built the chamber?"

"Yes, according to the Lady Harbinger's design. She assured us it would attract any potential visitor."

"Do you have anyone among your people called Amanda?"

Andrew could almost hear Arta frowning in the darkness. "A strange name. What does it mean?"

"I'm sorry?"

"I am named Arta because of the legacy of that name. The first 'Arta' was a great leader of our people. What does 'Amanda' signify?"

"Nothing ... that I know of."

"Is this 'Amanda' also a Harrower?"

Ronald snorted loudly. "No."

"Then it is a strange name," Arta said. "In all the pages of our writing, I have never seen it before."

"I have one more question for now," Andrew said.

"Just one?" Arta's chuckle held no warmth – his mood seemed to have been blighted by the visit to the top of the watchtower. "Usually I am not so fortunate."

Andrew decided to ignore this and pressed on: "You've talked about the Harbinger a lot. What was she like?"

Arta's reply was cold. "Another test, Harrower? Your recollection is surely better than our mouldy archives. You would be best talking with the Speaker Arcane. She is more versed in passing your trials."

Andrew bit his lip. "I'm sorry, but you said you were the Keeper. I need to know what is said about her."

In response, Arta sighed and stopped walking, almost causing Andrew to crash into him. "As you wish. I will answer this last question for today. Our records on the Harbinger are extensive. There are many descriptions of what she did, where she went, and the miracles that she performed. However, there is only one description of what she looked like. It says, '*Her eyes held a strange whiteness that mirrored the stark colour of her hair and her robes. In the darkened stone tunnels, she was the embodiment of a beacon of hope'."*

A sickening sensation gripped Andrew in the pit of his stomach and he heard Ronald barely containing a gasp behind him. "I see," he managed to answer at last. "Thank you."

Something Stable

"Ana's been here before us."

The blank stone echoed with the pacing footsteps of a frustrated man but, as he sat on one of the beds, Ronald Gibbs hardly heard the words. He was afraid.

Arta had led him and Andrew back to their room. He'd told them it was time to rest, though Ronald could see that the doctor wouldn't be sleeping – he was clearly agitated and excited by what they had learned. He was unsure what Andrew would do next, but he hoped he wouldn't keep pacing. He stared at the wall while Andrew thought aloud.

"Imagine: she promised these poor people salvation, then fucked off to another world, leaving them with an empty prophecy. She'd no intention of coming back for them. She left them here to die on this rock."

Ronald said nothing. Usually he didn't keep his mouth shut if he had the slightest thing to say, but now he stayed quiet. Fear kept him in check. He realised when this paralysing wave of emotion had first started: the moment Gideon had explained what had happened. *'Your death opened the portal,'* he'd said. A part of Ronald's mind refused to accept the words but, in his gut, he knew it was probably true. Despite this knowledge, he was desperate to cling on to what semblance of life he had left.

According to Gideon, he might cease to exist at any moment; his current state of being relied on an uncontrollable tic in his subconscious that would just stop if they visited the wrong world; any world that was too similar to home. The lack of control was terrifying; like a terminal cancer patient waiting for the end, except he had no peace to make with anyone.

"Are you even listening to me?"

He glanced up. Andrew was staring at him, his expression expectant. Ronald struggled to recall the last thing Pryde had said and failed, so instead opted for a general reply. "We can't be sure she's the Harbinger."

"Of course it was her! This stinks of her – using people ruthlessly for her own ends. She got them all lapping up this prophecy crap."

Ronald knew what the unspoken end of this comment was: *just like you*. He tried to focus, though he was feeling disorientated and dizzy. He was reminded of the conversation with Ana in his aunt's boarding house. "Gideon said someone came here recently. That's why he told us to go through the arch that led here."

Andrew's expression darkened. "What are you getting at?"

"These people said no-one's been here for more than seventy years, but what if something got through that their runes couldn't see?"

"What makes you think that?"

"I don't know. I feel weird. I can't get my head straight."

Andrew frowned. "I can't sense anything, for what it's worth."

"All the same, I can't shake the feeling that we're missing something."

Andrew stopped pacing and they both lapsed into a silence that Ronald was grateful for. Unfortunately, it lasted only a few moments.

"Do you really think it wasn't her?" Andrew asked.

Ronald sighed. "I didn't tell you earlier, but she talked about the Caer, just like Gideon. I think you've made a reasonable assumption, given the description."

"Makes you wonder how many worlds she's been to."

"Doesn't matter much now. We should be thinking about the things we can actually do something about."

"Meaning you changed your mind about doing the ritual?"

"Not in the slightest, but staying here doesn't offer much of a life – it's like being in prison."

Andrew smiled. "I can't see any other way out, unless you fancy taking a leap off the tower?"

Ronald glared at him and an awkward silence fell between them.

"I'm sorry," Andrew said. "That was uncalled for."

"You're making this harder. We need to know more about this place before we think about trying to escape."

"You want to leave them here?"

"Do you realise what taking them out of here would do?" Ronald asked. "According to Gideon, displacing five thousand people would bring your friend Candleswick down on top of us. You'd also be murdering millions of possible futures. Every one of them passing through would never diverge again."

"But look at their lives here!" Andrew said. "You said so yourself –

this is a miserable way to be."

"Better that than nothing at all."

"Existence or oblivion; that's a tricky one," Andrew mused. "Is it better to live a life of suffering or to never be born?"

Ronald could feel himself getting angry. "Listen, this isn't some academic debate with your class! These are real lives we're playing with – our lives! All of this scares the shit out of me."

"I'm just trying to get an idea of what you're basing your decisions on."

"It's all right for you: you're not dead."

"What do you mean?"

"You know what I mean. Every time we do this, I could cease to exist and there's absolutely nothing I could do about it!" His hands clenched into fists. "At least you have a chance of getting home. I've got nothing and no-one!"

Andrew gave him a pitying look. "Ronald—"

Ronald's temper snapped. "How dare you judge me!" he screamed. "I don't want your fucking sympathy!"

The harsh words echoed and faded, leaving behind an awkward quiet, and Ronald found himself staring at the floor. The situation wasn't Andrew's fault. If anything, he blamed himself for getting involved. "You don't understand, do you?" he mumbled, his eyes blurring as they filled with tears. "I have nothing. It's all so different. Everything."

Andrew sat down beside him. "I'm sorry. I guess change is easier when you have something familiar to keep hold of."

"But that's the point: I don't have anything left."

Andrew reached into his jacket and produced Ronald's bloodstained flick-knife. "Here," he said, handing it to him.

Ronald recoiled and dropped the weapon to the ground. "What do you think I want with that?" he demanded.

"I thought you might want it back."

Ronald stared at the blood-encrusted object lying before him. Andrew was right: he did want it back. At the same time though, it repulsed him. Flashes of remembrance sparked to life in his head and his chest went tight. "Take it away," he gasped.

Andrew picked up the knife, flipped the blade closed and tucked it back into his pocket. "I'm sorry."

"Don't be." Ronald's breathing suddenly became easier "You were right: I do want it back, but it's too tied up with everything."

"Your choice. I can keep hold of it till you're ready, if you want?"

"No," Ronald replied, and reached out his hand. "You're right again: it'll help."

Wordlessly, Andrew gave him back the knife. As he did so, his stomach growled. He smiled, stood up again and went to the door. "I'm starving."

"They said it was time to sleep."

"Still, surely all this homage and respect should get us fed."

Ronald realised he was hungry too. It was nice to have something else to think about. Andrew tried the door and they were both surprised to find it unlocked.

"I guess they're starting to trust us a little," Andrew said.

"Or they figured us out and they know we're not going anywhere."

Andrew opened the door. "Hello?" he called out.

"Yes, Harrower?" responded a male voice from the hall.

"We're quite hungry from our trip. We were wondering if there was any food?"

"Of course, Harrower."

Andrew left the door ajar and turned back to Ronald. "Seems we have us an assistant."

"More like a jailer. They don't want to lose us."

"All the same, he was happy to trot off and find us something."

Ronald shrugged. "I suppose you're right, although I don't fancy our chances of finding a way to escape."

Presently, they heard footsteps and the man returned. Andrew stepped back as he entered the room. Unlike the other people they had met, the attendant was dressed in plain brown trousers and a white shirt with a drawstring at the neck. It was his hair that drew Ronald's attention: braided locks and a decorated beard framed a weathered face. His huge hands carried two stone bowls that steamed in the cold air.

"What's your name?" he asked.

The man declined to meet his gaze. "Brodi, sirs," he answered, as though he were intimidated just to be in the same room. He placed the bowls on the ground and backed away, closing the door behind him.

Ronald stared after him. "He seemed almost frightened."

Andrew sat down and picked up one of the bowls. "I hope you're not fussy. This is pretty basic."

Ronald peered into the other bowl; it contained a thin watery liquid that supported several unappetising and unidentifiable lumps, floating in its midst, and a short wooden spoon. He had a momentary struggle to determine whether he was hungry enough to try the brew, but his empty stomach won out and he gulped down the contents, resolving to ignore any taste he might encounter in the process. He looked up to see Andrew fussily pawing at his bowl with the wooden cutlery.

"In my life, I learned to eat what I was given," Ronald said. "Might not be anything else for a while."

Andrew sighed. "I know."

"Besides, you were the one who said he wanted food."

"All right, don't rub it in."

*

After they finished eating, the room darkened and they decided to try get some sleep. Ronald couldn't fathom how the glowing torches worked. He'd noticed how each of the lights faded as they moved past them in the tunnels, but there didn't appear to be any wires or other electronics.

Now, he struggled to get comfortable on the stone bed. A woollen blanket was the only cover provided and he decided to lie on it to soften the unyielding rock.

It was too cold to take off any clothes, so he zipped up his battered parka and only took off his shoes, then lay on his back to stare at the ceiling. He realised then he was exausted. Events had taken their toll. He closed his eyes.

He let his mind drift as he tried to relax, remembering the corridors that Arta had used to lead them to the tower. That walk in the gloom, with the lights brightening and dimming around them, had seemed to go on forever. His thoughts took him back, struggling through endless passageways until, at last, he came to a door that hadn't been there before.

Andrew snored gently on the other side of the room. Ronald felt oddly remote and removed from both places, as though he were floating between them. He hesitated for a moment, hovering in the place between asleep and awake. Gideon's words about dreams came to mind: '*Dangerous things they are, and more dangerous once you know about them.*' He started to recall what Andrew had told him about his sleep adventures, but he was too tired to resist for long.

The dream took him. He walked further down the corridor and opened the door. The room beyond was the last thing he'd been expecting. The flickering light of a computer screen illuminated a messy bedroom that he recognised instantly as his own. Next to the cluttered desk, his CB radio wheezed, scanning the airwaves and randomly announcing transmissions from different sources. Everything was in the same place he remembered. There was even a balled-up piece of tissue paper on the table.

Yet, something had changed. He wasn't alone.

Sat in his swivel chair was an old man who turned to face Ronald as he entered the room, the monitor casting a menacing shadow across his weathered, ancient face.

"Who're you?" Ronald asked. "Why are you in my room?"

He was answered with a gap-toothed smile and a watery stare that offered no clues. The old man was clean-shaven and dressed in ragged scraps of cloth that seemed to be the remains of a ceremonial vestment. A thin metal band sat atop his bald head. *Like a crown.*

"Gideon?"

The old man shook his head and turned back to the monitor. Ronald followed his gaze. Tiny pixelated figures marched across the screen, from left to right and back again, carrying an assortment of boxes and other, stranger, objects. He stared at the old man, who seemed mesmerised.

"So, who are you, then?"

This time the man held a wizened finger to his lips and swivelled in the chair to face him. Ronald glanced down and bit back a gasp of revulsion. The flickering light revealed a mass of blood flowing freely down the man's legs, staining his emaciated knees and bony ankles, to pool on the carpet between his toes.

Transfixed, Ronald found he couldn't turn away. The old man exhibited no sign of pain from his hidden wounds. His ancient lips creased into another wide grin and, with wrinkled hands, he picked up an object from the desk and held it out for Gibbs to take.

It was a stone cup.

At that moment, Ronald realised he could move again. Without a second thought, he bolted back through the door, slamming it loudly behind him.

He woke up.

The chamber was completely dark now, the perfect silence of the night broken only by Andrew's snores and his own breathing. He was bathed in sweat, his heart pounding and he shivered as though he'd caught a fever.

The dream definitely meant something, but what? He couldn't guess. He regretted not taking the cup from the old man now; it would have been something tangible if he'd somehow woken up with it in his hand. He wondered briefly what was in it. *Unlikely I'll ever find out now.* But that didn't stop his mind from speculating.

A long time passed before he could sleep again.

Hunters and Hunted

Darkness. Lights gradually brighten to reveal a plain room with a long table at its centre. There are boxes lined up in pairs, all shapes and sizes, wrapped in different paper, like Christmas and birthday presents all at once.

I walk towards the largest and stop. I reach out.

"You can only take one," says a voice – a man's.

I look up. There is a figure standing in the corner of the room. He's wearing a porcelain mask and a silk shirt that glistens. He tilts his head to one side. "You must make a choice," he says.

"But why put all these presents here if I can choose only one?"

"Because that is the way of things; that is the game you were made to play." The man backs away and the shadows engulf him. "You must choose."

I open the largest box and it swallows me. I scream and …

*

Mike Underhill woke up to the sound of the phone ringing. He rolled over in his large, empty bed and fumbled for the receiver. It had been left out of the charger, so he had to get up, pick his way across the floor and find the handset in the spare room.

"Yes?"

"I need to talk to you before you get into the office." Emily's voice. She sounded pissed off. "Something's come up."

For you and me both, Mike thought, remembering last night's strange encounter between DI Davies and the dog. "Where?"

"The Gibbs place on Eleanor Avenue. You know where?"

"Sure."

"How soon can you be there?"

"Give me half an hour."

The phone went dead. He dropped it and went back to the bedroom. The alarm clock said six-fifteen. That meant he'd managed about five hours of sleep last night – *more than the night before.*

Mike dressed quickly in yesterday's clothes, leaving the tie. He didn't bother to shave or shower. He planned to meet Emily and come home afterwards. Davies would have to cut him some slack. He picked up his car keys and went straight out.

Twenty minutes later, he was outside the house. The street was cold and grey in the early morning, with a little mist in the air, but lights were on in the upstairs and he saw Emily's Mercedes parked across the road. He got out and went in. The front door was ajar and the living room had a discarded smell. He heard footsteps on the stairs.

"That you, Mike?" said Emily.

"Yeah."

She appeared in the hallway. Mike thought she looked as tired as he felt. Her eyes were hollowed with fatigue and her face bore the slack expression of someone who hadn't slept. She was holding a pile of papers in one latex-gloved hand and favoured him with her habitual scowl.

"How long you been here?" Mike asked.

"A couple of hours. Been a weird night all round."

"Anyone with you?"

"Two from Uniform for a while, but they got called off. Still waiting on forensics too."

"Why'd you call me?"

"Because Davies didn't answer and I wanted a chat."

"About what?"

Emily waved a hand around. "All this weirdness. You can't tell me last night was just another day in Durrington, surely?"

Mike chewed his lip, thinking about how much to say. He settled on, "No," then tried to change the subject. "You busy other than here?"

Emily shook her head. "Took me hours to get the paperwork straight; I was last in the office when the detail here got another shout. They waited till I arrived, then left."

Mike stared at her. "So, you decided to take a peek? That's illegal."

Emily flinched. "You think I don't know? Like I said, Davies didn't answer his phone. Worth it though. With everything going on, no-one'll remember afterwards."

"You found something then?"

"To start, I've got bills addressed to four different people, all recently opened. Could be a mistake, but I also picked up these;" She held up several small laminated cards; "Student IDs in each name, with the same photo. One of them says, 'Ronald Gibbs'."

"Pretty small-time for a murder suspect."

"Takes all sorts."

He nodded. "Anything else that can't wait?"

"Plenty. You might want to visit the rooms though."

He followed her up the darkened staircase. "No light?"

"Bulb's gone," Emily replied over her shoulder.

A flickering, blueish glow emanated from the room furthest along the landing. The door was ajar and he heard the familiar sound of a computer fan. "Study?"

"I guess you could call it that," Emily replied.

Mike went past her and pushed open the door, until it bumped against some unseen obstacle. The half-light of the monitor cast eerie shadows. The flickering was from a series of figures marching across the screen, carrying an assortment of boxes and other strange objects.

He glanced around the rest of the room. It was a mess. Dirty plates and crisp packets were strewn all over the desk and bookshelves packed the walls, making the little room even more claustrophobic. Discarded clothes lay everywhere and he noticed the door had caught itself on a pair of boxer shorts. After that, the swivel chair drew his attention. It was black, but stained with something dark. The same stuff was all over the floor. He recognised the scent.

Blood.

Mike knelt down. "This Gibbs' blood?"

"Don't know. If it was, there's no sign of a body or anything being moved. Whoever bled here got up dry and left no mess."

Mike glanced at the screen again. The marching procession was a screensaver. "You touch any of this?"

"No. Thought I'd leave it. We can dredge the hard drive. We'll probably get him on something from that; enough at least to threaten him with when we find him."

"Yeah." Mike nudged the mouse with his fingernail and the figures disappeared. A single window was open on a desktop covered in icons. *Some kind of chatroom*, he thought. Whoever had been sat here was logged on as 'ronhunter101'. All the users appeared to have logged out but, before they had, there was a page full of messages from different people.

Ronald, where are you?
Ronald, where are you?
Ronald, where are you? What's happening?

Mike checked the time and date of the responses. They went back to sometime midmorning of the previous day. Mike yawned and stepped away from the computer. "What time did you say Uniform chased away a couple of kids?"

"About an hour before lunchtime. I was sat out there."

Mike nodded and glanced around again. "Anything else in here?"

"CB radio, in the corner. I'm sure he'll have been scanning the police channels. But next door, well ... it's interesting."

Mike followed Emily into the second bedroom. This time she switched on the light. Mike blinked in reaction to the electric glare.

"See what I mean?" she said.

He shook his head and rubbed his face, trying to acclimatise himself, then looked around. It was a plain bedroom, with magnolia walls and a neatly made single bed. All around, brackets were fixed crudely into the plaster and on these were mounted a series of knives and swords. The weapons gleamed, casting reflections across the room. Mike was impressed – there must have been forty or fifty items, ranging from a simple cross-handled knife to an imposing Scottish claymore that hung suspended downward over the headboard.

"That's quite a collection," he said.

"A lot of people collect this stuff," Emily explained. "They're cheaply made. The steel shatters if you try to fight with them." She took one of the smaller swords off the wall. "People who collect these like to pretend. The edges are supposed to be blunted. But you may want to check the blade anyway."

Mike stepped forward and examined the claymore. There were marks along the steel; It had been sharpened carefully. Along the top, near the weapon's point, was a crusted red stain. "Is that more blood?" he asked.

"Yes. They're all like that." Emily gestured around the room. "Every fucking one."

Testing Times

"The first thing to do is get access to their books."

Ronald guessed it was the equivalent of morning in Corbenic. He'd been awake for about an hour, watching as the strange torch grew brighter. Andrew was up and putting his jacket back on, seemingly refreshed from his night's sleep. "What do you mean?" Ronald asked.

"Well, you were always talking to me before about how the book extracts were the key to making a rift work. We need to start reading their writings and that means a conversation with Arta."

"Listen, I wouldn't take anything I said before this as gospel," Ronald warned. "I'm not exactly sure what's right or wrong."

"All the same, we need to try. Remember what Gideon said: it's all about belief. We have that here in spades."

At that moment, there was a soft knock at the door. "Come in", Ronald said, and Brodi walked into the room. He nodded respectfully at Andrew and turned his attention to the large hourglass in the corner. Ronald saw it had run out. Brodi picked up the glass timer and flipped it over, before bending down and clearing away the stone bowls they had eaten from the previous night.

"Thank you," Andrew said. Brodi bowed before leaving the room, pulling the door closed behind him. "I want more time with him," he added wistfully, when the man had left. "It would be helpful to get another perspective on what's going on around here."

Ronald snorted. "He's so awed by us, it's unlikely you'll get much."

"All the same, can't hurt."

"I think they would prefer we just accepted the explanations they prepared for us."

"Exactly. All the more reason to try find out more about what's really going on." He walked over to the hourglass and scratched at its surface. "Any idea how we're supposed to read this?"

"None at all," Ronald confessed. "There are no markings."

"Makes me want to know what the time is all the more, even if it doesn't mean anything."

Ronald joined him and stared at the timer. Its shape reminded Gibbs of the stone cup the old man had tried to give him in his dream. For a moment, he considered keeping the story to himself, but the lack of any answers made concealment pointless. "Did you sleep?" he asked at last.

Andrew glanced at him. "Yes, actually. I was quite surprised. What about you?"

"Sort of," Ronald said. Andrew's face clouded with concern, so Ronald decided to tell him what he'd seen and how he had run away from the old man.

"Why did you do that?" Andrew asked.

"I was frightened, damn it! After what happened to you, can you blame me?"

Andrew shrugged. "Fair point. Are you hurt at all?"

"No. I didn't get injured in the dream, so I think I'm okay."

"I wish you'd taken the cup."

"Me too, but I can't go back."

"I wonder what it meant."

"We'll never know, so we'll just make do without it."

The conversation was interrupted by a firm knock at the door, which then opened to reveal the black robe of another Arcane who Ronald didn't recognise. "I am here to take you to the Council," he announced, seemingly ignorant, or indifferent to, the discussion he'd halted. "You must follow me."

"Must we?" Ronald said, bristling a little at the man's tone.

"It has been decided," the Arcane responded and strode from the room.

Gibbs looked at Andrew, who shrugged and followed the robed man out of the door. "What else do we have planned?" he said over his shoulder. "Judging by his mood, they're unlikely to let us set the agenda."

Ronald sighed and mustered as much patience as he could, then followed, closing the door behind him.

The man led them back into the stone tunnels, but any idea Ronald had of trying to remember their route was quickly lost; he chose passageways they hadn't been down before. Eventually, the corridor widened to reveal two large wooden doors that opened at the Arcane's rap of the knocker, allowing them all to enter.

At first, Ronald thought they had been taken back to the Arrival Chamber. This room was also circular and adorned with runes and bracketed torches. Yet, there was no stone arch at its centre. Instead, eleven seated, robed figures and one empty chair surrounded a huge round table. They had been brought before the Arcane Council.

As Ronald and Andrew entered the room, all the Arcanes rose from their chairs, bowing their heads towards the newcomers. Whether this was a gesture of obedience or respect, Ronald couldn't be sure.

"Be welcome, emissaries," said a female voice he recognised as belonging to Gwuina, the woman who had first greeted them. She removed her hood, confirming this with a smiling face. "We have asked you here to discuss the details of our imminent passage."

Ronald decided he'd kept quiet for long enough. "You didn't *ask*," he replied coldly. "Your friend told us we had to come."

Gwuina's smile slipped and she glanced around. "Well, we—"

"Gwuina speaks for us all," a strong male voice interrupted and a second of the robed figures cast back his hood, revealing a middle-aged man with sharp features and grey-brown hair. "But we each hold our own opinions at Council. You may not be familiar with our ways, but I caution that you do not dismiss them."

The man stepped out from his chair and walked towards Ronald. "I am Merhl, Lord Arcane of Corbenic and the Gedha. It is I who lead this council. Be welcome. Within these walls, all Arcanes shall speak their minds to you. It is an honour that you should be made part of our mind."

"Thank you," Andrew replied, offering his hand, which Merhl took hesitantly, as if he didn't know what to do with it. "I am Andrew. This is Ronald."

Merhl nodded. "The giving of names is also an honour." He let go of Andrew's hand and gestured to a stone bench that lay behind his seat on the far side of the room. "Please make yourselves comfortable and we will begin the deliberations."

Ronald followed Andrew to the place the Lord Arcane indicated and they both sat, prompting the Arcanes to return to their seats and remove their hoods. Their vantage point put them right behind Lord Merhl. On his left was Gwuina, with Arta some distance to the right.

"Forgive my interruption, Speaker," Lord Merhl said. "I felt a personal explanation was necessary, if presumptuous."

"I understand," Gwuina replied.

"Then we should begin," Merhl announced. "The matter in hand is one of the highest import."

"Indeed," said another Arcane further around the table.

Lord Merhl stood up and raised his voice: "Send for the chosen!" The sound of booted feet in the corridor indicated to Ronald that someone was attending to this request. He glanced at Andrew. "They have been picked according to your requirements, as laid out by the Harbinger."

Andrew's expression was a crafted mask of neutrality. "Of course."

"You will tell us if there is any unforeseen problem?"

"Absolutely."

Ronald bit his lip. He had no idea what all this meant and neither did Andrew. The situation was untenable; they couldn't continue to bluff without knowing what the Arcanes expected. "I have a question or two," he announced.

"Indeed," Lord Merhl said. "Please ask them."

"First, we must know what you recall of the Harbinger's visit."

"But the Keeper went through this with you, did he not?"

"He did," Ronald admitted, "but I need to see your documentation – one man's recollections are not sufficient."

"He is the Keeper," said another of the robed figures. "Surely this suffices?"

"No. I need to see your records."

Merhl turned back to the gathered counsellors. "What do you say, Arta?"

The Keeper shrugged. "I am happy to assist as always. The emissaries may visit the archives."

An angry murmur went around the table. "You realise what precedent this sets?" demanded a woman from its opposite side.

Arta smiled. "Would you wish to be the person who allowed our traditions to stand in the way of salvation?"

"The Keeper's answer is given," Lord Merhl said in a tone that brooked no argument. "The emissaries will be permitted to read our scripture."

At that moment, the wooden doors opened once more and Ronald looked up to see six men walk into the room. Each was stripped to the waist, their bare skin adorned with runic patterns like the ones on the walls of the chambers. Whorls of sky-blue paint swept across their chests and faces, attesting to hours of painstaking work.

"They have been prepared, just as the Harbinger requested," Lord Merhl explained, as the men filed into the room and formed a line near the doors. "Every man accepted his fate, as did those before them. They are prepared for your ritual."

"Thank you," Andrew replied.

Ronald could tell he was biting back what he really wanted to say.

Apparently, Lord Merhl was oblivious to his discomfort. "When will you be ready?"

"I'm sorry?"

"When will you begin the ritual?"

Andrew looked at Ronald again with pity. The doctor was having a hard time trying not to commit to anything that the two of them hadn't agreed, while also giving the Arcanes the impression that they understood what was required.

"A day, maybe two," Ronald answered, causing a rumble of approval. He held up a hand for quiet. "That is, providing we are given access to your archive and remain undisturbed until we are satisfied."

"These terms are acceptable to the Council," Gwuina said, her voice ringing with enthusiasm. "They are the same requests that the Harbinger made, and they too were approved."

Andrew smiled gratefully at Ronald and seemed to relax. "There is still much for us to do," he said.

"Indeed, and you will be extended every courtesy," Merhl replied. "After all, it is for the benefit of everyone."

A flicker of doubt crossed the Lord Arcane's face and, for a moment, Ronald thought the man might suspect how little they really knew. He turned away before Merhl could read his own expression. As he did so, he noticed a flickering distortion in front of him – it was like a symptom of the migraines he'd occasionally had in the past. He pushed his thumbs into his forehead – the last thing he needed right now was a headache. He stared at the stone wall, watching as the distortion rippled in the dim torch light, then saw it glide across to settle in front of the six tattooed men who had been led into the room before.

"Do they displease you in any way?" Merhl asked.

Ronald started, realising he was being addressed. He groped for a suitable answer. "I was wondering, why no women?" he asked at last.

"Another test?" Merhl replied, as a murmur of humour went around the table. Then his voice became serious. "We followed the Harbinger's directive to the letter: no woman should be selected. Mothers are far too important to the survival of our people. The act of sacrifice is not taken lightly. Each of these men is well aware that they will die to save their people."

Ronald felt sick, as though someone had reached inside him and whisked up the contents of his stomach. He heard Andrew cough to hide his own reaction. Lord Merhl's words confirmed what they suspected: it must have been Ana who had visited Corbenic before. She had to be the Harbinger. He could almost smell her hand in the ritualistic sacrifice of innocent victims to allow her to escape to the Caer.

"Well, if there are no more questions ..." said Andrew, leaving the sentence hanging for a response.

"I do not believe there are." Lord Merhl glanced back to the gathered council, giving them a final opportunity to speak. Their silence and the shaking of heads confirmed his statement. "We will leave you to your work."

Ronald left his seat and headed straight for the door. He had no wish to stay in the room any longer than was necessary maintaining the charade. He could feel Andrew close behind him.

"Please do inform us when you are ready to begin," Merhl said. "We will make the final preparations to gather the people."

"We'll let you know," replied Ronald as he reached the doors. He went through and walked quickly back to their chambers, his heart thumping in his chest.

The Source of Knowledge

Ronald felt seasick.

When he was younger, about twelve, his parents had taken him to France. The short ferry trip rapidly turned into an unmitigated disaster as the sea conditions grew worse. All he remembered was spending his time throwing up over the side or being told to stare at the horizon. He spent the entire week in Normandy dreading the voyage home. He could still remember his father's disapproving expression each time his stomach gave way; things had never been the same between them afterwards.

One thing made the trip bearable. He found a flick-knife in a small shop near the place where they stayed. They were illegal in Britain, so he smuggled it home in his luggage, almost hoping that he would be caught, just to see the look on his dad's face. But no-one had stopped him. After that, he hid the knife in a shoebox for years, until he was old enough to move into his own home.

He slipped a hand into his pocket now and touched the weapon. The nausea didn't completely disappear, but he felt better all the same.

He sat at a long rectangular stone table surrounded by shelf upon shelf of books. Andrew was busily thumbing through tattered volumes and had placed several more on the table for them to study.

"Seventy-seven years, they said. Apparently, they re-scribe things quite often, as the parchment doesn't keep. I wonder where they get it from?"

"What do you mean?" Ronald managed to ask.

"Well, to produce any kind of paper, you need trees or plants. You seen anything growing around here?"

The question reminded Ronald of the thin soup they had been given to eat the night before, which didn't help with his queasiness. His stomach threatened to rebel and he clenched his teeth to suppress it. "You're right," he chewed out the words. "I suppose not." He glanced briefly at one of the books Andrew had left open. The writing was unfamiliar, though some of the letters were like the English alphabet, or at least the older Greek equivalents. "You can read this?"

Andrew nodded. "Oddly, yes. Seemed like gibberish at first but, when I tried, it just made sense."

"So, this isn't a language?"

"It's a language all right, but not one I recognise. It's sort of *shaped* like English or French, but I'm not entirely sure how I'm reading it."

Ronald sighed and pushed the book away; he'd never been able to read whilst feeling ill. "You found anything?"

A self-satisfied smile appeared on Andrew's face. "A few references, but Arta said they kept a full record entry for each of the days of the Harbinger's visit. If we can find that, we can use it to make sure we do everything right."

"Great," Ronald replied weakly. Not for the first time, he wished Corbenic had more wooden chairs. The only ones he'd seen were those in the council chamber. All the other furniture seemed to be benches sculpted out of stone.

Once they had left the Council, they had been escorted directly to the archives and Andrew had launched into a quest to find the right records. Ronald had started feeling queasy then and it had only gotten worse since. He paced the floor, trying to keep his mind off being sick.

"Don't you want to understand anything about these people?" Andrew asked.

Ronald scowled. "Why would I? Bad enough they're emotionally blackmailing us."

"I just thought—"

"Thought what?"

"Well, after what Gideon said about you not being able to go back home, you might learn all you can and get to know them."

Ronald turned. Andrew was regarding him carefully from a vantage point near the bookcase on the other side of the room. "Listen," Ronald said, "just because we're going through the motions of helping, doesn't mean anything's decided."

"But I assumed—"

"What did you assume?"

"Well, that you'd agree to us aiding them so we can get out of here. From what you said to the Council, I guessed you'd chosen the latter."

"You thought I'd been persuaded by you?" Ronald shook his head. "No, not yet." He grimaced as another spasm gripped his guts.

"Besides, I'm not even sure I'm up to it."

"You don't look well," Andrew confirmed, compounding the obvious.

"I'm surprised you don't feel the same way. You do realise what they were saying?"

"Which bit?"

"You know fucking well which bit: they want us to kill those six men as part of the ritual."

Andrew sighed. "Yes."

"No wonder I'm ill. Poor bastards."

Andrew glared at him. "If you're trying to imply I don't care, you're wrong – I do. That's why we must find these records."

"Why?"

"Because you needed those extracts last time and the only reading matter these people have is here. If we're going to learn about any kind of power like that, it must be here."

Ronald frowned. "If they don't place much of a stock in writing, it may not work that way."

"What do you mean?"

"They don't do speculation – they do archives, which means they probably don't imagine things the way we do. The way they guard their runes, I doubt these books contain much about power."

It was Andrew's turn to frown. "All the same, the meeting will be over soon and Arta will be back. We need to find out what happened and how Ana got out."

"Face it, you know what they'll say: she killed me to get out of Durrington. I expect she did that here too; sacrificed some poor kid to make a portal."

"That doesn't mean we will, though," Andrew argued. "We need their belief. We must learn what she told them, then we can work out what will convince them not to sacrifice those people."

Ronald didn't answer. His stomach had started to cramp again and he doubled over on the stone bench, fighting a series of retches and heaves.

"You okay?" Andrew asked.

"I still haven't shaken off all that stuff from this morning. Did you get like this after you had that dream?"

"No, I was fine."

Ronald glanced around the room and became aware of the flickering distortion again. It seemed to be hovering over the bookshelves to his right. He blinked several times, but the shape refused to disappear, raising his suspicions once more. "I feel awful."

Andrew shrugged. "The soup?"

Ronald focused on the hazy shape. It wandered lazily across the room towards him. "I don't think so." It was almost in arm's reach. "I think it's something else."

He made a quick choice and snapped out his right hand. Surprisingly, his fingers clutched at something solid and he balled them into a fist as it tried to pull away. "What the—" Ronald was nearly yanked off his feet, but he kept a tight grip. Whatever he had a hold of felt like silk cloth, except that it was in some way less substantial. He closed his left hand over his right, pulling on the material as though it were a rope. "No, you don't," he yelled. "I've got you now!"

"Very well," said a cultured voice. "Indeed, you do – your eyesight is a little better than I gave you credit for."

With that, the air shimmered and a man appeared in the room.

Andrew dropped a book in astonishment. Ronald could see now that he was holding onto the stranger's left wrist. "Who the hell are you?" he demanded, as his stomach did cartwheels.

"Not your precious 'Gideon', that's for sure," the man replied. He was thin and bald, with a neatly trimmed goatee, and dressed in a tabard and knee-high boots over grey leggings. "You people always manage to impress and disappoint at the same time."

"Tell me who you are," Ronald hissed, twisting the man's arm to an angle designed to cause pain. "And why you're spying on us!"

The man regarded him with a cool stare. "Is that supposed to hurt?" I try so hard to get the three-dimensional biology accurate."

Startled despite himself, Ronald let go. The stranger placed his hands behind his back.

"You mean you aren't human?" Andrew said.

"Well done!" the man said. "You people! All the possible things you could learn from me and all you want is to give me a label and to state the obvious."

"You know us?" Andrew answered coldly.

The man laughed. "Yes, of course. I've been following you for some time."

"What do you want?"

"Aha – basic, but a little more interesting." The man clapped his hands. "At least that one has some legs. Essentially, I want what you want, for the moment."

"And what do you think that is?"

"To get out of here. To do that, you need to understand what you're dealing with."

Ronald ground his teeth, willing his stomach ache to subside. To make matters worse, his head wouldn't stop spinning. He got up from the bench and lurched away to the other side of the room. "What do we call you?" he managed to ask.

The man sighed. "Green will do." He tugged at his tabard and glanced around the room. "It's fitting. This place can trap you to fit its own image."

"They'll be back soon," Ronald warned.

Green shrugged. "Well, you chose to reveal me and force this little discussion. Any issue of us being discovered is down to you."

"I don't like being spied on."

"What makes you think I was spying? That's only one way of looking at it."

"We're wasting time," Andrew said. "Can you help us?"

Green smiled. "Yes, I can. We both desire the same outcome – we want out of here and, without you, I can't manage that."

Ronald decided it was best to set aside the questions this provoked for the moment. "We need to know what you can do and what you want in return."

Green stared at him and laughed, his eyes wide and staring, like a madman. "I just need you to get the rift open and I'll be on my way. I doubt you have anything else that would interest me."

"And what help do you think we need in doing that?"

"You forget, I heard most of your talk and have been in on your little meetings," Green countered. "You're both feeling squeamish about human sacrifice, which is understandable, given your limitations …"

Ronald couldn't help himself this time. "Limitations?"

"Yes, the boundaries of your form – you know, life, death." Green waved a hand. "You don't want to end up like your Spider." He smiled knowingly. "Yes, I know about her as well."

Ronald was struggling more than ever to hold on to the contents of his stomach. "How can you help us then?" he asked through gritted teeth.

"By giving you what you should have accepted before," Green said and snapped his fingers. Out of nowhere, the stone cup from Ronald's dream appeared in his right hand. "You have more friends than you realise," he said, wagging a finger at them. "And you really should have taken this the first time."

"What does it do?" Andrew asked.

"Objects from different places gain a resonance when they are used. It makes them all the more useful. You already have one item like this – your knife, which you were right to keep a hold of. This one has another use."

"And what's that?"

"Mix the essences of realities in here, drink the result and you will attain the power to force open your rift. It's a catalyst. It should be enough to make the people here believe strongly enough in your ritual, without the need for a sacrifice."

Ronald eyed him. "If it's that easy, why don't you do it?"

"Because this place doesn't work the same way for me. I take it that when you arrived you both appeared in the arrival chamber?"

"We did."

"And the lights flared?"

"Yep."

"Of course. Your friend The Spider helped the Arcanes' construct that room. The spell they created is a warning and a beacon for any traveller. The lights, as you probably worked out, are reactive to the presence of living creatures."

"But they don't work on you," Ronald finished.

Green smiled. "Much better. There's hope for you yet."

"Why not?"

"Because I'm not like you. That's why we need each other."

"Suppose we do this …" Andrew interjected, "… Suppose we take your cup and perform some ritual that opens the portal; what do we do then?"

Green laughed. "You step straight through – you'll have succeeded and you won't need to worry about me."

"It doesn't solve our problems though," Andrew replied. "If we go back to the woods, she'll find us."

"Or Candleswick will catch up with us, especially if we take nearly five thousand people through," Ronald added.

Green frowned. "Who's Candleswick?"

"Gideon told us he's like an antibody – part of the natural order trying to right itself and stop people like us jumping between worlds."

Green almost doubled over laughing. Finally, he stopped and wiped tears from his eyes. "When your friend Columbus discovered the world was round, or when Galileo realised that your planets revolved around the sun, do you think everyone believed them?"

Ronald frowned. "What do you mean?"

"That you humans always see yourselves as the centre of everything and you can't accept just how little you know and understand." He snorted. "Do you actually think the universe cares what you do? Just because you perceive the world in three dimensions and have a vague understanding of a fourth, doesn't mean that's how it is for everyone else."

"Look," Andrew said, sounding angry, "I don't care what you think; if we leave here, either we'll be walking right into *her*, or *he'll* be down on top of us."

"Then don't go back to the same place."

"We must; it's the only way to find somewhere for these people to go," said Ronald.

Green sighed. "Is there any reason why you don't want to just go back to a time before she arrived?"

"You mean we can do that?" Andrew asked.

"You need to stop thinking of limitations and start considering possibilities!" Green tapped the side of his bald head. "It's all up here. You must overcome your humanity and think about what could be possible, based on knowing nothing."

"Are you saying Gideon was wrong?" Andrew asked.

"I'm saying your friend was trying to advise you by projecting his own tired and paranoid perception. He's human, like you, but he holds onto his own peculiar set of inhibitions. They limit him, just like all travellers. It is time you judged for yourself."

Ronald thought about this last point carefully. "So, we can travel to any time we like?"

Green glanced at him. "What is time? I mean, really, what do you think it is? Human beings can make things wider, taller and longer. Is there any reason you can't control the 'when' state, or at least appreciate someone who can?"

"It's a lot to take in. So, we could transport everyone to another reality in the past, before The Spider learned of us," Andrew reasoned. "But what we're talking about is a previous time in her life, which she's lived in many worlds. It's a lot to take in. I can't make sense of it."

Green chuckled. "Then I'm afraid you'll find yourselves on a sharp learning curve from here. You must work out what you want and be prepared for what it might cost you."

Ronald glanced back towards the open archive chamber door; he could hear faint footsteps in the stone tunnel. It had to be Arta. "You had better go," he warned Green.

Green nodded. "We'll talk again. I'll find you." He pointed to the top shelf of the bookcase he'd been searching. "The book you're looking for is up there, fourth from the left."

Ronald glanced up. "How the fuck did you—"

Yet, when he turned back, the man was gone.

Making a Choice

"Can I trust you?"

Nine-thirty on a Wednesday morning and the Albany café was quiet. Mike stared at Emily across the table, two mugs of coffee between them. After finishing up at Eleanor Avenue, they'd both phoned in sick, leaving messages on DI Davies' answerphone.

"Of course you can; we're the police."

"I don't mean like that Emily. I'll be blunt: you're a brown-noser with an eye for making sergeant as fast as you can. The first and only step I've seen you take out of line was today's business in Gibbs' house."

Emily glared at him. "You any idea what being a woman in CID is like?"

Mike shook his head. "No, I don't, and I'm sure you've got your reasons for everything but, right now, I must know whether I can rely on you, above and beyond your self-interest."

"I called you out to an illegal search, which I performed. You could shop me."

"Yes, that's why we're here. I think I trust you, but you need to say it."

Emily shrugged, clearly still irritated. "All right, you can trust me. I'll keep your shit quiet so long as you're silent about mine. If we don't start sharing some of this weirdness, it'll eat us up."

Mike nodded. "Okay then." He told her what happened at Dene Street and about the strange car ride with Davies. He described the dog and the way their boss had behaved. "I couldn't hear what he said but, when he came back, he called off the search and sent me home."

"You think the dog spoke to him?"

"I think something changed his mind. I don't know what."

Emily sighed. She picked up the mug in front of her and took a sip of the tea, grimacing as she did so. "Been feeling ill all morning. I used to love these greasy spoon places when I was a kid. Not sure I have the taste for them anymore."

Mike leaned forward in his chair. "Davies made it pretty clear I was to keep my mouth shut, but all I can think about is those three missing kids."

"You think this is tied up with Gibbs and Pryde?"

"No idea. You're the one who pointed out how the town seems to be going nuts."

"Yeah." Emily stared at her tea. "What do we do?"

Mike chewed his lip. "There's plainly more going on than we're being told. We need to pick the battles we actually understand and win them."

*

"*Record of the after time – Entry two hundred and ninety-four after the burning.*

Since she joined us, it is as though hope has re-materialised from the depths of our darkness and despair.

Her appearance on After Day in the council chamber caused much consternation. At first there was strife among the Arcanes. The sacred rules were broken and violence came in opposition to her presence. Yet she quickly defeated all argument with a silver voice and magic unknown to us; no symbols did she draw or cast, but her power was assured and complete. Lord Myrhl was overmatched and the others were cowed into submission by her art and words.

She promised us deliverance; our resistance was calmed by her simple question: 'Don't you want to learn how I got here?' Immediately, she understood that we are a lore-wise people; her asking reached to the heart of our Council's quest."

"Sounds like her, doesn't it? And did you get the name of the council leader, Lord *Myrhl* – very similar to *Merhl* – the current Lord Arcane? Names must be hereditary."

Ronald glanced up from the dusty tome Andrew had asked him to read. They had returned to the arrival chamber, having left the archive room after Andrew had persuaded Arta to let them take some of the books with them. "Do I need to get through all of this?" Ronald asked. "Because, if I do, we'll be here at least a week."

"No, you're right. Once you've got to the bit about going through the opening, skip ahead – I've marked the pages."

"Does Arta know that?"

"No, and I'm not planning to tell him."

Ronald sat on the floor and read the sections he'd been told to. He sighed as he flipped through the tome. This kind of research used to excite him, but he couldn't muster any enthusiasm for it now. All he could think of was the ritual they would have to perform. Another ritual; something he was dreading.

"*'She walked among us for a long time, recorded in the old annals as three-score days. Her interest was predominantly in the records and the magic that defends Corbenic.*

The Arcanes were reticent at first but, once she passed their test for the gifted, they were more willing to share their knowledge. Yet, still the majority opposed her curiosity and her enquiries were treated with disdain.'"

"Doesn't sound like they got on," Ronald remarked.

"No. I guess that's why some of them weren't too pleased about us poking around the archives. They don't know that we don't like her either."

"They must think they have something to hide."

"*'The day she announced the intention of her visit – to provide us with a way of escaping the veyl – there was much rejoicing. Her hesitation, it seemed, was a test to judge our worth.'*"

"Bitch."

"Yes, she certainly had them fooled."

"*'She gathered up the Arcanes and bid them join her in a meeting in the Council Chamber. Some, like Mord, refused, calling her presumptuous and arrogant, but curiosity afflicted most enough to attend. Once there, she produced a young boy named Gauw and, in front of their eyes, she made him drink a potion. Suddenly he disappeared and was never to be seen again.'*"

"Right there; do you see it?" Andrew said.

"What?"

"What it says: she made the boy disappear. See?"

"Yeah. So what?"

Ronald could almost hear Andrew's frustration. "Now tell me what isn't mentioned."

Suppressing irritation, Ronald read the passage again aloud: "*'Once there, she produced a young boy named Gauw and, in front of their eyes, she made him drink a potion. Suddenly, he disappeared and was never to be seen again.'*" Then it hit him: "No death."

"Exactly. She didn't kill anyone," Andrew replied and slapped the table. Ronald glanced up to see him smiling triumphantly. "We can do this!"

"Maybe they missed out a passage," Ronald said, unconvinced. "Perhaps the boy died."

"If he did, we're calling their bluff."

Ronald thought about this. "If it's a lie and they know, they'll kill us."

Andrew sighed. "Do we have any other choice? If their ancestors covered up what happened, they probably don't understand the truth, or we'd already be dead. If she genuinely transported the child out without sacrificing someone, we can do the same."

Ronald frowned and flipped through more of the tattered pages. "How did she leave?"

"There's a long section towards the end. Apparently, she told them the ritual had to be more elaborate to work on her and that they had to agree to her needs or she wouldn't send someone back for them. In the ceremony, she made them build the arch, etch these runes everywhere and sacrifice a young male."

"Sounds familiar."

"Yes, disturbingly so."

Ronald put the book down and stood up. He walked over to one of the walls and traced the path of the writings idly with his finger. "You're still trying to talk me into this," he said softly.

"I thought Green had convinced you."

"He certainly said a lot of interesting things, but it isn't his skin on the line."

The words echoed around the chamber and faded away. Both men fell into contemplative silence. Ronald studied the runes carefully; they blended the angular lines of Norse symbols with ornate Celtic whorls and patterns. He fished into his pocket, pulled out his flick-knife, flipping the blade open. He was about to press the sharpened edge to the sculpted groove when a hand gripped his wrist.

"What's that?" Andrew hissed in his ear. He wouldn't let go, and was pointing with his free hand at the knife. A strand of white hair was caught in its hinge.

Ronald reached out and pinched it between his fingers. "Must be one of hers."

"We can use it."

"For what?"

"Remember what Green said – objects from different places gain a resonance when they are used – take it and put it in the cup."

Ronald considered this for a moment, then made a decision and plucked it loose, before carrying it to where he'd placed the stone cup on the dais, next to the book they had borrowed from Arta. "I guess it can't hurt."

Andrew chuckled. "You're doing a good job for a man who isn't convinced."

"Let's just say I'm hedging my bets."

Andrew shrugged. "Some academics believe philosophy is about understanding how to die and, by accepting the inevitable, becoming free."

"That's comforting," Ronald said sarcastically.

"Discussing death is one of the biggest taboos of our society; we do everything we can to avoid it, because we don't understand what it is and we can't escape it."

"The difference is, I don't get a choice. I'm dead and the risk you're asking me to take puts everything I have left on the line."

Andrew nodded. "Is it liberating?"

"What do you mean?"

"Well, you've an advantage over the rest of us. You get what's at stake and what you stand to gain or lose. One of the things that defines mankind is its need to understand its own circumstances. Your perspective is unique on that because you can actually measure the outcomes."

"That doesn't help. If we're talking about some lab rat experiment maybe I could think of it like an academic, but we're taking about what's left of my life."

"No," Andrew countered. "If Green's right and the mind is what makes most of the rules here, then we aren't. You're second-guessing yourself."

"Am I interrupting?" said a familiar voice. Both men looked up to see that Arta had entered the chamber.

"A bit," Ronald said. "We did say we didn't want to be disturbed."

"I will not stay long," Arta replied. "The Council asked for an update on your progress, and we must renew the runes."

"We're doing fine," Andrew answered. "We're discussing your records."

Arta glanced at the book on the floor. "Our archives are a precious treasure. The plants we used for making paper now die when we try to grow them. These may be the last copies of these documents. Please take care with them."

"History is only of use when we can learn from it," Andrew said. "Don't worry – in my own place, I am a keeper of records too. I will return this as soon as we are ready, in good condition."

"Very well." Arta turned his attention to the walls. "If you will both wait a moment, I will replenish the chamber's magic."

"What are you going to do?" Ronald asked.

"A simple rote to renew the energies that are already there. The initial casting would require the presence of all of the Arcanes. It was done soon after the Harbinger's departure – our forebears carefully retraced the symbols from her ritual, etching and empowering them in the rock. Ever since, we renew them regularly and have expanded much of the work according to her instructions. We maintain it so that it will function as you wish."

"Please, go ahead," Andrew said.

Arta strode over to the wall and placed his hands on the wall. The lamplight dimmed. Lines of light spread out from his palms, tracing along the etched symbols and illuminating the magical writing in all its intricate beauty. Then he let his arms drop. The air crackled with energy, the lamps brightened and the rune-light gradually faded away. "It is done," he announced in a tired voice. "Hopefully for the last time – provided you are successful."

"Thank you," Andrew said in a quiet voice.

"Yeah, thanks," Ronald echoed.

The Arcane removed his hood and smiled briefly at them both. "I will trouble you no more. An attendant will remain outside of the chamber, should you need anything."

Andrew forestalled him: "One more thing, Arta."

"Yes?"

"I read the passages about the Harbinger's visit. The boy – Gauw – did you ever see him again?"

"There is no mention of him," Arta replied. "His family grieved for his passing, as did we all. He was gifted with the magic as well – he would have joined the Council when he was old enough."

Ronald frowned. "But you must be happy for him; he got to leave here."

"Indeed, but it was not a life that his people could ever share."

Ronald wasn't satisfied with this and was about to press further, when he started to feel sick again. The symptoms were painfully familiar and he glanced pointedly at Andrew, who took the hint.

"I see," Andrew said. "Thank you again."

The Arcane bowed in response, turned and left the chamber.

When he was gone, Andrew shut the double doors behind him. "Right, we had best get started."

Once more, the air tensed and Green appeared on the dais next to the stone arch. "Apologies for the delay. I thought it better to wait until he left."

"No problem," Andrew replied. "Good choice."

Ronald clenched his teeth against the cramps in his stomach. "You knew him, didn't you?"

Green frowned. "Who?"

"Don't play games – the boy, Gauw – you knew him."

"Why do you think that?"

"In the archive, they said he 'drank a potion'. It was from the cup you gave us. That's how you got it."

Green shrugged. "Well now! Very perceptive of you. All right; yes, I met him."

"So that means you've managed to leave here before."

Green sighed. "I never said I had been trapped here all along; only that you were my only way out now. The cup is partially made of stone from here and partially from somewhere else. That is why it will help you: resonance, as we discussed before."

"You're evading the point." Ronald was angry. "Why were you here?"

"I had my reasons."

"And where were you just now?" he pressed. "I can't imagine you have many other friends to visit."

"That's my business," Green replied defensively.

"Not if you want to get out of here, it isn't," Ronald shot back. He felt Andrew's hand on his shoulder and tensed even further, sensing that the doctor might be trying to let Green off the hook, but Andrew surprised him.

"You need to tell us," he said simply.

Green sighed again and ran his fingers through his hair. "I was looking for something that your associate Ana took from me. When she came here, I followed her, and helped her, much like I am helping you. When she left, she stole an item of mine."

Ronald scowled. "You helped her kill those people!"

"I didn't ask for your good opinion. I'm not trying to be your friend."

"No, but you *do* want our help," Andrew retorted, "and getting it just got a lot harder."

Surprised by the support, Ronald glared at Green. "What did she take from you?" he asked.

Despite not being human, Green at least had the decency to approximate discomfort. "I can't say."

"Then we won't help you," Ronald said.

The man's eyes bored into him. "Your aid will get me out of here swiftly, but if you choose to withhold it, eventually, someone else will come. I can wait – my people live far longer than yours do.

"We're not going anywhere either."

Green smiled. "You say that, but if you don't give these people what they want, then your fate is sealed. They will kill you."

Ronald flinched. "All right; I'll do it. I'll perform the ritual, but not for you; for them and for us. If you gain from that, I can't prevent it."

Green nodded and a thin smile crossed his face. "Fine." He stuck out his hand. "Agreed."

Ronald ignored the gesture and turned away.

*

By mid-afternoon, Linda Frakes didn't know what to do with herself. She sat on the sofa, but couldn't stay there. In the last hour, every five minutes or so, she'd got up and found something else to clean or organise. Three wine glasses had already ended up in pieces. One of the shards of glass had sliced her right index finger, which now sported a plaster.

She'd slept a little, but her dreams had been terrible. Being awake wasn't much better. She'd put on makeup to hide the drawn, tired look around her eyes, but staring at herself in the mirror led to more soul-searching and, when that was done, she felt ready to get out of the house, but there was nowhere to go.

Oh George, why did you—

The doorbell went, its sing-song tone cutting through her grief. She went into the hall and stared at the shape on the other side of the distorted glass. It seemed familiar, so she opened the door. Detective Inspector Davies stood there.

He gave her a nervous smile. "Sorry I couldn't drop by earlier. It's been quite an evening."

"Do you need me to come to the station?"

"We're a little busy there, so I thought it'd be better if I came to you, if that's all right?" When Linda nodded, he added, "Can I come in then?"

"Of course. Sorry."

They went through into the living room. Davies hesitated for a moment, but then made for the armchair by the window. As he sat, he glanced at the police tape on the street where George's car had been. "Can't be nice having that out there as a reminder."

"I—I didn't think about it." Linda returned to her place on the sofa.

"Oh ... well, sorry for bringing it up."

Davies produced a notepad and a pen, setting them on the arm of the chair. He leaned forward. "Mrs Frakes, you may have seen on the news, we had something of a difficult time last night."

"I don't watch television much, but I heard what you and your colleagues were saying when you got here."

"Yes, a lot of things happened." Davies chewed his lip and his gaze roamed the room. "Are you religious, Mrs Frakes?"

Linda stared at him. "I'm sorry, what does that have to do with George?"

"I'm trying to get an idea of his motive. I'm afraid conversations like this are never easy."

Linda sighed. "I guess I didn't expect a question like that. I suppose I'm like most people; Church of England but, well ... I believe there's something out there. Whether it looks like what's in the Bible ..." She shrugged. "George was a choir boy when he was younger. His parents brought him up going to service every Sunday."

"Was he C-of-E too?"

"Yes."

"I grew up near here, just out of town," Davies said. "My parents took me to church too, although their reasons were different, I think.

Did George carry on going?"

"He went early on Sundays. I'd go with him at Easter, in the day, and for midnight mass at Christmas."

Davies nodded. "Seems strange that a man with faith would give up like he did. Forgive me for asking, but were there any problems between you?"

"Some. He didn't like me speaking to Andrew."

"This recent business can't have helped then."

"No, it didn't, but I ..." Linda swallowed and took a breath, her gaze straying to the scene outside the window. "I didn't think he felt like this."

Davies caught the look. "Do you need to be anywhere this afternoon?"

"What? Err, no, I don't think so."

"Then let's go for a drive; get you away from all this for a few hours." Davies stood up. "We could both do with a break and sitting here won't help you."

Linda stared at him. Her first instinct was to say no. *My husband just died and now a stranger's asking me to go somewhere with him.* But she realised he was right. *What else am I going to do? Sit here and blame myself, that's what.* "I think I'd like that," she replied. "I'll get my coat."

*

Andrew was worried. He'd lost track of time again, but he was sure they had been reading for hours. He slumped against the wall of the arrival chamber and stared intently at Ronald.

Green had been true to his word, advising them constantly on what would work in the ritual and what wouldn't. He had questioned Ronald painstakingly about their previous attempt and expanded on his ideas. At his instruction, candles now lined the floor around the arch, trailing across the stone to the great doors. Andrew carefully cleaned portions of the etchings and requested cloths to cover some of the others. In places, he'd been forced to dig out dirt and grime with his fingers, clearing away centuries of filth and disuse. "Why did they let it get like this?"

"Because these weren't the symbols they were instructed to maintain," Green explained. "Your friend The Spider never intended for them to discover a way out for themselves."

Andrew sat staring tiredly at Ronald. He had to be just as exhausted, but continued arranging the room and mumbling the phrases he had been told to memorise long after Andrew had stopped. Now he sprawled on the dais, scraps of paper arranged all around him, scribbling notes incessantly with a broken pencil.

"We must have been at this all day," Andrew said.

Ronald stared up at him. His pale complexion, lank, straggly hair and watery blue eyes, belied any confidence Andrew may have gleaned from his newfound resolve. "Well, no-one else is going to do it," he said.

Andrew nodded. "I know. I was just wondering how you were holding up."

"I'm fine. Why wouldn't I be?"

Andrew shrugged. "No reason. It's just that I, for one, am tired."

Ronald turned back to his work, but Andrew continued to stare at him. The terse conversation didn't convince him. Ronald wouldn't be able to cope with the strain of the ritual unless he found a way to calm down.

"This is all I have left from my old life," Ronald said finally. "Pieces of paper, vouchers, receipts, tickets, loyalty cards; I guess they mean nothing now."

"A Durrington bus pass might be valid in lots of places."

"Hardly likely to be anywhere we go."

"Depends who you believe: Gideon or Green."

"Or something in between." He smiled weakly.

Green returned at intervals, predominantly to test Ronald on the words and symbols he'd taught him. For some reason, the obscure intonations refused to stay in Andrew's mind each time he heard them, but Ronald seemed to grasp them readily enough.

"How do you do that?" he asked Ronald.

"Do what?"

"Remember everything."

"I don't know; just sticks."

When Andrew spoke to Green about this, Green had laughed. "Haven't you worked that out yet? You two are chalk and cheese. This ritual is Ronald's part of the task. Yours is to guide them once you step through."

"Then what do you need to teach me?" Andrew asked.

"Nothing," Green had replied. "You'll either manage it, or you won't."

Andrew was surprised, but Green hadn't elaborated and went soon after, leaving Andrew to think about it on his own.

As he cleaned the runes, Andrew cast his mind back to their last journey, trying to work out what he'd done. It seemed so long ago. Yet he couldn't think of anything he could do beforehand to prepare for his task.

"You all right?" This time, Ronald was eyeing him from his hunched position on the dais.

"Yes, I'm fine," Andrew replied, smiling broadly despite his misgivings.

"I think we're done. I'm all for sleeping in here."

"Makes little difference in terms of comfort."

Ronald chuckled. "You hungry?"

"Enough for another bowl of wallpaper paste? I think so."

Ronald got up and walked to the wooden doors. A quick word sent the warden scurrying away. "I don't think there's a menu. Must be hell to eat such crap all your life."

"One of the reasons why helping them is the right thing to do."

"Yeah, I guess."

They sat quietly for several minutes before Andrew decided to talk about what was on his mind. "You know he's going to abandon us?"

Ronald frowned. "What do you mean?"

"Green. After you transport us out, we're on our own. That's why he's spending so much time with you and none with me."

Ronald was amused by this. "You sound jealous."

Andrew smiled humourlessly. "Hardly. I'm more concerned about avoiding Candleswick once we pass through. We've done this once, but this is on a different scale. It's a lot to take in."

"You're getting cold feet."

"No, nothing like that. I guess I'm worried about us trying it though."

"The whole thing's fucked up," Ronald replied. "There's no comfort zone. I'm surprised it's taken you this long to realise it. No-one has all the answers – even Green. We just hit and hope."

"I just wish we could get more from him."

Ronald shook his head. "I don't. We can only trust him as far as his interests coincide with ours. Remember, he helped Ana; that means everything else he says is suspect."

Andrew shrugged. "I suppose you're right."

The warden returned with two steaming stone bowls and the woollen blankets from their room. After he left, Ronald said, "I told him we'll be staying here till tomorrow."

"Good." Andrew got up and walked over to the food. The stoneware was hot to the touch and disturbingly similar in design to the cup Green had given them.

"I can sense it," Ronald said. "When the right runes are uncovered and each time we put a candle in place, everything feels right in some strange way. I can't explain why."

"Like you said before," Andrew said, walking back to his spot against the wall, "no comfort zone. I guess we'll never learn it all."

"But we must try. That's what makes us human."

"I'm not so sure." Andrew pawed at his food. "Rousseau writes about how society can blind us to the truth of what we are. If we seek to understand based on ideas of right and wrong, we'll fail, but if we accept what we discover and move on from there, we may have a chance. I think acceptance is a whole lot more important than understanding. People fear change but, you and me, there's no choice for us. We're living in it. If we resist, we die."

Ronald frowned. "We're going to need to guess a bit though, so we at least have some semblance of choice."

"We must make decisions with whatever information we have at that time, not measured against our old lives. All other things being equal, the simplest solution is the best – we'll go with that."

Ronald didn't reply at first but, when Andrew looked up, he found the younger man smiling. "That's possibly the most sensible thing I've heard you say."

Andrew chuckled. "Not my words – Ockham's Razor. A detective at the police station reminded me."

Rite Work

"That's impossible."

Mike stared out of the window of his car at the garage on Dene Street. There was no sign of last night's incident. The metal door he'd seen ripped apart wasn't even dented.

"You sure this is the right house?" Emily asked.

"Of course I'm sure."

"Okay ... well ... I don't know what to say."

They'd left the café and both headed home, agreeing to meet up here in the early afternoon. Now, Emily stood on the road staring at the same thing he was staring at: a pristine, three-bedroom semi on the end of the street that bore no evidence of the events he remembered; not even police tape – the minimum he had expected to find.

"Forensics are never that fast and they wouldn't have got the door repaired."

"Do we knock and ask about the missing kids?"

Mike chewed his lip. "I'm not sure."

Emily stared at him for a moment, then turned and started walking up the drive. Mike's stomach lurched. He got out of the car and caught her up. "If I'm wrong, she'll think I'm mad."

"Well, *I* already think you're mad but, if we don't ask, we'll never know'."

They reached the door and Mike's belly cramped again. "I'm not feeling good about this."

Emily pressed the buzzer. "Keep quiet and let me do the talking."

The door opened and a blonde thirtysomething woman peered out at them. She was carrying a small child on her hip. "Yes, can I help you?"

Emily pulled out her warrant card. "I'm Detective Constable Jacobs. This is Detective Sergeant Underhill. Sorry to disturb you, Mrs?"

"Edwards," the woman replied.

"Mrs Edwards, we're conducting a house-to-house check after a few incidents last night. Did you notice anything suspicious?"

"No, nothing."

Mike stepped forward. "Mrs Edwards, do you have a son?"

"Yes. Steven's at school."

"Is there a Mr Edwards?"

"Not anymore."

"I'm sorry."

Emily laid a hand on Mike's shoulder. "Thanks for your help, Mrs Edwards. We'll leave you to it." They walked back to the car. "Either you're mad, or everyone else is."

Mike scowled. "I saw what I saw. I don't understand how ..."

"Who else was here?"

"Me, Davies and a couple of uniforms who stayed for a few hours, with the mum and the baby."

"You remember which officers?"

Mike shut his eyes, trying to recall as his stomach throbbed. "I was really tired and pissed off. I remember speaking to them, but ... no ..." He frowned and looked at Emily. "I didn't know them."

Emily's face clouded. "You sure you were—"

"No, you don't get it! I'd recognise anyone from our station. I remember the faces. They weren't ... they weren't ours."

She nodded. "The two at Gibbs' house weren't faces I recognised either. You think Davies or the super called in another force because we were stretched?"

"If they did, they kept it quiet. Not a whiff on the radio."

"Then who were they?"

"I don't know."

*

The hall was packed. For the second time, Andrew found himself the centre of a crowd in the arrival chamber. Wardens and Arcanes lined the walls and doors as people crammed into the room and the corridor beyond. As he and Ronald went through the final preparations, they were a surprisingly quiet audience.

Ronald stood by the dais, arranging the council members around him. Andrew was struck by how much older he seemed from when they'd first met, but he moved with an energy that belied his lack of sleep.

The arrangements for the ritual were similar to those from the library before, but this was much a much grander affair. Ronald placed the stone cup and the flick-knife near the arch and stood in front of them. Chanting from the Arcanes filled the room as the wardens organised the people into a great line. Andrew sensed their awe at the occasion. A feeling of power, intoxicating in its essence, gathered in the room.

The chosen sacrifices were next to enter the room. The runes on their bare chests blazed with light, as though fired by the potency of the ceremony. When they reached Ronald, he offered them the knife. Each took it and cut their hands, shedding blood into the bowl. Lord Merhl seemed perturbed by this and stepped forward to intervene, but Ronald held up his hand, stopping him in his tracks. Then he turned to Andrew.

"We have to prove to them that we don't need their deaths, so you must go first."

The request came as no surprise, because it made sense. Andrew believed he was guiding them in a last transfer; letting him go first, before the others, gave them a chance to test that theory. If correct, it was their best possible hope of getting where they wanted to go.

Andrew walked over, picked up the stone cup and held out his left hand. Ronald carefully pricked his thumb with the blade, causing a drop of blood to fall into the mixture. Andrew dipped his little finger in the contents and touched the residue to his tongue. "Ready," he announced.

"Good," Ronald replied, taking the cup from his hands.

The chanting of the Arcanes gripped the room and many voices amongst the crowd joined in. Yet, try as he might, Andrew struggled to add his voice to theirs; the words slipped from his mind even as he heard them. He turned towards the stone arch.

The space between the pillars seemed to expand and contract in a way that defied any conventional explanation and he became intensely aware that there was something there. Ronald's creation was alive with potential, the air heavy with purpose and a faint breeze stirred the hairs on the back of his hand. The arch became the gateway it was intended to be – a portal to another world.

This time Andrew didn't hesitate, and walked boldly into the void.

*

Jennifer Samms knew she was in trouble the minute she drew the burly Northman's attention. Three hours of fighting in full chain mail on a summer afternoon, coupled with weakness from her previous 'deaths', had left her exhausted.

When she saw the horned helm turn in her direction, she hefted her broadsword from the dirt, ignoring the dull pain in her right side, and brought her shield up into a guard position.

The Northman clambered over the dead and wounded towards her, just as he might ford a river – a strong and powerful stride that made Jennifer feel even more tired. Briefly, she thought one of the corpses might yield some help – there was always a chance of a knife from a dying man when you were one of the last survivors of a battle – but she had no such luck, as the Northman advanced without hindrance and closed into the reach of her sword.

Jennifer swung the heavy weapon with as much strength as she could muster. Steel clashed as her foe brought up his battle axe in response and caught her sword between the metal and wooden haft. He pulled the tangled instruments wide to his right, pulling Jennifer forwards and onto her knees, before stamping down, snapping her blade beneath a booted heel.

After that, time seemed to slow, just as it always did when she was going to die. Somehow, Jennifer twisted and brought the broken sword upwards, stabbing it into the Northman's thigh, bringing a roar of pain from him. A mailed fist smashed into the side of her head, crushing her metal helmet and sending her back into the dirt. Jennifer counted the breaths as she lay face down, waiting. Surprisingly, she got to five before she felt the axe bite into the back of her chain mail, severing her spinal cord and pinning her into the mud.

Instantly, everything went numb and, as her mind spun away, she clung to a faint hope that the Northman would remove the weapon once he was done. Then the world flashed white and, for the third time that day, Jennifer Samms died.

She was used to this; it happened every time. The world evaporated and she became weightless, floating outside of her body. She found herself asking the same questions as before: *Is it the end this time? Is there a heaven or hell?* She was aware of something out there, watching her. An undefinable presence that gave no indication of approval or condemnation. It seemed closer to her each time, reaching out and—

Then she snapped back onto the battlefield, face down in the dirt. The pain of the axe blow was still there, a dull ache that reverberated down her legs, but it didn't stop her struggling to her knees. She glanced around and saw a mist over the land. The echo of steel-on-steel came to her from far away. The fighting had moved on, leaving her alone among the dead.

Bemused, Jennifer struggled to her feet and picked up her shield. The round wooden panels were chipped and battered, but remained unbroken. Her sword had fared worse. Only the hilt was visible in the bloody muck. Strewn around it were corpses of soldiers from both sides. The broken-horned helms of the Northmen were all that set them apart from the fallen Seacsan warriors with whom Jennifer had fought. The low groans of the injured and dying chilled the air.

She remembered the Thegn's words as they had gone to war: *'We shall not break and it will be they who fall under our swords.'* The evidence around her said otherwise, but she couldn't tell who had won.

Jennifer located the man who had murdered her. As she hoped, the thigh wound had slowed the Northman down, until someone else had finished the job. His corpse lay stretched across a mound of the dead, armour pitted and rent from the blows he'd taken. Jennifer allowed herself a small moment of satisfaction.

She clambered over bodies of men and women, seeing faces hollowed by pain and death. The smell of war was the smell of an open latrine. A year ago, such an experience would have horrified her, but life since then had been harsh and unyielding, hardening her like a soldier. She knew she would never forget moments like this, but other things had become harder to remember; sometimes she forgot who she was, even her own name.

Jennifer reached under the sleeve of her chain mail and touched her fingers to the shirt beneath. She'd worn it ever since the first time she'd found herself alone in a strange world. It was little more than rags, but it still meant something important. A number nine, for her team: the Boston Terriers. It was an anchor to her memories – *all I have left from back home.*

She started up the hill, back toward the muster field. The mist grew thinner as she moved away from the River Aven to the east and the sounds of battle faded.

Above her, two dark shapes loomed out of the fog. The great

stones, silent eight-foot sentries that guarded the barrows, were all that survived from a forgotten age. A third rock spanned them, forming an archway.

She remembered pictures of henges on postcards from England, back in her own world; they were exactly the same, but she knew this was not that world.

"Still alive, then?" said a man's voice from the mists. Jennifer tensed instinctively, but she knew who it was. She looked around to see a familiar set of yellowed eyes staring down from the ridge.

"Yes, no thanks to you," she said roughly, trying to remember the man's name.

"I would have helped if I could," the figure answered solicitously. "But we all have our own tasks. Now it is time to move on."

"What if I like it here?"

"We can go through this again if you like? You know nothing about why you are here or how any of this happened to you. The only chance you have of returning home is through me."

"So you say. When will that be?"

The figure emerged from the mist. Jet-black hair and dark eyes adorned a serious face that showed no evidence of humour. The man's clothes were simple but also monochrome; a charcoal shirt and tight trousers tucked into knee-high boots. The only colour came from an angry red scar that ran down the side of his pallid left cheek. A physical malevolence seemed to emanate from him – a promise of danger that never ceased to unnerve Jennifer.

"It will be, when my tasks are done." A thin finger reached out and almost touched her nose. "Don't forget, my purpose is to fix problems like you. So long as you are useful, you remain my ally and not my enemy. I will return you to your home when I am ready."

"Suppose I want to stay here?"

The man licked his lips. "You don't have that option. Try it if you wish, but be warned – my largesse is not inexhaustible." He walked towards Jennifer, who flinched. "It would be interesting to test the limits of your resurrection."

"You bastard."

"I am as I am; nothing more or less. Now, to business: did you get him?"

Jennifer ground her teeth in response. She couldn't bring herself to speak, but nodded curtly.

"Good. Then our work here is over."

*

Once she was in Davies' car, Linda's mood improved.

The Inspector drove in silence. He'd said nothing since checking she'd put on her seat belt, but Linda didn't mind. She wound down the window and the cold air was a refreshing purge, washing away her guilt and shame for a while. George and Andrew disappeared from her thoughts and she was back to being a child, out for a drive with her parents. She remembered those trips fondly, her father driving their Morris Marina Coupe and singing along to Fleetwood Mac. A tune came back to her and she found herself humming it and smiling.

"You okay?" Davies asked.

"Yes," she replied, turning to him. "Thank you for this, I feel so much better."

Davies smiled, his lips thin and his expression schooled. "I'm glad."

"Where are we going?"

"A place that means a lot to me; it's not much further."

Fifteen minutes out of town, they drove along a narrow street with terraced houses on either side. The road wasn't wide enough for two cars and Davies slowed down to pick their way along. At the end was a church. He braked as they neared it and pulled into a small car park. "We're here," he announced, before switching off the engine and climbing out. Linda got out as well and went with him through the lich gate into the grounds. There were a few gravestones near the path, mostly old and neglected. On one of them, she saw the surname 'Smith', with the first name worn away.

Davies didn't stop, but carried on to the door and went inside. Linda noted the long key in the lock as she followed him.

The shadowy church interior seemed empty. She looked around. The fading sun revealed dusty air and neglect. Her footsteps echoed on the worn floor and she noticed marks, faint symbols drawn on the stones.

Davies walked down the aisle and took a seat on one of the pews. Linda followed, sitting in the row behind him.

"I used to come here as a child," Davies said. "I never sat here with the congregation. I'd be brought in by my parents and left, late at night. They would come back for me in the morning."

Linda frowned. "They left you here on your own, all night?"

"Many times. But I was never really alone." He turned towards her. "I need you to tell me what you know."

Linda stared at him. "What do you mean?" she said, confused.

"Andrew Pryde confided in you. What did he tell you?"

"What I told your officers: that he was meeting this man, Ronald, who claimed to know all about the case."

Casually, Davies took hold of her wrist, a seemingly innocuous gesture, but his grip tightened around it in front of the protruding bone. "What else did he say? You need to tell me, Linda."

"Nothing! Please, that hurts."

The crushing grip relaxed a little, but he didn't let go. "I should never have let Pryde leave the station," he said, his gaze becoming distant. "Unfortunately, there's only so much you can do with police procedures. Ignorance is always a two-edged sword. Helps protect what we have, but ... well ... gets in the way too."

Linda put her other hand on his and began trying to peel off his fingers. "I don't understand what you're talking about or why you brought me here. Let me go or I'll start shouting."

Davies chuckled. The sound was mirthless and hollow in the empty space. "No-one will hear you. I'll ask you one more time: what else did Pryde say?"

"I told you everything."

Davies sighed. "That's a shame. I can't take the risk either way, I'm afraid."

He stood up, dragging her to her feet and towards the vestry door. For a moment, Linda let herself be pulled along, then she regained her balance and yanked her arm in the other direction as hard as she could.

Her heels slipped on the stones, but she was free and ran for the exit. Straightaway, she realised her disadvantage and kicked off her shoes, picking one up as she did.

She reached the door, but Davies was only a beat behind. He grabbed at her shoulder. She spun, brandishing her shoe, and caught him across the jaw with the heel. He howled and stumbled back, letting her slip out of the church. She pulled the door closed and held it as she turned the key, pocketing it and backing away. He'd find another way out soon enough, but it gave her a momentary advantage.

"Help! Someone help!" She ran barefoot down the path, towards the row of houses. A stone caught her toe, but she ignored it and didn't stop. Over the road and she was at the first gate, through the garden and hammering at the window. The curtains twitched but no-one came out. "Help! Please! There's a man chasing me!"

Still no-one answered. Linda felt like she was making all the noise in the world. Between her shouts and banging, there was nothing, only eerie silence and a faint mist rolling down the street, like a translucent blanket, creeping towards her.

"Linda!"

She spun around. Davies was at the door of the church and hurrying after her. Linda wondered if he was armed, like all the American police in the movies. *No time for that!* She ran across the grass and forced her way through the thin hedge into the next garden, knocking on another window. "Help!" No movement this time, but the light was on and a television murmured and flickered inside. "Please, help me! I know you're in there!"

There was no reply.

She ran along a stone path and climbed over a fence. The cold tarmac of a garage driveway scraped the soles of her feet, but she didn't dare stop. The doorbell rang loudly in the hallway but again, no-one answered.

"They know not to interfere."

Davies stood at the end of the drive, a bloody gash on his cheek. He held out a hand to her. "I'm sorry about all of this, but when breaches like this happen, we scorch the earth; round up everyone who's been in contact with those affected and ... well ... quarantine or cull."

Linda retreated from him, until she had her back to the door. "Which am I to be?" she asked, blinking back tears.

"Quarantine, thankfully. But you must stay here, at the church, until we're sure. Please, you need to trust me."

"What about George? Was he culled?"

"I'm afraid so, and his death led us to think we needed to intervene with you." He took a step towards her. "Mrs Frakes, if Andrew said anything else to you, tell me now. It'll make it easier."

"He didn't say anything." She was breathing heavily. "Why can't you let me go?"

"Because we can't take the risk; you may have subconsciously learned something and they'll use that to come here." Davies was edging closer. "I spent my whole childhood being dragged to that church for my own good and the good of everyone else. The least you can do is spend a few nights in—"

He didn't get to finish the sentence. Linda's shoe hit him in the side of the head. His glasses flew away into the bushes and he went down hard on his backside.

Linda didn't hesitate. She charged past him and unlatched the garden gate, then slammed it into his temple. Davies yelped and reached for her, but she skipped back and swung the gate at him again and again until he stopped struggling and went limp. She smacked him one more time for good measure, and waited.

He didn't move.

Linda knelt down and patted his pockets, until she found his car keys, then got up and left him, making her way back to the car.

*

Andrew smelled grass again; a tangy, musky scent that instantly arrested his nostrils. The time underground in Corbenic had made him wistful for a glimpse of the sun or a chance to walk in the outdoors again. He blinked once and his eyes cleared, focusing immediately upon a familiar object. Another stone archway stood straight ahead of him, set into the green hilltop. Behind it, he saw another pair of pillars and another a little further away down the slope. The land around him was covered in henges. This time, unlike before, the sky was the clear blue of a bright summer's day. Only the sound of birds was missing.

It was a very reassuring sight.

"You took long enough," said a gruff voice. Andrew glanced to his right. Gideon walked up the hill towards him. "I was beginning to think you'd lost your way."

Instantly, Andrew was disappointed. "Then you remember me? That means I've failed."

"Why, what are you trying to do?"

"Go back in time to before we arrived, to avoid The Spider."

Gideon raised his eyebrows and frowned. "That won't work here."

"Why not?"

"Because you aren't *anywhere* at the moment."

"What do you mean?"

"Well, you're between places, like I told you before; in the middle of your choice of direction. The only consistency the Caer relies on is what you imagine to be. It doesn't exist beyond your thoughts."

"Surely that makes it easier."

"No. You don't have a frame of reference. You can't go back in time without knowing what you are going back to."

Andrew looked around. "Okay, so I find an arch and concentrate on a memory—"

Gideon shook his head. "No, that won't work either. Your subconscious will always know the chronological order of things." His frown deepened. "Besides, you could meet yourself ..."

Andrew sighed. "I guess that's bad too?"

Gideon nodded. "It always is in all the science fiction stories."

Andrew was annoyed. "You should have told me that when we met before."

"It wouldn't have done any good. You weren't ready to listen. Wherever you went to, it's opened your mind."

"What about you? Are you just a part of my psyche, then?"

Gideon chuckled. "No, I'm afraid not. If I was, you might be able recreate a version of me that existed before we met. I'm as real as you are and I'm in the same between-place. The only difference between me and anyone else is that I want to talk to you and you want to talk to me, so we can share the same in-between space."

A thought occurred to Andrew and he reached forward to take Gideon by the shoulders. "We need to stand clear of the arch. Ronald is bringing others through."

"How many others?"

"Four or five thousand."

Gideon laughed loudly. "You don't do things by halves! Well, at least it's a refreshing change." He slapped Andrew on the back. "Good for you." Silence fell between them, before the old man's expression became quizzical. "Are we waiting for something?"

Andrew frowned. "I don't understand it – they should be right here; right behind me."

"Oh, I see: you mean the others you're bringing with you? They're not here because you don't want them to be. Trust me, that's a good sign. If you had them all here, your mind wouldn't cope."

"Okay." Andrew still felt a bit unsure about everything he was being hearing and was aware that Green had told them differently. "Does that mean we have a limited amount of time to talk?"

"You're guiding a very large group of people, which may or may not be a strain. You remember what happened last time?" Andrew nodded. "Good, then look out for the signs," he added. "You should recognise them again."

"What about the people we were trying to avoid – The Spider and Candleswick?"

"They can reach you just like I can, unless you are capable of blocking them out."

"Did she get through after we left?"

"She did. You weren't really stopping her; just existing between the point in which she followed you and the moment you arrived at your destination. If she's between places now, she may choose to contact you. It is possible you could resist her – it depends how strong you are."

"And him?"

"Candleswick?" Gideon became serious. "Well, if you didn't attract his attention already, you will have by now."

*

"What have they done?" The man turned away as if smelling the air. "This can't be countenanced!"

Jennifer was surprised. It was unlike her companion to become distracted. She glanced in the same direction. "What's up?"

The man turned back towards her, his yellowed eyes full of dark purpose. "Nothing you need concern yourself with. You will wait here."

"But—"

"I didn't say that you had a choice."

In a flurry of movement, she found herself pinned to the ground. Her baleful gaze held his own as the man knelt on her chest. "Unfortunately, I require your special talents once more." A pale hand filled her vision, black nails growing impossibly into sharpened tips; three-inch blades that shone with deadly intent. "To work powerful magic with no preparation requires sacrifice. I hope you don't mind."

For the fourth time that day, Jennifer Samms died.

Confrontations

Linda got into the driver's side of the car, then closed and locked all the doors. The mist was closer now, rolling over the windows.

"Hello, Linda."

She jumped and looked around. George Frakes was sitting in the passenger seat. She stared at him, unable to speak.

"I'm so sorry, Linda," he said.

Linda could barely breathe. She reached out a trembling hand and touched his shoulder.

"Yes, I'm real; as real as I can be."

"But ..."

"Yes, I died, Linda." George sighed. "I sat and watched you in the house from the car. I took out a pistol loaded it with bullets and put it on the dashboard. I turned up the radio and thought about ending it, but then decided I was being selfish. So I sat there and just stared, until the car door opened, and someone grabbed the gun and shot me. That's the last thing I remember."

"I found you ... you were—"

"I didn't kill myself. I didn't want to die."

Gradually the knot in her chest eased enough for her to speak. "The detective said ... they ... you ..."

"I don't understand it either, love." He smiled sadly. "All I know is, I've a chance to speak to you now and I wasn't going to pass up on that." He turned and pointed out of the window. "It's the mist. There's something about it that allows us to be together." He gazed at her. "That's all I ever wanted, really."

"I ... I ..." Linda swallowed, trying to get a grip on what was happening. "The man who brought me here, he's still out there. He'll come for me."

George nodded. "I know. I can't stay either. The mist ... it'll fade."

"What do I do?"

"You have to make a choice. They'll be after you wherever you go. Start the engine."

"A choice? What choice? I don't—"

"Linda, please, start the car!"

Something slammed against the back window. She screamed, jammed the key in the ignition and turned it. The engine roared into life immediately and she stamped on the accelerator. The car bucked against the handbrake and leapt forwards, smashing through a wooden fence and into a farmer's field. "Where do I go?" she yelled.

"That's your choice."

"Tell me what you want!"

"Aim into the mists, where its thickest and you can't see; right into the middle of it!"

Linda swung the wheel and the windscreen filled with dark grey cloud. "What happens now?"

"Hopefully, we escape."

*

The sky's brilliant azure blackened, as if the light of the world were fading all around them.

"So, what's the plan?" Gideon asked Andrew.

"I don't have one. I was hoping Candleswick wouldn't get anywhere near us, because we'd be going to a place before he wasn't aware of me."

Gideon scowled. "A risky strategy."

"I understand that now, but there wasn't much choice."

"You should have stayed put."

"Wasn't an option."

Gideon stroked his straggly grey beard. "Then you're in serious trouble," he pronounced tersely. "Candleswick's been at this for years, centuries even."

"Can you help me?"

"Not really. I'll be lucky enough if he leaves me be." The old man glanced up into the gloom. "He knows you're here."

Andrew looked around. "I can escape through an arch. There's time."

Gideon shook his head. "He'll still catch you there, before you make it anywhere else, and then he gets to make the rules. Where would you rather face him: in a place of your choosing, or one of his?"

Andrew thought about this. "The rules of this place are mine to command?"

Gideon nodded. "More or less, but that doesn't mean you can use them to hurt him, unless he believes that to be the case. It's the same for you. Here, your physical form is just an extension of the mind. He can only hurt you if he can find your weaknesses."

"Pretty cryptic."

Gideon sighed. "Sorry."

The sky was almost pitch black now, yet Andrew could still see the old man quite clearly despite the absence of light. The henges, however, disappeared into the gloom. He shuffled backwards to place his back against the reassuring presence of the stone arch he'd just come through. "If you're going to stick around, stay close."

"You got a plan now?" the old man asked.

"The beginnings of one."

The air tightened around them. The space between the stones dilated and two small yellow lights appeared between them. Andrew recognised them immediately. The orbs of the creature's eyes grew quickly and he felt the familiar stirrings of fear. Candleswick had arrived.

From beneath the arch, the shape appeared, hulking and hungry; a ravenous, dark creature bent on murder and hate. As before, Andrew's right hand began to ache with a dull, throbbing pain that emanated from the centre of his palm. He rubbed at the puffy scar with his thumb. This time, things had to be different.

"Hello, Janus." The familiar voice reverberated in Andrew's skull.

Janus? Is that the old man's name? thought Andrew. But there was no time to stop and ask now.

A form coalesced in the blackness and he was surprised when a gaunt-looking man, dressed in black, emerged from its depths. He wore a plain shirt and his trousers were tucked into high boots. His face was deathly pale. The only contrast came from his yellow eyes and a red scar on the side of his cheek.

"Hello, Candleswick," Gideon said.

"This is of no concern to you." Candleswick's glared at the old man. "You should leave."

"I'm fine here," Gideon replied.

"If you stay, you will share his fate."

He chuckled. "You won't kill me, Candleswick. You haven't figured me out yet."

Candleswick cocked his head sideways. "You do not live, Janus; you exist. Your reflections are long gone and you no longer resonate anywhere. Therefore, you are of no use."

Gideon flinched and the mirth died on his lips. Andrew took his cue. "Your argument isn't with him, it's with me," he said, edging to his right and away from the stone arch.

"Ah yes – you." Candleswick turned towards him, oozing menace. "I wish I'd dealt with you the last time we met."

"You killed Amanda Baines," Andrew said.

The man smiled. "Yes, yes I did. She made the mistake of leaving the place she was supposed to be. That made her mine."

"She didn't deserve to die."

"I'm afraid she did, as do you. What you are doing threatens the entire weave."

"Says who?"

"Me."

Gideon chuckled at this. "I think our friend is well aware assertions like that are lacking in substance."

Candleswick's gaze didn't waver. "I am not concerned with what either of you believe."

"Perhaps you should be," Andrew warned. He'd circled and positioned himself between Candleswick and the portal that he'd emerged from. "Belief's about the only thing that's important around here."

Candleswick laughed. "Well, your trip is at an end. It's almost a shame; your reality yielded a substantial harvest."

Andrew frowned. "Is that why you were in the street when I saw you?"

"Yes. I found three children experimenting with a strange magic. I wonder what could be causing it all?"

"The Spider, perhaps?" Gideon suggested.

"She was in their world?"

"Yes, for some time; at least a hundred years."

"She has been unhinging them."

"You could put it that way."

Candleswick shrugged. "Once you two are dealt with, I will go back to your world and find her."

"What will you do with the kids?" Andrew asked.

"Kill them."

"Like you did Amanda?"

"Yes, and as I will do with you." Candleswick yawned, but his eyes blazed and the throbbing in Andrew's hand intensified. "This is tiresome – you know this place is your own fiction. It will suffice for you to die here. I will ensure your physical form returns to where it belongs."

Andrew gritted his teeth. "That's not going to happen."

Candleswick smiled, his eyes glinting hungrily in the gloom. "Really? We both know I marked you – the knife wound from the carnival. Dreams can be just as dangerous as reality."

Andrew couldn't move. The yellowed eyes fixed him in place as the pain in his hand spread into his chest, clawing at his heart. He felt it labouring, struggling to pump blood through his strangely resistant body.

"A heart attack. It will seem natural to anyone who chooses to investigate. I did learn a lesson from dear Amanda. A shame that I won't gain anything from your death, but you've proved you're altogether too dangerous. By getting rid of you, I can dispose of all those on your little trip, too."

Andrew dropped to his knees. His breathing came in deep gasps. He tried desperately to focus, but the throbbing filled his head, surging into a howl that crashed against his clenched teeth.

He heard Gideon's voice. "Andrew—"

"Shut up, old man," Candleswick hissed. "Interfere again and you join him."

The moment of distraction gave Andrew a chance. He fought to tame his lungs, subduing his panic, at least for a moment. "There's one more thing I want to know," he whispered hoarsely.

"You don't get to negotiate!" Candleswick snarled, walking towards him.

"Where did you find Amanda? Where had she gone?"

Andrew coughed and leaned forward, staring at the grass; the pose of the condemned at the executioner's block. Candleswick loomed over him, his breath a faint heat on the back of his head. "I tell you what; I'll show you," he growled. "It can be the last thing you experience."

Andrew screamed as thin fingers pressed into his neck, and scalding nails dug into his skin.

And he saw.

*

Images swirled in his mind. He was in the courtyard of a walled manor, crouched low in the bushes beside the wall of the house. A woman walked across the cobblestones from the walls to the house entrance – he saw a pair of oaken doors, guarded by a man in leathers, emblazoned with the symbol of a white stag on green.

"He is overdue, Gamm."

The man nodded. "Yes, my lady. He must have been delayed."

"I will be upstairs. Make sure he is informed when he arrives."

Without volition, he glanced up at the sky. Twin suns blazed down from above. Somehow, he knew it was nearly noon.

He ducked back into the shadows, avoiding the eyes of the guards as the doors slammed shut. The woman disappeared into the house. The scene blurred and he found himself upstairs, in a bedroom, near the terrace entrance. The woman from the courtyard was in the centre of the room, looking at him.

"How long have you been standing there?" she asked.

"Moments only," Andrew heard himself reply in a strange voice. "Although, such measurements are relative."

"Are you here to take me back?"

Andrew laughed; an unfamiliar tone, full of throaty scorn. "In a manner of speaking. Goodness! After all this time, is that all you managed to learn?"

The woman retreated a step. "Was that what I was supposed to do: learn about what happened to me?"

Andrew shrugged. Neither the gesture nor the words were ones he had chosen. He was a passenger, witnessing these events through the eyes of a stranger. "No. No rules. In fact, your ignorance makes my part easier – no preconceptions to deal with."

He strode across the room towards her. For the first time, Andrew got a good look at the face of the woman – Amanda Baines. She was older than he had expected. Faint lines of care framed her solemn, oval face. She appeared to be in her late twenties; certainly, more than the seventeen years she'd lived in his own reality.

"Please don't complicate matters." The brusque tone of his adopted voice continued. "We could do without difficulties, and time is short."

"I wanted to wait for my husband ... and the children," the woman protested softly. Her solemn veneer of innocence cracked a little with emotion, but the protest was dismissed with a shake of his head.

"I am afraid that isn't possible. They are still days away. This must happen now."

Andrew watched her acquiesce, burying her feelings beneath poise. "Very well. What must I do?"

The stranger held out his hand. "You must accompany me onto the balcony. You may take one last look upon this place."

She took the proffered hand carefully and modestly – a light touch resting upon alien fingers – and strode forward, her boots echoing on the floor. "Will it hurt?" she asked.

His eyes flinched from her gaze and Andrew knew the stranger was struggling to lie. "Perhaps. These things are never easy."

She turned to face the window, moving quickly out of the room and into the light of the twin suns. The purity of her spirit seemed to shine through her body, as though she were lighter than the air.

"I am ready," she announced.

"Good," he replied, and let go of her hand.

A moment before it happened, Andrew realised what his host was doing. He railed against the action, but it was no use. The stranger stepped backwards and gathered himself before rushing at Amanda. He crashed into her, causing her to lose her balance and pitch forward towards the rail. A split second later, she smashed through it and fell the thirty feet to the courtyard.

When Andrew heard her scream, his own mental voice joined in.

*

Abruptly, the vision shattered and Andrew was back in the Caer, kneeling on the damp grass of the hilltop, with Candleswick standing over him."

"You see? I keep my promises."

The fingers on Andrew's neck were a lancing pain; the nails dug into his skin and seemed to ignite a fire in his flesh, but he couldn't move away. His body remained paralysed as he struggled to master his breathing. Again, his heart lurched, each beat an exhaustive effort as he fought against Candleswick's will.

Agonised, he wrenched his head to the right. Gideon stood looking horrified, but seemingly unwilling to intervene. *Perhaps you've already done enough*, Andrew thought. *I hope I understood.* With every last ounce of energy he could muster, he tried to focus. *Gideon said I make the rules here and resonance is important. Let's find out how important.*

"Let go," Candleswick chided. "There is no point resisting me."

Andrew saw flickering lights in the unnatural gloom. He shut out the pain and ignored everything around him, reaching instead for something else that he wanted to be there.

"Ronald!"

For a minute, he thought he'd failed. The shout in his mind was little more than a hoarse whisper in his throat and it quickly died in the gloom; but it had touched something.

"Ronald!" Everything around him echoed with the name as it became both a howl and mantra.

*

Finally, the arrival chamber was empty.

Flick-knife in one hand and stone cup in the other, Ronald continued the chant alone, just as he'd been taught. The etched runes shone in response to the conjured magic – *my magic!* Some part of him found it difficult to accept – it always would, he suspected – but the sense of achievement he felt at making the ritual work far outweighed any lingering misgivings.

He was exhausted beyond measure; the effort of maintaining the portal for nearly seventeen hours would have been impossible alone but, once it was established, the Arcanes had taken over most of the task. This ritual had been rooted in a lore similar to their own magic so they were able to understand its workings. Lord Merhl had been the last to leave only moments before; trusting his people to the spell, he'd finally set aside his responsibilities for Corbenic and joined them in the portal, leaving Ronald alone in the city.

Almost alone.

"Well done, Ronald."

The air shimmered and the smiling figure of Green materialised on the stone dais.

Ronald inclined his head towards the arch. "Just you ... and me ... left," he managed to say between lines of the chant.

Green nodded. "Yes, of course." He extended his hand. "My cup?"

Continuing to intonate the required phrases, Ronald passed him the receptacle.

"Well, I won't keep you," Green said with a sigh. "Hopefully we'll meet each other again."

Ronald shrugged in response. Green smiled again and stepped beneath the pillars, and vanished.

My turn.

He took one last look back. The lights of the chamber dimmed, making it seem as though the walls were closing in. Fleetingly, he thought about the danger. Each transport could be his last, but what was the alternative: staying in Corbenic alone into old age? *No. Time to take a risk*, he thought. *Time to go.*

He stepped through the portal.

*

Ronald's eyes blurred for a moment, then refocused. The first thing he recognised was Gideon; the old man stood a few feet to the left of the stone arch, his face fixed in a panicked and powerless expression. Ronald followed his gaze and saw what was troubling him.

Directly ahead, Andrew was on his hands and knees. Over him was a hulking, dark shape, vaguely human in appearance, its intentions unmistakable.

"What's going on?" Ronald demanded, running towards his friend.

The figure turned towards him. It had a coal-black body, coarse hair springing from its muscular back, teeth shining behind black lips in the unnatural gloom. But it was the eyes that drew his attention: black pupils shone like miniature voids in a yellowed gaze that overpowered his own; a malevolent stare that revelled in hate and thirsted to destroy life.

Ronald halted, his knees going weak under the assaulting gaze. He couldn't blink or flinch from it. His heartbeat fluttered and echoed in his head. The creature brought back memories of dark corners in his childhood bedroom and half-seen figures in shadowy alleyways. The malevolence in those eyes appalled him, making him want to flee.

I can't leave Andrew!

From somewhere, he found courage. Yelling, he charged at the beast. Ebony claws lashed toward him, but he ducked under them and barrelled into it, driving the bloodied flick-knife deep into its chest.

The creature howled. A powerful blow ripped Ronald's feet from under him. He slashed out with the knife again. Hot, black blood spattered across his face. He sprung to his feet and brandished the weapon, but all fight seemed to have left the beast, and it remained huddled and whimpering on the ground.

Strength coursed through Ronald, primal and heady; a mixture of adrenaline and bloodlust. The terror from before had become something else, violent and fatal. The knife burned in his hand, urging him to strike again.

Yellow fire glowed in the creature's eyes, but it held no sway over him now. Nevertheless, it remained a threat. Ronald's hands trembled, but he stepped forwards, making sure he was between it and Andrew.

Now what do I do?

Deliverance

"Now, are you going to explain why you are giving me so much trouble?"

Ten year-old Andrew Pryde swallowed nervously; he'd never been kept behind after class before. Mrs White was usually so nice, but today she was angry with him and he didn't know why.

"I'm sorry, miss," he managed to mumble. "I only asked—"

"It was a stupid question, Andrew. Surely you understand?" Mrs White's tone was curt. "Maths is maths." She held up her hands. "Look at my fingers. Two plus three equals five."

"But, miss, I wanted to learn *why* it does."

"There isn't a *why*, Andrew."

She'd kept him behind twice more after that for *wasting time*. It had made him feel guilty about raising his hand and, years later, he had chosen his courses to avoid any whisper of mathematics, finding more comfort in the variable answers of the arts. He had never thought of that moment as being pivotal to the rest of his life.

Until now.

*

"Andrew, get up."

Andrew opened his eyes to find Gideon's concerned face a few inches from his. "There isn't much time," the old man said. "Your parlour tricks got you further than I thought they would, but you're pushing the limits. You need to sort all of this out."

Andrew sat up. The sky had brightened once more, comparable to a fading summer evening. He was lying near the stone arch he'd travelled through, exactly where he'd been before. Metres away, a man lay on the ground with Ronald standing over him.

Candleswick.

The man moaned, his arms clutched around his waist. By contrast, Ronald was visibly angry. He held his flick-knife in shaking hands while the blade dripped black blood onto the grass.

"Nothing excuses what you are and what you've done," Ronald spat at the figure on the ground. "I ought to—"

"Ronald, wait!" Andrew gritted his teeth and hauled himself to his feet. "Don't do anything stupid."

Ronald glanced up and looked at him in surprise, as if noticing him for the first time. "Andrew, you're all right!"

"Just about." He tried to grin. "Thanks for your help."

"Glad I got here in time."

Andrew nodded. "There's a lot to talk about, but time isn't our friend."

"Where is everyone?" Ronald asked, looking around. "You already sent them through?"

"No – it's complicated," Andrew replied and pointed at Candleswick. "We want rid of him."

Ronald frowned. "Yeah. I stabbed him, but I'm not going to kill him – I don't think I can."

"I'm glad. But we need to do *something*, or else he'll just come after us again."

"What are you thinking?"

Andrew walked carefully over to where Candleswick lay and prodded him with his foot, attracting a malevolent, yellow-eyed glare. "Let's leave him in Corbenic."

A flicker of recognition crossed the pale man's face. "No, please—"

"Good idea," Ronald interrupted.

Together, they grabbed him and hauled him to his feet. Candleswick struggled, but had no strength left to fight. They dragged him to the Corbenic archway.

"You'll regret this," he whispered hoarsely.

"Oh, I don't think we will," Ronald replied.

Ignoring the protests, they reached the arch and shoved him through. For a moment, Candleswick hung suspended in mid-fall between the stones. Then he vanished.

"I hope that place is secure enough," Gideon coughed.

"I think it will do," Andrew said and glanced at him in concern. The old man seemed to be having trouble breathing and leaned heavily against one of the other stone archways. "You're out of time," he breathed. "You're carrying a lot of people and you're tired. I'm not sure you'll make it."

"We must," Andrew insisted.

"Then go through *his* portal." The old man pointed at the shimmering henge that Candleswick had used. "It's still resonating, so it should be easier."

"But I know where Amanda is!" Andrew protested. "Candleswick pushed her off a balcony and killed her in another world."

"Then come back and find her afterwards," Gideon rasped, sinking to his knees.

"Do we really want to go where *he* came from?" Ronald asked.

"We may not get a choice," Andrew replied. He was feeling the strain now, like the beginnings of a migraine, distorting his vision and clawing at his forehead, "Come on."

They crossed the grass quickly to the other arch. Andrew gestured for Ronald to go first.

"Are you sure about this?" Gibbs asked.

"No, but I don't think we have any option." His head began to throb.

Ronald stepped through and vanished. Andrew glanced around one more time; Gideon was lying on the ground motionless. "There's always a price, even if you don't expect it," he shouted hoarsely. "Now go!"

Andrew gritted his teeth and followed Ronald.

*

As he stepped under the stone lintel, the hilltop and standing stones fell away, leaving Andrew alone with the universe.

Since he'd been there before, he was better prepared for the transfer. He became weightless and slipped out of his body. He was staring into a storm of black that revealed nothing of itself, but he knew it was endless and alive.

Once more, he marvelled at his own insignificance in the vastness of the void. The darkness seemed to writhe and he found himself falling into the depths of the infinite velvet expanse.

A pinpoint of light appeared in the deep; it had to be where Candleswick had travelled from. He focused on it and when he did so the journey became much easier.

A sensation of speed overtook him. He was being pulled inexorably towards his beacon-lit destination. He recalled what Green had said: *Just because you perceive the world in three dimensions and have a vague understanding of a fourth, doesn't mean that's how it is for everyone else.*

The idea that the universe was both vast and dimensionally incomprehensible had always frightened and appalled him. He remembered fevered dreams as a child, struggling to find any sense of himself in an infinite nothingness. Something within him laughed bitterly. Humanity was less than a speck in this expanse. Believing otherwise was folly; another piece of human arrogance that he would need to give up.

He fell, deeper and deeper but, unlike the first time he'd travelled like this, he knew now that there would be an end to this journey. He could sense himself beginning to faint; it was only curiosity that helped him resist unconsciousness.

He let go …

*

Andrew became aware of the cold. The air was chilling and he began to shiver involuntarily. He was lying on hard ground this time – rock beneath a thin layer of damp mud.

"Where the hell are we?" said Ronald from somewhere nearby.

Andrew opened his eyes. They were on a stony hilltop in a deep fog, the other side of which descended gently into the gloom. "Where's everyone else?" he managed to ask.

"We are here," said a heavy voice, and Lord Merhl emerged from the mists. "It is wondrous – we are delivered."

"Are they all here?" Gibbs asked.

"I can't be sure yet," Merhl replied. "We must wait and see."

Andrew heard more voices around them; the hum of nervous talk and noise confirmed the presence of a substantial group of people on the hill. He got his feet under him and stood up. The effort made his head spin.

A hand gripped his shoulder and Ronald's face appeared out of the fog. "Best you stay there; you must be knackered. I'll go take a look around."

Andrew nodded and glanced around. Shadowy shapes moved in

the grey. He caught fragments of conversations and whispered words as people gathered together.

"This doesn't feel any different to Corbenic," said Andrew. "Maybe we haven't gone anywhere?"

"No, it *is* different." Merhl took his shoulder, guiding them both gently to their knees. The damp ground soaked into Andrew's trousers. Merhl took his hand and, together, they touched the wet soil beneath them. "Soil, grass and plants. We are saved!" said Merhl.

Other voices cried out in triumph. Andrew stayed where he was as the people around him celebrated. He realised he was exhausted in mind and body. The victory wasn't something he could share. There was still too much left to do.

The hands and the presence of others disappeared and suddenly, he was alone. He tried to get up, but slipped in the muck. He peered into the heavy air and could just see the sun – a forlorn sentinel hugging the hills on the horizon.

"Andrew, where are you?"

Hands took hold of his arm and he was helped gently to his feet. It was Gwuina, accompanied by two men. "Come, Harrower," she said kindly. "You are needed at the bottom of the hill."

Andrew leaned heavily on her and one of the other men as they descended. His legs felt weak, as though he'd run a marathon. As they picked their way down, the fog was beginning to clear. "Is everyone all right?" he asked.

Gwuina's reply was buoyant. "They seem to be, thanks to you, Harrower."

"What is this place?"

"Ronald has found someone who he thinks can help."

Gwuina took him down a steep, twisting path, until finally they reached a gathering of people. Andrew made out the black robes of the Arcanes among a larger crowd swathed in the mist.

"—I don't give a fuck who you are, no-one gets to go through my stuff while I'm still alive."

"My apologies, but we thought you were dead."

"Yeah, I hear that a lot."

The first voice shocked him; the girl's American twang was unmistakable, sending a bolt of electricity up his spine. His fatigue evaporated. *Where are we?*

A new strength pushed him past people. Ronald's distinctive parka coat was easy to spot and he pushed through the crowd to his side. "What's going on?"

"That's my question too," said the unfamiliar American voice.

Andrew stared at the stranger. Unkempt blonde hair and blue eyes framed the worn, freckled face of a girl in her early twenties. Light lines suggested she was a person who usually smiled easily, yet now that smile was a grimace.

"My name's Jennifer Samms. Who are you?"

*

Mike Underhill kept his head down and attention on his phone as he entered the station, avoiding the friendly greeting of the desk sergeant and eye contact with anyone else. He marched straight through to the main staircase, took the steps two at a time to the office floor and made straight for his desk.

Within moments, he was logged into the central database and browsing staff profiles, looking for photo IDs of the police officers who'd attended the disturbance at the Edwards residence.

He had browsed identikits for many years, chasing down suspects and witnesses. He'd developed a skill for remembering faces, noting individual turns of the nose, cheekbones, scars ... anything memorable; but every time he tried to recall the officers he'd seen, none of those things came back.

After an hour, he gave up and looked up the incident reports, searching for the logs related to the Edwards call out.

Nothing.

He closed the database and opened another – school records this time – looking for Steven Edwards' name in the local catchment area. He found three and checked their addresses, but none of them matched the house on Dene Street. Had Mrs Edwards lied about her boy? He remembered her face at the time – no, she had given the name straight away, without any hint of her hiding something.

What's going on?

Mike leant back in his chair, finally allowing himself a moment to look around the office. It was all but empty, with a figure similarly hunched over a computer on the far side. He glanced towards Davies' room. The door was shut and blinds drawn. No-one at home there either.

His gaze returned to the person at the end of the room. Mike got up and slowly began to walk over. The figure remained stock-still in the chair, no sound of typing or a mouse clicking.

"Who are you?" Mike asked.

The man stood up and stared at him. He wasn't in uniform, but was wearing a shirt and tie. He had a strangely forgettable face – grey eyes, light brown hair, a small nose and mouth – making him seem almost featureless. But Mike did remember him.

"You were at the Edwards' place, weren't you?"

The man didn't reply, but kept staring as he eased away from the chair. When Mike stepped forwards, he stepped back towards the staircase.

"Hold on a minute. I can't let you go," Mike said. "You know that, don't you?"

Again, the man didn't answer, but a thin line of saliva oozed from the left corner of his lips. He didn't appear to blink.

"Who do you work for? What's your badge number?"

The man reached the doors and pushed them open, but lingered in the entrance way. He raised his left arm, his hand open, palm facing Mike, fingers extended, as if giving some kind of strange greeting.

Then he stepped back and the doors swung shut. His hand balled into a fist and snapped out, punching the fire alarm on the wall, shattering it. Sirens blared out all around the station. Mike leapt for the doors, but the man leaned against them, holding them closed. Their faces were inches apart, separated by glass as each strained at the door. Over the noise, Mike heard the latch turn and suddenly the man was racing away down the stairs, leaving him to fight the lock.

Shit!

Mike ran back to his desk, snatched up his office keys and hurried back to the door. He got it open just as people started to appear at the other office exit.

"Hey, what's going …"

Mike didn't wait to hear the rest. He rushed down the stairs, catching sight of the stranger a flight below.

"You, stop!"

The man ignored him, broke into a sprint, and leapt down the last few steps to the ground floor. Mike almost slipped as he tried to follow, but managed to keep his feet and reached the doors as the stranger elbowed his way through reception.

"Someone stop him!"

The man crashed through the front doors, turned left and pushed his way past the evacuated police officers. Strangely, no-one made an effort to stop him. Mike spat a curse and scrambled after, trying to keep pace. As he ran, he fished out his phone and dialled Emily's number.

"What's up?"

"Need some help! I'm after one of them. He followed me to the station!"

"One of ... Oh, right, okay. I'm parked up on Ragthorn Road."

"Make for the supermarket on the corner. I'll meet you there!"

Mike didn't wait for the answer. He sprinted down the street, rounded a corner and cut down an alleyway between two shops. He caught up with the stranger just before the end and leapt at him, grabbing his shoulder. They tumbled to the ground. Mike landed heavily on his knees and yelled out in pain, but didn't let go.

"Who are you?" Mike panted.

The man didn't reply, but squirmed in his grip. Mike straddled his back, pinning his arms to the concrete. He heard tires squeal at the end of the alley and a car door slam. He glanced up to see Emily running towards them, a pair of handcuffs in her hands. Together they restrained the man, propping him up in a sitting position against the wall.

Emily knelt down in front of him. "Whatever you were trying to do, you must realise you've failed."

The man stared at her, giving no indication he'd heard or understood what she'd said. Then he blinked and looked at Mike. "You need to let go," he said.

"What?"

"You are in transition; the memories you're holding on to won't help you. Eventually, you'll die."

Mike glared at him. "I know what I saw. I'm not mad!"

"It doesn't matter; you need to let it go."

"Right now, you should be thinking about yourself," Emily said. "We'll be taking you into custody for impersonating a police officer, and worse."

The man looked at her. "Your rituals are unimportant," he said. "Our nature is to be ignored. You have seen it already. People forget who I am; I fall from their minds even as they notice me. The minute you turn your back, I will disappear. Write and record what you wish; it will all be changed."

"Like the house?" Mike said. "What happened to the three kids?"

"He took them."

"Who?"

"The guardian of ways and doors. He who prevents trespassers." The man's gaze lost its focus. "You are beneath his notice, but he will come for you if you cling to what you were."

Mike grabbed him by the shirt. "Listen, you better start making sense soon or …"

"Or what?"

Mike found himself staring into the man's glassy eyes. There was something unnatural about them that reminded him of the dog he'd seen with Davies. "What are you?" he hissed.

"An editor," the man replied. "Nothing more." He went limp and slumped forwards into Mike's arms.

Emily's hand went to his neck. "He's got a pulse. He's breathing too; just unconscious. What do we do with him?"

"Put him in the car. I've got an idea."

No Place Called Home

The car bumped and bounced across the ground. Linda peered into grey fog and clung to the steering wheel, her knuckles white. She could see nothing beyond the glass and every moment she expected to drive into something. Fortunately, she didn't.

"I don't know how much longer I can keep this up, George," she said. She wasn't sure how long they'd been driving anyway. "My nerves won't take—"

Something screamed outside, followed by a loud bang, and the car lurched to the right. Linda strained against the wheel and got the vehicle back under control. Formless shadows and dark shapes gathered around the windows and she heard scraping noises. "George!"

He gripped her arm in reassurance. "Not much further," he breathed. "These are the threshold wardens; we can't let them stop us."

"What happens if they do?"

"It'll be like we never existed!"

Linda pushed the accelerator to the floor. The car vibrated and shook in protest, but increased speed. Far away, above the sound of the engine, she thought she heard a roar, as if a huge creature was crying out in anger at their escape.

Gradually, the sounds faded and the car settled down. With no point of reference in the endless fog, any sense of speed disappeared.

"Slow down now," George said. "We're clear of them."

Linda relaxed her right foot and the speedometer needle dropped from eighty to sixty, then forty and thirty.

Suddenly, a dark shape loomed out of the mist and she swerved to avoid it. Two more appeared and the ground became bumpy once more.

"You can stop here," George said, just as she was about to slam her foot on the accelerator again. "We've arrived."

Linda hesitated for a moment, before pulling up in front of one of the shapes. She uncurled her fingers from the steering wheel and sat back with a sigh. "Oh, George, I don't understand any of this! Where are we?"

He opened the car door. "I'll show you," he said and got out.

It seemed like madness to venture outside with those things – those *wardens* – out there; but what other choice did she have? Where else could she go? She took a deep breath, pulled the handle and inched the door open. Nothing grabbed her. She climbed out and walked around to the front. She was standing on wet grass. The strange shapes were huge stone pillars, barely a metre from the car where they'd stopped. A third piece of stone bridged them at the top, forming an arch. She reached out and brushed her hand along the rough rock and her fingers tingled. "What is all this?"

"A place between places," George explained. "We passed through the boundary and this is what's beyond."

It wasn't cold, but Linda found herself shivering. "Am I dead?"

George smiled, walked around the car, and took her hands. "No, you're not dead. But you would have been if you'd stayed where you were. Judging by what they did to me, those people would never have let you live."

Linda squeezed his fingers, then let go and sat down on the bonnet. "I don't understand any of this," she said. "But you talked about us finding somewhere we can be together."

He nodded. "I think it's possible. Most of the things I thought were rules about life, death and everything else don't seem to apply." He gestured at the stones. "I've been here before, for a little while, after …" he swallowed. "I went through one of these and found myself in the fog around the church graveyard. I saw you and the car and … well, you know the rest."

Linda looked around. The mist began to recede, revealing a flat grass field dotted with more and more of the stone archways. "Where do we go?"

"We choose an archway and pass through it."

"Are all of these doorways to somewhere else?"

"I guess so," George said.

"Well, how do we choose which one to go through?"

"I've no idea."

*

Ronald wasn't sure what to do.

After about an hour, the fog had cleared. Jennifer had been acting as an impromptu tour guide since they met. She'd told them that the locals called this place the Valley of Aven, near the river of the same name, in the south of Albion.

The American's easy drawl, along with some tired insistence from Andrew, quickly helped smooth over any ruffled feathers from the earlier confrontation. However, Ronald had noted the lingering, angry glint in Lord Merhl's eye. The Lord Arcane appeared to have little time for the newcomer.

Corpses littered the ground – hundreds of dead and dying men and women abandoned to the scavengers and elements; the result of a massive battle between rival tribes. Jennifer told them that the victorious army – the Saecsens of Thegn Cerdic – had already marched further south to burn the raiders' ships. "They must," she'd explained. "Since the *Romanii* left, this land is anyone's to claim. All that holds back the raids are Saescsen swords and shields."

Lord Merhl had been quick to spot the opportunity this presented. He divided the Gedha into groups who buried corpses and cared for the injured. Bodies were stripped and washed for burial, while the refugees shared their possessions.

All of this had left Ronald alone with his thoughts and he'd mulled long and hard over everything that had happened. His mind burned with questions. Andrew was still exhausted from the portal and sleeping amidst the wounded, so Ronald had told Jennifer that they needed to talk. The American had become instantly busy. The demands of nearly five thousand people on her local knowledge had intensified when they discovered language differences between the Saescen survivors and the Corbenii. Someone had to translate between them.

Ronald admired her diligence. As soon as she realised she was needed, she adapted and took the situation in her stride. Her blonde hair bounced as she moved among the Corbenii, giving help and advice. She reminded him of that popular, sporty kid at school: bright, happy and attractive, everything he'd hated back then, but also everything he'd always wanted to be. He quickly realised that he was attracted to her, in the way moths obsess with a flame. Jennifer brought decisiveness and action with her; she didn't overthink things.

The air was still cold and a breeze picked up as the sun set. The countryside was uncomfortably familiar to Ronald; this particular reality was quite similar to home. He'd lived in and around Durrington all his life, so noticing all the similarities and subtle little differences in this land was strange. He walked back up the hill to the stone arch and tried to visualise where it would sit back in his own world. He guessed he would be standing somewhere near the golf course. The main difference was the lack of roads.

He thought back to what Gideon had told him the first time they'd met. Despite Green's contradiction of the old man's advice, the warning against travelling home still hurt. *This could be the nearest I'll ever get.*

Ronald zipped up his parka and put his hands in his pockets. The reassuring cold metal of the flick-knife calmed him. Much as the corpse-picking below was disgusting, he couldn't fault Merhl's reasoning. Winter was fast approaching and, without additional supplies of food, clothing and shelter, the Gedha wouldn't survive.

"What you doin' up here?"

Ronald glanced around to see Jennifer making her way up the slope. His gaze lingered, until he realised what he was doing, became embarrassed and looked away towards the horizon.

"Good place for some privacy, and the view's pretty good."

"What did you want to talk about?"

"A lot of things."

She spread her hands. "I've met a few travellers in the last few years. The way we've always done things is to help each other a bit before going our separate ways. No harm, no foul."

"I'm sorry, but we can't do that this time."

Jennifer frowned. "Then we *do* need to talk."

Ronald stared at her, carefully this time, and noted her injuries. She was wearing rusted chainmail and leather armour crusted with mud. Huge rents and tears covered the garments, each of them stained with blood. "You had a chance to sit down since we got here?" he asked.

She chuckled bitterly. "I'll sleep when I'm dead." Her eyes narrowed. "If he sent you, I ain't going back."

It was Ronald's turn to frown. "What?"

"If *he* sent you to babysit me while he goes off doin' something, you'll find you got more than you bargained for. I ain't going back."

"You mean Andrew? He's asleep."

"No, not him."

"Then who do you mean?"

"The Gaoler – I'm not going back to him. I'm outta here first chance I get."

A thought occurred to Ronald. "This *'Gaoler'*, did he leave before we arrived?"

"Yeah."

He tried to appear calm, but inside he was shaking. "What proof can you give me you really are Jennifer Samms?"

"What?"

"I know who Jennifer Samms is, and what happened to her in my world."

Her eyes widened. "Hold on – are you saying you think you're from my world?"

"I'm not sure," he admitted. "Where I come from, you're dead."

Jennifer laughed. "Happens a lot."

"You said that earlier, when we first met you." He scowled. "Didn't make sense then and doesn't make sense now."

Jennifer's smile faded. "Buddy, how long you been out here?"

"We've made a few trips."

"And, apart from being able to do all this weird shit, you haven't worked out how it's affected you?"

"What do you mean?"

"You and the other guy: Andrew, right? We each have a different gift. I couldn't have brought that many people through from another world."

Ronald stared at her. "You mean that's part of it?"

"Yep. My gift is that I can't die."

"You keep coming back?"

"Yeah. That's why I mentioned being dead a lot."

Ronald frowned. "How do I trust you're telling the truth though? Like you said, travellers don't stay together."

Jennifer sighed. "You think I cut myself up like this for show?" She took hold of both edges of a huge tear in her leather jerkin and pulled it open. Whatever had made the rent had also ripped her chainmail. "Last one went right through me; a guy trod on my back and put his axe into my spine. The blood's mostly mine … from that and the other stuff." She lifted her chin and pointed at a livid red scar on her neck. "And the Gaoler did this to open the arch."

"We were followed by someone called Candleswick."

"Yeah, I've heard that name. Same guy," Jennifer replied heavily. "The older travellers acquire a lot of names and shapes." She opened the torn leather further to reveal a tattered red top underneath. "See this? Last thing left from before. My Boston Terriers football shirt."

"You played, then?"

"If you say you know me, then you know the answer to that."

Ronald relaxed; the answers felt right and he was more confident that she was who she claimed to be, but he needed to be thorough. "What happened to your book?"

"My book?"

"The one you were reading when you were transported."

She grimaced and ran her fingers through her hair. "Oh shit. I can't remember. It was ages ago. I picked up a cheap paperback after I got in from some other girl's dorm. I was bored and trying to avoid study. When I first came through, he took it off of me."

"Who?"

"Who d'you think? Gaoler. Told me I didn't need it. I didn't learn till later about the whole resonance deal. You saying it was important?"

Ronald nodded. "We think so. The book was the key to your transport and to at least half a dozen others. It's also how we created our first portal."

"You mean you got out intentionally?"

"Yes."

Jennifer stared at him. "Not quite what you thought it'd be, is it?"

"No," he admitted. "You're right."

They lapsed into silence, but it wasn't an uncomfortable one. For the first time, Ronald sensed he'd met someone who understood him. The newfound sense of kinship he felt was palpable.

"We fought Candleswick after he left here. I stabbed him with this." He reached back into his pocket and produced the flick-knife.

Jennifer let out a low whistle. "Yeah, I can feel the power in that thing. Did you kill him?"

"No. We put him in another world; one he shouldn't be able to escape from."

"Well, I wouldn't count on that," the American drawled. "He's powerful. If he wasn't, I'd have run away long ago."

Ronald turned to face her. "Why did you stay with him?" he asked.

All at once, Jennifer's natural confidence seemed to shatter, her face clouding with self-doubt and remembered pain. "I had no choice," she mumbled. "He said when he was done with me he'd let me go home."

Ronald sighed and rubbed his face with his hands. "Candleswick's our enemy. You were with him and we've only your word you were coerced. We don't know for sure you're telling the truth."

Jennifer glared at him and tugged at her torn leather jerkin. "Were you listening to me? You think I faked this shit?" she demanded. "Bastard cut me from ear-to-ear. You think I'd make that up?"

Ronald flinched and looked away. "No, I don't. But I've seen so much in the last few days, perhaps you'll understand why I'm hesitant."

A strong hand gripped his shoulder and Jennifer turned him around. Her blue eyes were like chips of ice. "Listen, the thing you call Candleswick kept me in a cage for a long time, using me like some kind of pit-fighting animal. It got so bad that I couldn't remember my own name. He took me to all sorts of worlds and made me hunt down other travellers like you, or even just potential travellers – people who might one day make it, but hadn't broken through. He said he was enforcing the rules, that people like you and me shouldn't exist and that we endanger existence. Hell, I didn't have any choice, but he said that didn't matter. For a while, I believed it, but there's only so much blood you can wash off your hands before you start to wonder what's right." She jabbed a finger into Ronald's chest. "From what you told me, you guys had options, so if I was still buying into the Gaoler's little dream, I should be gutting you right now."

"So, why aren't you?"

"Perhaps it's because I *don't* believe it; or maybe I value my freedom more." Her face was two inches from his. "Now I'm happy to work with you for a bit, but don't cross me. You want my help, you ask. No tricks and no other shit. You can keep what secrets you like, but I walk away when I want to. You got it?"

Ronald flinched again and wished Andrew was with him. "Fine," he managed to mumble in response.

She scowled and turned away. "Glad we're straight. I best head back." Her gruff tone made Ronald feel guilty.

"So how long you been here?" he asked weakly.

She turned back and regarded him grudgingly. "About a year. Gaoler was waiting for someone; he left me here to do a job." She pointed down at the battlefield below, where the Gedha were still clearing away bodies. "There was a guy, one of them down there, who'd started dabbling. Our friend wanted to make sure he stopped."

"You killed him?"

"Yeah. Well, he killed me and I left him injured enough that someone else finished him off." She sighed and looked down at her hands. "You kinda get numb to it after a while."

They both fell silent again. Jennifer shaded her eyes and gazed back down the hill. "It's getting dark and cold. We'll need to organise a group to walk to the village and see what help they can find."

"What's the village called?"

"Dureton."

Ronald chuckled. "I thought it looked familiar."

"You been there before?"

"No, but in our world, this is where Andrew and I live." He gestured around him. "All this is a golf course now. This looks like some time in the distant past."

Jennifer laughed. "Really? Is this the Middle Ages?"

"At a guess, some version of Dark Age Britain. A time between the Roman Empire and the Norman Conquest."

"That figures; *Romanii* equals Roman. Good to learn, thanks. I wasn't a history major."

"Me neither," Ronald replied, "but it helps when it's your own country."

"Yeah, I suppose."

They both started back down the hill but, before they got too far, Ronald pointed at the stone arch. "What do you know about those?"

Jennifer shrugged. "Not sure. They appear in a helluva lot of worlds, but I've been to places without them."

"Andrew thinks each place has a trigger – a set of rules that you need to overcome to open a portal."

"Could be, but Gaoler never hung around long enough to work out that shit. He always popped from place to place saying sacrifice was the key – murder, you know? I think that's why he kept me around. To him I'm like a battery."

Ronald swallowed hard. "Must be horrible."

"Put it this way: if I'd got at him with that little rabbit-sticker of yours, he wouldn't have got up." The American's expression was stony.

"Do yourself a favour and get something bigger to cut him with."

Ronald nodded. "We're not planning on staying too long."

"Good to hear. Neither am I."

Night Notes

"Stop here," Mike said.

Emily nodded and pulled over. It was early evening and they'd been driving for more than an hour out of Durrington. The cars on the roads were switching from sidelights to headlights and the layby he'd chosen was deserted.

It began to rain; a steady downpour that quickly coated the windows. Emily switched off the engine and the lights. "What are we doing here?"

Mike nodded towards the man sprawled on the back seat. "He was right when he talked about rituals; we can't take him in. We'll get nothing and it'll only make things worse."

"So, what do we do?"

"We wait." He took out his mobile phone, opened the voice recorder app, touched the record button, then turned in his chair and stared at the man. "While we do, you're going to tell me what happened last night."

The man raised his head and shrugged. "Someone performed a ritual in the library and transported out of this reality. It caused several rifts elsewhere and edits had to be made. Unfortunately, you both got caught up in the inconsistency. Still, the changes were made successfully and most people have accepted them."

"Does this happen a lot?"

"Not really. The people who got away found an obscure loophole involving books. It's been closed in the latest correction."

"What about Davies?"

"The inspector called us in; he informed the technical supervisor before we began work." The man's lips thinned in an approximation of a smile. "He's been one of our more successful operatives for some time."

Mike glanced at Emily. "So, what you're saying is that everything I saw – the attack on the Edwards place, the big dog, the bloody knives in Gibbs' home – it was all real."

"Oh yes, they were, but now they're not." The man turned towards the window. "My associates have arrived."

"I was counting on that," Mike said. He looked at Emily again. "Stay here."

He climbed out of the car, into the driving rain. He pulled up the collar of his jacket and hunched over, but it did little good and he was quickly soaked.

Three figures were walking up the road and turned into the layby. Mike clenched and unclenched his fists. In America, or the movies, this might have become a gunfight, but he knew that kind of solution wouldn't bring any more answers.

Two men and a woman approached. They seemed barely affected by the rain, their clothes damp, yet not sodden like his. He recognised the woman immediately by her freckles and curly hair.

"Hello Miriam," he said.

"Hello Mike."

"Are you part of all this?"

"I wasn't, but I am now."

"Who are your friends? Going to introduce us?"

"Names don't really matter."

Mike stared at her, but she didn't flinch. "How long since you joined the new team?" he asked.

"Last night."

"Good. Would hate to think you'd been ratting on me."

"I wouldn't do that."

"Even now?" Mike smiled. "Then why are you here?"

"We have to take him, Detective Sergeant," one of the men said.

"I know," Mike replied. "Before you do though, I want to know why."

"It won't help you," the other man said.

"And why's that?"

"Because you won't remember any of this and neither will your friend."

"Not unless I join you?"

"We're not offering you that."

Mike nodded and stared at the men. They had the same kind of featureless faces as the man in the car. "I still want to know. Tell me what happens."

"We take him, and you go to sleep here in the car and wake up with the past we need you to have," Miriam said.

"And what if it doesn't take?"

"You disappear."

"That's it? It's all that simple?"

"Memories are like a new carpet. You barely miss the old one. Believe me, the preparation that goes into this kind of exercise isn't simple," Miriam said. "They had to prepare something very special for you and DC Jacobs."

"What about the reasons for that?"

Miriam tapped the side of her head with her finger. "You already got your answers, Mike. We know what you know."

"I see." He stepped around the car, putting it between him and them. One of the men followed.

"Don't make this hard, Mike," Miriam said.

"Sorry, I really don't mean to." He edged towards the road, watching the headlights of the passing cars, waiting for his moment. When a lorry got close, he dashed out in front of it.

A horn blared and something clipped his foot, sending him sprawling into the oncoming traffic. He leapt up and ran for the grass and trees beside the road. He heard Miriam shouting, but didn't look back.

He didn't dare.

*

Andrew woke up.

It was dark and a wind whipped through the canvas of the crude shelter he found himself in. Outside, in the darkness, he could see the flickering light of a fire struggling feebly against the chilly air.

He sat up. Low moans echoed in the night. He guessed he'd been taken to the makeshift infirmary with the injured that the Gedha had recovered from the battlefield. Their resourcefulness and ingenuity surprised him. Then again, they had been waiting for decades to escape the remains of their trapped city.

He gazed out at the fire. Dark shapes huddled close around the wavering light, while others moved around in the gloom. They seemed in good spirits and he could make out snatches of singing and laughter.

It was a gratifying scene and he allowed himself a moment of pride in his part in bringing it about.

When he tried to stand, his legs shook and rebelled. His skull throbbed too, the same headache from the Caer, but it was marginally less severe now and the pain settled into an irritating throb as he got to his feet and stumbled out of the shelter towards the firelight.

"Ah, Harrower! How are things with you?" Arta's voice ghosted out of the dark and the Keeper Arcane appeared next to him at the edge of the gathering.

"I'm feeling better, if that's what you mean. Thanks for asking."

Arta seemed relieved. "Good news then. Ronald explained in detail your part in the proceedings. I hadn't realised so much of this magic relied on your strength."

"Yes, well, we weren't too sure on the details either, before we tried."

"He also said we wouldn't be travelling again."

Andrew nodded. "Yes, I hope there'll be no need. You're a strong people. You just needed a chance."

Arta chuckled. "You have faith in us?"

"I think you're worth the trust."

"Thank you. This will be a large task. The woman named Jennifer says this land is wracked with war."

"Yes, not easy," Andrew admitted. "But there is no such thing as an ideal world."

"She calls us 'Keltoi' – they are a native people, older than the Saescsen and the Dene, who fought here."

The words sounded like those from Dark Age British history books: Saxon, Dane and Celt. "If these are a similar people, I think you should accept the name. You may find it easier to integrate."

"Indeed. Though it grieves me that our story will fade from memory, we must change if we are to survive here."

"Your own past is still important, but you need to be accepted and find allies."

"Indeed. I think my people will understand; yet, for me personally, this is difficult. The archives were my life."

"How much did you bring with you?" Andrew asked.

"Very little. Most of our scriptures remained behind."

"You left them in Corbenic?"

"Yes, we locked the doors and abandoned everything." Arta's face clouded with concern. "Should we have done something differently?"

Andrew thought about Candleswick. Sooner or later he was sure to find the rooms. He could only hope the documents wouldn't help him escape. "No, I'm sure it'll be fine," he answered, forcing a smile. "But it does mean we will be leaving soon."

"Oh." Arta seemed disappointed. "We thought you would stay at least a few days, so that we might show our gratitude."

"Probably best that we don't. There are others to help."

"Your tasks are arduous. I hope you do not tax yourself too much."

Andrew smiled. "We'll be okay."

He turned and stared into the flames. Someone started singing again and other voices joined in. He noticed Brodi, the servant he'd met in Corbenic. The young man stood proudly, singing at the top of his voice. Andrew looked at the other men and women in the crowd and was struck by the expressions of hope on each face he saw.

"The Seacsan tongue is strange to us. It will be difficult to learn."

Andrew frowned. "When we found Jennifer, how did she sound to you?"

"She spoke like you. You have an odd accent, though you speak the same words as us."

"Did she talk to the wounded?"

"Yes, she told them we would help."

"Did she sound different then?"

Arta thought about this for a moment. "No, I do not believe she did. They seemed to comprehend her just as we do." He frowned. "I do not understand."

Andrew sighed and turned back to the fire. "Neither do I."

*

Ronald yawned and blinked rapidly, fighting to stay awake as he walked. Next to him, Jennifer seemed untroubled by fatigue. The American's eyes scanned the darkness, her hand gripping the hilt of the sword at her waist. Its selection from among the pile of weapons removed from the dead warriors had taken the best part of an hour after they had finished talking near the stone arch, by which time it was dark.

Now, Ronald guessed, it was around eight or nine o'clock at night.

Lord Merhl had asked them to accompany Gwuina and some of

the wardens tasked with visiting Dureton village, and now they were on their way back. Jennifer had introduced them to the people – the Keltoi – and Ronald had come to the same perplexing conclusion as Andrew: for some reason, he and Jennifer could understand the speech of everyone they met, yet the villagers seemed to struggle to comprehend Gwuina's words at first, although they did eventually manage to communicate. The requests for aid were grudgingly accepted and one of the elders decided to go with them back to the camp.

Now they walked cautiously in the dark, the wardens spread out in a wide circle around them, their eyes piercing the gloom. Ronald got the sense Jennifer would be more comfortable with them, instead of being one of the protected.

"How come they can understand us? How does that work?" he asked her.

She grunted. "I'm not sure. Kinda strange though. You and me speak and everyone understands every word we say and we get everything they say, no matter what language."

"That's what I thought was happening. But why?"

"Like I said, I don't know. Maybe it's the transportation or something. Doesn't happen everywhere though. I've been to places where I ain't had a clue what people were saying." She stared out into out the night. "When you do understand though, it sure makes things easier."

Ronald chuckled. "Yeah."

"Trust me, I've talked down plenty of shitheads who wanted to gut me. Woulda been more painful if I'd had to play phrasebook with 'em."

The firelights of the camp ahead came into view, miniature candles in the velvet black. The small group headed towards them, picking their way carefully over the unfamiliar ground.

"Are we likely to be attacked?" Ronald asked.

"I don't think so," Jennifer replied. "But you can bet the Saescans heard that these people are here by now, or that they will have heard by morning."

"Will they come to fight?"

"I'm not sure. They took a lot of casualties when they defeated the Dene, and the Keltoi aren't their enemies; they may leave them alone."

Ronald allowed himself to feel a little relieved. He didn't doubt the courage of the Gedha, but they were ill-prepared for warfare, having only recently arrived. If accosted, they would be fighting for their survival.

Gwuina joined the conversation. "Our scouts have already begun patrolling the land to the south. They will tell us if there is any cause for concern."

"What will you do if they come?" Ronald asked her.

"Lord Merhl will decide. We are not defenceless; the lore that protected us in Corbenic can be used to defend us here."

"I wouldn't rely on it," Jennifer said. "Things tend to change when you walk between worlds."

Gwuina seemed confused. "I do not understand."

"We will speak to all of the Arcanes about this when we return," Ronald said. "Jennifer and I must talk to Andrew first."

"Of course."

A short while later, they reached the camp. Ronald and Jennifer left the rest of the group and headed to Andrew's shelter.

"You never mentioned how you'd met me before," Jennifer said, as they walked.

"We didn't meet. You're a famous case, on a list of peculiar disappearances – an integral part of my research."

"Great." She smiled at him. "I'm a nerd's wet dream."

He frowned. "I spent years researching cases like yours. The people I work with aren't some conspiracy cult."

"Sorry, I didn't mean—"

"Yeah, but my *nerdiness* was what got me here and got you your freedom."

"Okay. Glad we're straight."

"Yeah."

"What about your friend?" she asked. "What's his story?"

"He was sat in a library when a girl who disappeared, like you did, turned up dead. He got accused of murdering her. He's out here for answers."

"You found any yet?"

"Some. We think Candleswick took her."

They soon located the shelter and made their way towards it. Ronald ducked inside and saw that Andrew was no longer in the litter where they had left him.

"Over here," said a tired voice and he turned to see the doctor sat alone on a broken box some distance away, illuminated by the firelight.

"Feeling better?" Ronald asked him.

"A bit. Still got a headache, although it's eased off a little."

Ronald nodded, "Perhaps you should rest some more?"

"I don't think I can right now. There are too many things we need to straighten up." He glanced at Jennifer. "Good to see you again."

"Likewise," Jennifer said. She drew her sword and placed it on the ground, before sitting cross-legged in front of Andrew. "So, according to Ronald, I owe you both."

"Candleswick was keeping you here?"

"Yeah, but I 'don't call him that. To me, his name is 'Gaoler'. Pretty sure he's the same guy though, and you getting rid of him means I'm free."

"Let's hope so," Andrew replied. "What are your plans?"

Jennifer shrugged. "Well, I don't want to stay here too long. I'll come with you guys, if that's okay."

"Where do you want to go?"

"Home, if I could," she confessed.

"We're not sure if that's possible. You were found dead in Los Angeles about a year ago."

"Never been there."

"Well, we don't know how you got there," Ronald said, sitting down next to her. "We aren't even sure you'll be able to go home. I'm in a similar situation; I was stabbed before we got out."

"So, you're worried you'll die if you go back?"

"Yep."

Jennifer shrugged. "I guess we can't find out unless we try, and we're screwed if we're wrong. Tough call."

"For you *and* me."

"We'll find a way to return you both if we can," Andrew promised quietly. "But, right now, we need to look at what we're going to do next."

"We can't stay here," Ronald said. "'Even if it's an improvement on Corbenic and it gives Merhl's people a good chance, it's not for us."

"No, you're right," Andrew replied. "Plus, Candleswick may not be as contained as we thought. He has Corbenic's archive to work with."

Ronald scowled. "I thought they'd burn the books or bring them here."

"I thought so too. I doubt Arta could bring himself to destroy them. He locked up the archives and kept the keys."

"That means Candleswick can find them. Eventually, he'll escape."

"We need to face him again anyway," Andrew continued. "He showed me where Amanda is and how to get to her, but he also kidnapped three kids from Durrington – we must find them."

Ronald turned to Jennifer. "Any idea what he might do with them?"

"He'll be keeping them somewhere safe until he works out how useful they can be," she replied. "This whole 'protecting reality' thing is convenient for him at first but, if they've got nothing he can use, he'll kill them."

"Then we go back and find him, so we can rescue them," Andrew said.

"I'll help," Jennifer growled. "After that, you can leave him to me."

Ronald shared a look with Andrew. They both knew what the American meant. "We can worry about that later," he said. "When do you want to go?"

"First thing in the morning," Andrew replied.

"What about the Gedha?"

"If we stay any longer, they'll get more and more dependent on us."

Ronald felt a hand on his shoulder. "He's right," Jennifer said. "From what you told me, you need to leave. You gave these people a chance. Now it's up to them."

"Jennifer, do you know why they can all understand us, but not each other?" Andrew asked.

"We were talking about it earlier," Ronald said. "It's weird, particularly as it doesn't seem to happen for Gwuina and the others, but their language is similar to the locals in the village."

"Could they manage without us?"

"I think so. The Arcanes will learn."

"They'll learn much quicker if we're not here as a crutch," Jennifer said.

"I agree," Andrew said. "We head out to find Amanda, then go back to Corbenic."

"How are you going to help her if Candleswick's already killed her?" Ronald asked.

"Before you arrived, I shared his memory of the event," Andrew explained. "Based on what Green told us, I think I can transport us there to a moment before she died."

"So that's your gift, then?" Jennifer asked. "You can travel in time?"

"I don't think it quite works like that," Andrew replied. "All I understand is, I have a talent for finding the way between places, just as Ronald is good at opening portals."

"Okay."

"What do we do then?" Ronald asked. "If we stop Candleswick from killing Amanda, she'll never appear in the library and you'll never meet me, or find your way to another world."

Andrew sighed. "Yes, it's messed up, but I'm not sure we have all the answers yet. If there's a chance to help the poor girl though, I need to try."

"Why?" Ronald pressed.

"You know why. It all leads back to her."

Ronald frowned. "What if trying this gets us killed?"

"We'll ask Gideon about it."

"Who's Gideon?" Jennifer asked.

"We're not really sure," Andrew answered. "Whenever we travel, we seem to meet him in between."

"Weird," Jennifer said. "I've never met anyone in between; I just step through and I'm on the other side."

Ronald ignored her. "Why do you think Gideon can help?"

"Because, when Candleswick came through the portal, he didn't call him Gideon. He called him Janus. Janus is the Roman God of gates, doors, beginnings and endings, a two-headed god; one face stares into the future, one into the past."

Ronald wasn't convinced. "It's a bit weak."

"We can't do anything until we're sure. We leave here and talk to Gideon, then we decide what to do."

Gifts

"We need to make a decision."

The fog had lifted and Linda stood in the grass field surrounded by stone arches. The sky was grey, with no visible sun; the kind of bleak autumnal day everyone forgets.

She and George had walked a few hundred yards from the car. She could see it parked beside the pillars, the only irregular feature of the landscape.

What must I look like? she thought and smiled to herself. No shoes, smudged makeup, muddy tights and a torn dress. Even in her student days, she'd never found herself looking like this.

"The arches all seem the same. I've no idea which one we should choose," George said.

She licked a finger and wiped away the last of her lipstick. "What about the car? Can we take it through?"

"I'm not sure. I don't think it would fit."

She turned around, shading her eyes and staring at the horizon. "When we came here, we didn't need to pass through an archway; we just drove."

He frowned. "You think that'll work again?"

She shrugged. "I'm not sure, but what harm can it do?"

They walked back towards the car and George took her hand. "I never said thank you."

"What for?"

"For making this choice; coming with me."

"It wasn't a choice."

"I always thought it was – between Andrew and me."

"I made that decision long ago."

George laughed, a sound that made her stop in surprise. She hadn't heard him laugh like that in years. "I get that now," he said. "I worked it out for myself before they came for me in the car. You were just trying to help him and I couldn't see that because of your previous relationship." He gazed at her. "I don't own you; I never did. That's why I wanted you to choose earlier to come out here. I think I forgot all that."

Linda took his hand and tugged him forwards. They resumed walking. "Like I said, it wasn't a choice. You always were the only one for me."

"I see that now."

"Good."

*

Andrew stood outside in the dark. For a moment, he thought he'd woken up after sleepwalking from the shelter, but he didn't recognise any of the shapes and shadows from before. The refugee camp had become a large sprawl of windbreaks and campfires that carried the low hub of conversation and snatches of song, but he could see no-one about. There were two lights some distance away and then he heard the faint noise of a cheering crowd.

He made his way towards the sound and the twin fires. They were torches, burning on long poles, and suspended high above the ground. He walked between them and made out dim shapes in the gloom – wagons, parked in a line. Beyond them, more lights and a glow from a huge tent, from where the crowd noise also seemed to emanate. Somehow, the scene was familiar.

He moved closer and peered at the wagons. They were gaudily painted, with bars on the windows. He noticed large padlocks on the doors at the back. They were built to keep something in.

He heard whispers and froze.

"It's been hours."

"Shut up! He might be just outside! He told us not to talk!"

"I'm not scared of him."

"Liar. You crapped yourself when he got in your mum's garage."

"Shut up!"

Andrew recognised the voices. He remembered what Candleswick had said – *I found three children experimenting with strange magic.* Now, Andrew realised they were the same ones he'd seen in his dream the night he was at Ronald's house.

Booted feet paced nearby. Fearing discovery, Andrew hurried back into the darkness. When he was a fair distance away, he dropped flat on the ground and chanced a look back. Two figures approached the wagon that he guessed contained the children. One was human in size and shape, but the other was at least three feet taller and just as wide.

"Check 'em. Gaoler'll be wantin' to make sure they're fresh."

The large creature grunted and went up the steps to the door, unlocked it and entered, stooping so he could fit through.

The night echoed with the sound of children screaming.

*

Mike ran and didn't look back.

Over a grass verge into the scrubland beyond; across a field, up a hill, into the woods, scrambling up slopes and down through mud and dirty brackish water, wet dewy fields; over anything and everything as fast as he could.

He could hear his pursuers, or at least thought he could. Every sound, shadow and shape that emerged from the darkness fuelled his loping sprint. *If they catch me, it's all over. I won't remember. I have to remember!*

The last time he'd run like this, he'd been thirteen years old. The third year of secondary school had seen him lining up for the fifteen hundred metres against the popular sports kids. After two laps, one of them tried to slow the race down, but the teenage Mike had burst into the lead and never looked back. At the end, they'd had to shout at him to stop running. He'd been in a world of his own.

How ironic.

Thorns caught his ankles, making him stumble. Office shoes weren't made for cross country running, nor were his work jacket and shirt. As it grew darker, he struggled to avoid the brambles and bushes along the way. His breaths came in great heaving gasps, a sort of panicked exhaustion, making him move slower and slower.

Eventually, he realised his pace had become a walk. He stopped, leant against a tree and focused on breathing. Any pursuer would catch him and overpower him in an instant, but he couldn't go on. His clothes were torn and soaked, with long scratches on his forearms and calves.

When he'd recovered a little, he listened. He couldn't hear anyone, only the rain and wind as it stirred the woodland. He shivered, stumbled over to a fallen log and sat down. *Why would they give up?*

He pulled out his mobile phone and accessed the recorder app, holding it to his ear to listen to the playback. The interview in the car came back clearly, the rain outside interfering with a few words here and there, but all the information was intact. However, the conversation between him and Miriam outside was barely intelligible.

Damn.

He walked on for a bit, using the phone as a light. Bedwyn Forest was a huge place. He remembered visiting as a child. A museum to the nineteenth century lumber industry lay in the middle of it somewhere. He'd been dragged around it by his parents, but he couldn't recall where it was.

Ahead, he spotted something white. As he got closer, he realised it was a piece of torn canvas that'd been strung between an old oak's branches. Underneath, he found a damp sleeping bag and several crushed lager cans. He squatted down here, grateful to be out of the rain. He ran his hands over the ground and found something else – a small plastic box. He pulled it out, brushing away leaves and dirt. Under the light of the phone, he opened the lid. Inside was a small book with a plain cover and a pistol, with a bag containing six bullets.

Mike opened the book and read the title page – *Mythago Wood by Robert Holdstock*. He remembered what the strange man had said: the people who had managed to get away had found an obscure loophole involving books.

He turned off his phone and gazed out into the night, feeling guilty for leaving Emily in the car, but there'd been no option. Trying to find his way back to the road would be difficult and could mean he'd be captured. Finding his way to anywhere else would be impossible.

The last of the sunlight faded and he sensed there was something out there in the dark. The shadows and shapes of the woodland were like silent watchers all around him. In his mind, the trees became monsters, the swaying of branches and leaves their arms, legs, hands and claws.

He sat with his back against the old oak, picked up the gun and the bullets and began loading them. When he was done, he dropped the weapon in his lap and closed his eyes.

*

Ronald stood over the mountain of discarded equipment.

At Jennifer's behest, Lord Merhl had told the Gedha to strip the bodies of the dead before burying them. Many had worked through the night and mounds of earth now covered Dene and Saescen alike. The usable items were appropriated quickly and what remained was a mixture of broken weapons and armour. Smashed shields and battered horned helms adorned the piles. The wardens and other able-bodied men and women took the best of these; Lord Merhl intended to organise them into a militia to defend his people as they searched for a suitable place to settle.

It was early morning and both Jennifer and Andrew were still asleep. Ronald made careful use of the time, picking over the remaining arms until he'd collected a small pile from which to work. He sat on the floor with the items and drew out his flick-knife.

He examined the weapon. The long, black, hollow hilt was decorated with swirls of bright silver shapes like cartoon waves or gusts of wind, an unmistakably cheap, modern piece that held little material value. Still, it meant a great deal to him. The knife had become a friend over the years; every scratch and nick on the handle a memory. It was completely impractical – lacking the tidy size of a penknife or the multitude of tools that might come with a fold-away army blade – yet he didn't feel whole without it. The knife meant more to him than almost anything else he owned. That day in France had been his first adult decision, buying something for himself because of what it represented.

He'd gone on after that. The court settlement from the transport company whose truck had run over his foot made for a sizeable house deposit and kept him with a regular income for years. When he had his own space, he decorated, buying replica swords, axes; all sorts. Waking up and staring at the weapons fired his imagination.

"You wanted to see me?"

Ronald glanced up. Arta was making his way towards him, a tired smile on his face. "Thanks for looking after Andrew."

"It was the least we could do, after the two of you did us such service," Arta replied.

"Well, thank you anyway. I need another favour."

"Of course. How can I assist?"

Ronald weighed the flick-knife in his hands before flipping the blade back into its sheath and passing it to Arta. "You should take this."

Arta accepted the weapon. "For what reason?"

"I want you to melt it down. It'll require a hotter forge than your blacksmith's normally work with. Then I want you to use the metal to make something else." He picked up one of the broken blades he'd found in the pile. "You'll need to spread it along the edge of something like this."

"You want a newly forged sword, edged with the metal from this?"

"Exactly."

Arta frowned. "This will take time. There are no such tools available. It can't be done straight away."

"No rush. We're leaving later today, but we'll be back one day. I want you to keep it safe for me."

"You are departing so soon? That is unfortunate."

"We must go," Ronald said. "You should take care of yourselves."

Arta examined the knife, tracing his finger over the decorative swirls. "These patterns, are they significant?"

"You mean like your runes? No, there's no power in them."

Arta sighed. "A shame. I also have something to show you."

He led Ronald away from the piled weapons and took him back to the makeshift shelter they had rigged up for the battle-wounded. They picked their way over the sleeping forms of the Gedha folk. Here and there they found people awake, who nodded quiet greeting to the Arcane and bowed their heads to the Harrower.

After a few minutes, they reached the shelter and Arta gestured for Ronald to enter. Arta took him across to one of the litters. Ronald noted less people than before, when they had brought Andrew in to rest here. "What's happened to all the others?"

"They receive treatment and recover," Arta replied. "But I am vexed that we can't do more."

"What do you mean? Some of these wounds should take months to heal, if at all."

Arta smiled. "I am feeling strong. I will show you."

The woman lying on the makeshift bed was listless and sweaty; her eyes shone with a fever and a wrap of stained bandages swathed her ribs and belly. "A bad wound," Arta muttered. "We left her as we knew she would live, but we didn't anticipate these problems."

He began to unwrap the wound, plucking at the cloths as firmly as he dared. The woman's gaze locked on him and she hissed between clenched teeth. Strands of unkempt hair flicked across her face as she struggled feebly, but she was too weak to put up much resistance.

The first thing Ronald noted was the smell: sickly sweet and stomach-churning; a stink of putrefying flesh that stoked rebellion in his gut. He found himself gritting his teeth and staring into the woman's eyes, trying by sheer force of will to impart some sort of strength and resistance to the pain.

Arta knelt down beside her and Ronald couldn't help but stare. The wound was bare, the woman's skin a pale white in the cold morning gloom. She'd been slashed apart from the ribs to the middle of her stomach. The tear was crusted and clotted with dark blood. Yellow puss oozed out from the broken scabs and the remaining flesh was discoloured and corrupt.

The Arcane placed his hands carefully on the damaged skin, spreading them outwards around the wound. Ronald forced himself to watch, suppressing revulsion, as Arta wetted his index fingers with her blood and puss and traced patterns over her body. Ronald recognised the symbols as runes, like the ones from the walls of Corbenic.

The air became tense and hot. Ronald stared at Arta mumbling incantations, his face pinched with strain. *Magic.* The sensation was like the first time amidst the stones, when Gideon healed his knife wound.

Then it was over, and a faint breeze stirred the shelter. Ronald glanced at the woman again. She slept, her flesh repaired itself and the corruption vanished. He turned to Arta again. The archivist was doubled over and his breath came in gasps as he hugged himself on the floor.

Ronald bent down. "Are you okay? How can I help?"

"Water!" Arta gasped. Ronald moved quickly towards a small table and picked up one of the stone flagons that the Gedha had brought from Corbenic. He hurried back and sat down beside Arta, who accepted the vessel with shaking hands. Together, they guided the bowl to his lips and he drank heavily.

"Thank you," he breathed. "My work gets harder every time."

"You mean the magic?"

"Yes. Soon I fear we will lose our art and all that we dedicated our lives to learning will be gone."

They sat in silence for some time, the quiet disturbed only by the now regular breathing of the injured woman. Eventually, Arta recovered something of himself and struggled to his feet. Ronald helped him, and they moved back outside the shelter.

"What will we do?" Arta asked quietly. "Our magic is what defends us. In a world as dangerous as this, we will need it."

"Other people live without."

Arta sighed. "It is difficult to accept. Perhaps you do not understand my position in this. Can you picture a life in which you know you were set apart from others and that your gifts would require you dedicate your efforts to their care? The runes and the archives were my life. With both taken away, I find it hard."

"No, I can't imagine being like that," Ronald replied. "I'm sorry, Arta. My life is very different to yours."

"I struggle to learn my place here. I almost miss Corbenic."

"Maybe you need to see it another way?" Ronald reasoned. "What if you'd lived believing you were in some way special and gifted, but ended up frustrated because the rest of the world didn't believe in you?"

"If that had been so, I would be a different man."

Ronald nodded. "You would have spent your time trying to prove you were right, searching for the truth about magic, or whatever. You would have been lonely."

Arta sighed again. "Yet, l I do not wish to be the same here. Clinging to old lore would be just as bad."

"Then you need to find some new lore."

"Perhaps, but saying such a thing is easy. I find myself at a loss as to where to begin."

Ronald thought about this for a few moments. He gazed out across the countryside. The morning mist from the river Aven was gradually fading as a bright, bleak sun rose from the hilltops. "Look over there," he said and pointed. A twisted tree crouched on top of a hill some distance away, its leaves stirring faintly in the breeze. It was hardly a prime specimen, gnarled and hooked in upon itself. Ronald had never been knowledgeable about trees and had no idea what type it was. "You ever seen a tree before?" he asked Arta.

"Not like that. I've seen many in drawings and pictures, but the tunnels of Corbenic couldn't accommodate such plants."

"Well, you never would have if you'd hadn't come here."

"You are right."

"There's a lot of beauty in the world, Arta; a lot of beauty everywhere. We just don't take the time to look around. Everything has a secret, or a special gift, but if we don't take the time to appreciate that, no-one will. What I'm trying to say is that at least you were able to use your gifts. Sometimes life requires sacrifices. Far better to live a little and maybe help someone, or see a little beauty, than just exist and risk nothing. If you had stayed behind, perhaps you would have kept your magic, but at what cost? Think of the people you're helping here. You had years of pursuing your love for writing and learning the runic powers. Other people only dream of getting the chance to fulfil their potential."

"Indeed." Arta smiled faintly. "There is a danger in dreams."

"You better believe it," Ronald said ruefully.

Leave

"Who are you?"

Mike awoke to find a pair of eyes staring at him in the half-dawn light. They belonged to a girl, crouched in the dirt. She was in her twenties and wrapped in a sleeping bag. She had curly hair, a freckled face and reminded him of someone.

"Detective Sergeant Mike Underhill, Durrington police. You?"

"Gwen."

He was in a woodland and they were both under a white sheet of plastic canvas. He vaguely remembered getting here but not much else. He squirmed, trying to stretch his back against an old tree.

"This your place?" he asked.

"Yeah."

"I see." Mike glanced down and found a gun and a thin paperback in his lap. He stared at both for a while, trying to recall where he'd found them. Then he held up the gun in his palm. "I'll need to confiscate this."

Gwen shrugged. "It's not mine."

"And the book?"

"Nope. Never seen them before."

Mike stood up. His clothes were damp. He looked around, not recognising anything about the place. "Where am I?"

"Bedwyn Forest." She pointed to her right. "The bypass is about a mile that way."

He saw four or five empty lager cans on the floor. *Is that how I got like this?* The girl was staring at him expectantly, so he nodded his thanks, fished in his pocket and dropped some loose change in her hands. Then he started out in the direction she'd gestured towards.

As he walked, he stuffed the gun and the book into his jacket pocket and tried to piece together the night before. He remembered running from something and thinking he'd got away.

He put his hands into his trouser pockets and pulled out his phone. He turned it on. The battery was nearly empty, but it still powered up.

Two voicemail messages appeared and he saw there was a large audio recording file saved on the drive.

He listened to the voicemails first. One was from DI Davies at the station asking his whereabouts; the other was from DC Emily Jacobs, which cut out after fifteen seconds. He realised he was worried about her, but he wasn't sure why. He dialled her number.

After three rings, she picked up. "Where have you been?"

"Bedwyn Forest, sleeping rough; not sure why. Can you pick me up?"

"I guess. What's happened to your car?"

"I don't know."

"How do I find you?"

"Head down the bypass. I'll be on the roadside."

"Okay."

He ended the call and carried on walking.

*

"So, you asked yourself the obvious question yet?"

Andrew rubbed his eyes and glanced up at Jennifer. It was early in the morning and the American woman was standing beside the stone archway, scraping at one of the pillars with the end of a short knife.

"No. What's that?" he replied.

"Is this real? I mean, what if I'm just dreaming you up, or you're dreaming me up? Surely it's more likely than all this shit being true."

Andrew thought about this for a moment. "It's like the colour red," he said at last.

"What?"

"You identify red the same way I do, but I don't know if you see the same thing as me. We just agree it's called red."

"How's that like all this?"

"Well, we could be seeing and sharing the same dream or reality, but that doesn't really matter. What matters is that we identify things in the same way. Everything feels real, so how are any of us going to benefit by denying that it is?"

"So you're saying the question's irrelevant?"

He shook his head. "No, it's very relevant. I mean, I find myself wondering all the time, *what is real?* But we can't let that question distract us from another one: how should we behave? If we don't have a definitive answer to the first question, we deal with the here and now."

She chuckled. "Pretty well-adjusted philosophy."

He smiled at her. "Part of my job."

"You a therapist or something?"

"No, I teach at university."

"Right – and Ronald's your student?"

"No, he just met up with me after all this started. It's a hobby for him."

She laughed. "I guess that's one way of describing it."

Andrew got up and went over to the stones. "So how do we do this?"

Jennifer shrugged. "Like I said to Ronald, Gaoler never hung around long enough to work out the rules."

Andrew nodded. "He just used you."

"Yep, sliced me up to power his portals." She shuddered. "I come back, but it's like a little bit of me is lost each time. Sometimes I struggle to remember my own name. If you need to though, I could ..."

"I don't want to do that to you."

"Hopefully, you won't need to."

The sounds of people approaching interrupted them and he turned to see Ronald leading six of the black-robed Arcanes up the hill to the stone arch. He recognised Lord Merhl and Arta among them.

"Hail, Harrower," Arta called out. Andrew waved in response and walked over to meet them.

"A long climb," Arta remarked as Andrew offered him a hand up. "Much steeper than I remember from when we arrived."

"It's always easier going down," Jennifer drawled in reply.

Wardens flanked the small party and each man and woman carried swords and wore armour. They spread out around the Arcanes as they gained the hilltop, their eyes scanning the horizon.

"We came to wish you well on your journey," Lord Merhl said stiffly.

"Kind of you," Andrew replied.

"The least we could do," Arta responded with genuine warmth.

Merhl ignored him. "Where will you go?"

"We have another task to perform," Andrew said.

"And what of us?" The question was spoken lightly, but Andrew could sense the Lord Arcane's disquiet.

"You should be able to make a new life here – that is what you wanted," he answered carefully. Lord Merhl's eyes were icy black, like the most dangerous parts of a road on a frosty night, as he stared at him. Andrew held his stare.

"You won't remain?"

"We can't."

"What if something happens to you?"

"What do you mean?"

"What if you are captured or tortured? Will we be in danger?"

Jennifer laughed. "If any traveller wanted to come after you, it wouldn't make any difference if they caught us. They'd sense where you are because this isn't your world."

A ripple of dismay passed through the group and Andrew saw people whispering to one another. "You mean they could find us anyway?" someone asked.

Jennifer nodded. "It's not difficult for some of them."

An uncomfortable silence descended. Andrew wondered what Lord Merhl was trying to achieve.

"I intend to come back," Ronald said.

The tension eased. Lord Merhl's expression broke into a wide smile and he turned away from Andrew towards him. "Yes, and of that I am glad. Arta spoke to me of the gift you granted us."

Andrew glanced at Ronald in surprise. "I gave them the knife," Ronald explained. "I'll come back for it."

"Why?" Andrew asked.

"We need a bigger weapon than that. Arta agreed to forge one from the metal."

"It will be some time before we can do this," Lord Merhl said, "but we will make a blade worthy of your gesture."

Andrew frowned at Ronald. "You didn't tell me."

"We shouldn't need it for where we're going."

Andrew turned to Jennifer, who shrugged. "Fine," he said at last, "but we can't wait. We must get going."

"So how do you want to do this?" Jennifer asked.

"I don't think we'll need to do anything too difficult this time," Andrew replied. He turned back to Ronald. "We'll use the same spell as before."

Now it was Ronald's turn to frown. "What do you mean, not too difficult? It took days to get ready back in Corbenic."

"Yes, but that was building from scratch. Remember when Ana opened the portal from Durrington?"

"How can I forget."

"Well, that didn't take long to organise."

"I don't think that will work here. The rules are different."

"I think it will," Andrew said and looked at Lord Merhl. "Especially with your help."

"We will assist, of course," he agreed. "A small favour in return for what you did. How many people will you require?"

"Just those of you that are here. But we'll need a moment to prepare." He drew Ronald aside and walked away from the rest of the group. "Are you all right?" he asked.

"I'm fine."

"Happy to do this?"

"Yes. You're right: we can't stay here. I'm comfortable with the risk, but how can you be sure this will work?"

"The Arcanes' power from Corbenic is fading, but it's not gone. We aren't trying to transport all of them back; just to get ourselves out."

"We don't have the stone bowl."

This was a surprise. "Why not?" Andrew asked.

"Green wanted it back before he left."

"Arta has the knife and the Arcanes will support the ritual. Jennifer offered to let us kill her to invoke the magic – I don't want to do that, though."

Ronald flinched. "Me neither. Okay, we'll try this. Better than the alternative."

They walked back to the arch, where he picked up a short stick and began to draw runes in the dirt around the pillars. As he worked, he mumbled the broken phrases Green had taught him. Once again, Andrew recognised the words, but they slipped through his mind like grains of sand.

The Arcanes took up the chant, gathering in a half circle around Jennifer and Andrew. When he was finished drawing symbols on the ground, Ronald walked over to Arta, who handed him the flick-knife. Wordlessly, he flipped out the blade and drew it across his palm. Arta did likewise, before they pressed the open wounds together. Another

Arcane, Kai, who Andrew remembered from the healing shelter, took up the knife. He too pressed his bloodied hand to Ronald's before passing the weapon on.

When all seven of the Arcanes had performed the rite, Ronald stepped forward and held the knife to out to Jennifer.

"This makes a change," she muttered as she accepted and cut her own palm, wincing as she did so. She clasped Ronald's hand tightly and a bright red trail ran down their arms, dripping onto the dirt.

Andrew glanced at the stone arch and thought he could see a flickering between the pillars.

"Your turn," said Ronald over his shoulder. Andrew took the blade without hesitation, slicing through the puffy scar on his left hand before grasping Ronald's hand and facing towards the arch once more.

The air began to dilate and distort.

"Here we go," Andrew said and walked purposely towards the henge.

*

"So, what can I do for you?"

Doctor Andrew Pryde negotiated his way through the shared office to his swivel chair. It was rapidly becoming his best friend on a day that already felt like the longest of his life.

The girl followed him through the open door. She was in her mid-twenties, with blonde-brown hair scraped back into a severe bun, plucked eyebrows and a pinched expression on her face. She would have been attractive if she was less self-conscious.

"I just needed to talk to you, without the rest of the class."

That put him on guard. In the three years since he'd started this job, he'd always been careful about being alone with students. Tutorials were by arrangement and sometimes involved difficult personal conversations. "Some questions about the assignment?" he asked, trying to keep his voice light. "There are appointment times."

"No, something else."

He reached the chair, putting his desk between them, and picked up a file – his class lists. He flipped through the pages. "I'm sorry, first week of term; you are?"

"Sarah Templeman," the girl replied. "I was in your morning

seminar today."

He managed a weary smile in response. "Well, if you're not here about the lesson, what can I do for you?"

"You talked in the lecture about the need to re-examine things – to establish a truth for yourself, no matter how impossible that may be?"

He sighed. "Yes; the *lex parsimoniae*. A lot of people find the idea a bit disconcerting at first but—"

"Did you mean what you said though?"

Andrew frowned. "Of course I did. Ockham's Razor is a very important starting point for any student; we spend far too much time relying on other people's ideas of fact and fiction."

"And you apply this reasoning to everything?"

He ran his hand through his hair. "Listen, I've had a pretty full day; we can discuss this next week in class—"

"I think you might understand my problem." Sarah's expression pinched further and took on a vulnerable, pleading caste.

Help with what? He moved out from behind the desk, and grabbed another wheeled chair. "Sit down," he said, putting on his best reassuring voice. "Whatever's on your mind, we can talk through."

"Do you have any water?"

Andrew went to the dispenser, plucked out a plastic cup and filled it. The tank gurgled. He could feel her eyes on him. He turned back to his desk, handed her the drink, and dropped back into his chair, which squeaked in protest. "What I was getting at was that you should avoid making assumptions, and keep yourself open to new ideas."

"What if those new ideas go against what everyone else believes?"

"Well, then you must be brave. People thought the world was flat until they were proved wrong."

She leaned forward, resting the cup on the desk. She hadn't even had a sip. He leaned back, maintaining the distance between them.

"So, you think people should hold on to their truths, even when they're ridiculed?"

"*Especially* when they're ridiculed; those are the times when you most need courage. In time, the evidence always finds its way out and proves who's right."

She held his gaze. "And you'd do that in the face of any resistance or oppression?"

He frowned. "I'd like to think I would, though I can't be sure. I hope I never have to find out."

Something in her seemed to break; the pinched expression vanished and she leaned back in her seat, leaving the cup on the table. "Suppose I tested your belief now; found some value you hold dear and showed you it could be wrong?"

Andrew shifted in his chair. "I'm not sure how that would help you."

Sarah smiled knowingly, and a hot flush crept up his neck. This conversation wasn't going at all as planned.

"You'd be helping me, all right," she explained. "We'd be doing an experiment – a test."

"Okay," he replied, wary of what he might be agreeing to.

"I'll use a common example, like your flat world thing: take, say, water; you heat it to boil it, right?"

"Of course. Water's a basic component; its liquid state on our planet is fundamental to our existence."

Anna smiled. "I know that."

"Oh, right; sorry."

"What if you didn't have to make it hot? What if you could boil it at room temperature?"

Andrew's gaze dropped to the plastic cup. It quivered, bubbles forming at the bottom and rapidly rising to the surface. Steam curled around the lip and clouded the air.

"How—"

"That's not the right question," Sarah interrupted. "You might as well ask why water stays liquid. There are plenty of reasons; the water is an example, or a symptom, not the problem."

His mind baulked at what he was witnessing. "You put something in it; baking powder?"

"I've done nothing," she replied, staring intently at him, "other than believe a little more than you."

The cup shook violently as the liquid fizzed. Andrew wasn't sure what to say.

"But it's not—"

She stood up. "Thank you for your time, Doctor Pryde. Hopefully we can talk again."

"Wait a minute—"

"No! I'm sorry, but we've no time for more than one lesson today."

With that, she marched out of the room.

The cup continued to shake on the desk. Gradually, the bubbling water settled until it was gently trembling, before ceasing altogether; by the time it did, around half of its contents had dissipated.

For a moment, Andrew considered going after the girl, but he sensed she wouldn't give him any more answers. Hesitantly, he reached forward and dipped a finger into the water. It was still cold, chilled even; somehow, he'd already known it would be.

He never saw Sarah again.

*

The world Andrew emerged into was a surprise.

He was standing at the edge of a small pool, not more than ten feet from side to side, in a wood. He had a vague feeling that he'd climbed out of the water, but his clothes and skin were dry. The trees were drawn close together, shrouding him in a leafy canopy that blocked out any glimpse of the sky. The only thing that seemed familiar was the air: it had the same crisp feel he remembered from the Caer; a freshness that banished any thought of rest and demanded his attention.

He began to walk. The thick foliage obscured his sight so he had to carefully pick a path through the silent undergrowth, until he came across an almost identical pool in a clearing only a few yards away.

"You took your time again."

He recognised the voice and wasn't surprised to find Gideon sitting on the far side of the pool. The old man was crouched over and clutching a long wooden pole with a rope tied to the end that disappeared into the gently rippling surface. Andrew voiced the first question that came to mind: "Why is this all different? Where are we?"

Gideon's rheumy gaze lifted towards him. "You're still between places like before, but you see everything differently now; you're starting to understand how all of these things are interconnected."

"Where are the others?"

"Exactly where you want them to be right now."

Behind him, Andrew heard rustling bushes and Jennifer Samms emerged from the same direction he had. The American's face split into an easy grin. "Good job. Who's the fisherman?"

"This is Gideon Smith. Where's Ronald?"

"Right behind me."

The slighter figure of Ronald appeared, a surprised expression on his face. "Where are we?"

"This is still the *between*," Andrew replied. "Gideon says I made things different."

"You have," the old man said. "Remember, this place isn't *anywhere* precisely; only the junction or crossroads."

Jennifer glanced around. "If we were in my mind, I wouldn't have chosen trees."

"It's what Andrew imagines," Ronald said. "The journey's all part of his gift. I just open the portal."

Andrew looked at Gideon, who was still sat on the other side of the pool. "So, why are you here this time?"

Gideon shrugged. "I decided to help. I thought it best to keep an eye on the place you were going to."

"This the right place?"

"Of course. I saved you a little time looking."

"Thank you," Andrew said and beckoned Ronald and Jennifer over to the water's edge. "You need to hurry."

"What's the plan?" Ronald asked.

"You're going through, with Jennifer. Candleswick will push Amanda out of the balcony window; she dies from the fall. I need you to make a portal right underneath, so she can be transported out."

Ronald looked doubtful. "We've never been to that world. How can we know it'll work?"

"Because I'll be here, holding the way open from the other side. I think that'll make this easier."

"You're staying here?" Jennifer asked.

"Yes. Once it's done, you can both follow her back here and we'll figure out what to do next."

Jennifer seemed to accept the idea, but Ronald still looked unconvinced. "Weren't we going to ask him about it?"

Andrew turned to Gideon. "Will this work?"

Gideon hesitated and grimaced. He opened his mouth to answer, but Ronald interrupted him. "I'm not sure it will work. We've never tried these things before."

"It's just an extension of what we've already done," Andrew said.

"All the same, our luck's got to run out with this—"

"The principles of your plan are sound," Gideon said loudly, cutting through Ronald's doubts, "but you are wise to be cautious."

"This may be our only opportunity," Andrew urged. "We need to try."

Jennifer placed a hand on Ronald's shoulder. "Listen, even if it doesn't work, you and I get the chance to save this girl's life. The way I see it, we can't lose."

"We could be stuck there."

"So? Might be the greatest place ever."

"Might be the worst."

"But we won't know until we go."

Ronald glared at her. "It's all right for you. You come back when you die. Each time we go, it could be the last time for me."

"Might be the same for me too. You said I'm dead in your world," Jennifer countered. "I don't know what'll happen when I travel – I never do." She shrugged. "I just deal. Trust me, you don't want to swap your shit for mine."

Ronald sighed. "Okay, maybe I'm just being paranoid. I'll do it."

Andrew smiled. "You're sure?"

"Jennifer's right and so are you. If we can save her, we have to try." Ronald turned back to Gideon. "What do we need to do?"

The old man set aside the fishing pole and gestured towards the water. "Jump in."

Ronald glanced at Andrew. "Someone has a sense of humour."

"I didn't create it consciously!" Andrew protested.

"I bet."

Jennifer moved to the pool's edge and helped Ronald down after her.

"Move out into the middle," Gideon instructed them. "And relax. Let the water take you."

"Easy for you to – shit, that's cold!" Ronald gasped. "The bottom slopes away fast."

Gideon chuckled. "Indeed, it does."

Ronald turned back to Andrew as he edged into the pool. "You going to be all right here?"

"I'll be okay. I'll have Gideon for company."

Jennifer waded in up to her waist and swam away from the bank. She seemed to have no trouble doing this, despite her armour. "C'mon, it's fine!" she called out.

Ronald was hesitant but followed and eventually kicked out into the centre. "What now?"

Gideon smiled. "Just wait."

"For what?" Jennifer asked. "I can't tell if – whoa!"

Abruptly, she was dragged underwater. Ronald yelled out, before he too was yanked from sight into the pool's depths.

Andrew gasped and turned to Gideon. "What did you do?"

Gideon shook his head. "It's your magic. So, the question is, what did *you* do?"

A Rescue

Ronald had avoided deep water his whole life. He wasn't a strong swimmer. Whenever he got into a pool, he would struggle not to panic. The sea was something he'd always hated and feared. Even bathtime had terrified him as a small child.

Now, the water poured into his mouth, submerging the panicked scream in his throat. He clamped his lips shut and kicked feebly against the force pulling him into the deep but he knew, even as he tried, he was powerless.

He remembered stories of the strong undercurrents in Australia that had claimed the lives of surfers and swimmers completely without warning. Desperately, he flailed his arms and legs, trying to find something to grab, to push upwards from or hang onto. Above him, he saw the rippling light from the leafy glade fade into inky darkness as he was pulled further and further down.

Everything went black. His lungs burned and he closed his eyes. Even as he fell into the depths, his thoughts began to wander, curious as to the final outcome of his existence. He wondered what would happen, where he would go beyond the physical world (*or worlds* – he corrected himself). *Is there really a god, a heaven, or anything after death?* The last vestiges of panic drained away and unfettered his mind.

Ronald had never been religious, although his mother had taken him to church as a salve for her own conscience. Once he was old enough to think about it, he'd made a different choice. The price of his personal excommunication was her disapproval, but she never went to the services again and he'd been too young to point out her hypocrisy.

In later years, he searched for his own truth, but he always felt ashamed entering any holy place, and that feeling would boil into righteous anger. What right did those silent stones and crosses have to judge him?

Now, at the end, only regret remained. At first, he thought about all he'd learned in the past few days, the deliverance of finding magic and visiting places he'd never thought could exist. So many answers warming him and yet raising many more questions he knew he'd never understand – *unless there's someone out there waiting to show me what happens behind the curtain.*

His sense of regret deepened. He wished he'd said goodbye to his parents when they'd left Durrington. The early stages of his father's lung cancer had demanded a move nearer to the specialist hospital and closer to sea air. He'd never phoned and told them nothing about his life anytime they phoned him. The resentment of their interference in his life remained a barrier he couldn't bridge. Now, he realised the futility of the grudge that had defined him.

Other memories lit up the darkness as he sank into the abyss: breaking his school friend Sam's watch in primary class, stealing twenty pence from another boy, Jonathan, who had asked him to keep it safe. Then, at secondary school, being too scared to kiss Mary, a girl he'd fixated on for months, when she'd sat next to him and said she liked him in front of the whole class. It went on and on, each memory like a cut to his heart, urging him to let go and set himself free. He remembered the story of judgment day and its scales. He made his decision. *I know who I am. If there is a god beyond death, I will meet him unafraid.*

He opened his eyes. He was standing in the courtyard of a walled manor, near brickwork to the right of a house. A woman had her back to him, and was staring up into the sky. Near the manor entrance was a man wearing leathers and a sword belt.

A hand clamped over his mouth and wrestled him into a shadowy corner under the parapet.

"Jeez, will you listen?! I said shut up and get outta sight!" Jennifer's silhouette loomed over him, the harsh words softened by her habitual drawl. "This place has some serious security. If we're gonna get anywhere, you have to take orders. Can you do that?"

Ronald fought her grip before nodding curtly. She released him and touched a finger to her own lips. He glanced up. The wooden boards of the parapet above creaked as a booted foot pressed down on them. The footfall over their heads was reassuringly regular, giving no hint that they had been discovered. When they faded, he struggled to his feet and rounded on Jennifer angrily.

"How dare you—" he hissed.

"You wanna bust the job before we've even started? You were

standing out there daydreaming, for fuck's sake!"

"I was—"

"What? Count the fucking suns? There are two of them – great. Now, let's get on with it." Jennifer pointed to the manor house. "See over there?"

He glanced in the direction she was pointing. What he saw immediately drained all anger from him. Crouched in the bushes by the wall was a hulking figure he instantly recognised: *Candleswick*.

*

"It won't work."

"What do you mean?" Andrew asked.

Gideon sighed and picked up the fishing pole again. "Sending them to rescue your friend Amanda; it won't work."

"Why not?"

"She already died. Your ability to circumvent your linear perception of reality is impressive, but you can't change what happened."

"What makes you think that?"

"The very fact that you're still here. When I first met you, you said you wanted to find out who'd killed her. You did but, if you succeeded in saving her, you'd never have come here in the first place – a paradox of choices, which can't happen."

Andrew was angry. "Then why did you let me send them?"

"Because they'd be in danger if they remained here."

Andrew ground his teeth in frustration. Gideon's habit of providing answers that prompted more questions allowed the old man a means of leading the conversation just as he wished. He knew the next question he was supposed to ask: *'Why, what danger am I in?'* But that wasn't what he needed to know. He took a deep breath and buried the obvious response – *for now* – to ask something else.

"Why did Candleswick call you Janus?"

"What?"

"Candleswick called you 'Janus' before. Why?"

Gideon sighed and Andrew noticed his knuckles whiten as his grip on the pole tightened. "We all get those names."

"The names of mythological gods? You mean like 'Arachne' – the name you gave to the woman we called The Spider? You said at the time it was her real name."

"It is. It was given to her when she became one of us."

"So, Janus is your *real* name?"

Gideon glared at him. "Define 'real'. Janus is my name to other travellers. Naming is a power that transcends sounds and syllables. In some worlds, your name explains what you are." The old man gazed out over the water. His eyes seemed far away. "I'm called many things: Gideon Smith, Patrick O'Reilly, Pomeranze, Clark Johnson – all names I went by when I walked beyond the Caer. I've seen light, darkness and shadow; yet, above all, I have lived."

"Why Janus?" Andrew asked softly.

"Because it is who I am: the lord of gates and doors, beginnings and endings, and caretaker of the corridor and the passageway."

"Janus was a god to the Romans and the Etruscans before them. Who thinks you are a god? Were you alive back then?"

Gideon chuckled. "Theistic functionalism. Worlds like that are much easier for us – where people find religion in what you do or represent. They soon find you out though; people want something more tangible than smoke and mirrors."

Andrew frowned. "You didn't answer my question: how old are you?"

"I don't remember. Truly, years don't matter. It's the lack of them that counts in the end. I could be here forever. Back when I came here, I planned to be, when my time ran out – my own ambrosia – though now I'm not so sure it's what I really want."

Andrew rubbed his face with a hand, trying to place the revelation into a context he could understand. "Are you saying you're a mythological god from history?"

The old man shrugged. "I guess so, yes."

"In retirement?"

"You can call this 'retirement' if you like. It is still part of the theistic function I was given." Gideon stood up. "My problem was that I ran out of time, of life. Much like your friend, if I pass through into another world, I will age and, not long after that, I'll die. At least if I stay here, I won't."

"Even the gods die?" Andrew chuckled. "That's ironic."

Gideon looked at him sharply. "Oh yes, we all die. But each person finds their own answer to death. You just happen to have learned about mine."

*

"We don't need to fight him," Ronald said. "We can hide here till he's gone."

Jennifer nodded. "Okay, we stay put, then move to the wall. Once it's clear, you run around to the front and do your thing. I'll keep them off you."

The woman he'd seen before walked across the cobblestones to the house entrance. The guardsman stepped forward to meet her.

"He is overdue, Gamm," she said.

The man nodded. "Yes, my lady. He must have been delayed."

"I will be upstairs. Make sure he is informed when he arrives."

The woman disappeared into the house and Ronald ducked back into the shadows as the guard gazed in their direction. After a minute or so, Jennifer tapped him on the shoulder and gestured towards the wall. Ronald glanced up. The hulking figure of Candleswick clambered up the brickwork at an impossible rate. "How come no-one sees him but us?"

"No idea, but it's not usual. People crap themselves when he stares at them."

Candleswick reached a ledge on the second story, opened the small window above it and slipped inside.

"There's no way he should fit through that."

"*You* probably could."

"Yeah, but he's huge."

Jennifer glared at him. "What do you see?"

"A hairy black beast, like a cross between a dog and a man. "Don't you see the same thing?"

Jennifer shook her head slowly. "All I see is a thin man, dressed all in black."

*

The old man stood and stretched, flexing his toes in the wet mud at the edge of the water. Andrew noticed for the first time that Gideon's feet were bare.

"What happened to you when you saved those people?" he asked Andrew. "When you got to the other side, how did they treat you?"

"It was a bit uncomfortable. They believed we were saviours."

"Exactly," Gideon said, crouching down again and leaning towards Andrew, until they were inches apart. "Imagine what that's like after years of interfering in the lives of people, saving them from danger and peril they can find no other way out of."

"Surely you correct them?"

"Why should I? Belief drives magic. It's only natural for people to worship miracle workers; those who are able to do what they can't."

"That's wrong."

"Is it?" Gideon sat down again and dipped his index finger in the water. "Do you think what you did for those people you 'saved' was a good thing?"

"Absolutely."

Gideon stared at his wetted finger. "Did you consider the consequences? Every person who travels is cast out of their natural place in reality. Millions of possibilities were sacrificed for your act of kindness."

"Those people had no hope, no chance of getting out," Andrew protested.

"Was it so bad the way they lived?"

"Stuck underground in tunnels and caves? Yes!"

"But they didn't know any different."

Andrew thought about this carefully. "No, you're wrong," he decided. "They did know different. They wanted out. They had a hope that life would be better somewhere else. They sought to be free, so we gave them freedom."

"Would you have left them if they hadn't had a dream of this?".

"No. I'd still have freed them. No-one deserves to live like that."

"Who are you to make that determination?" Gideon laughed. "Power over the way we live and die – what is that, if not the power of a god?"

"I couldn't just leave them!"

"Of course not; I understand. In your mind, you did a good deed." The old man gave him a poisonous smile. "Yet you share in the blame. If you were innocent, you would be powerless. You see now why you can't judge me?"

Andrew looked away. A wave of guilt washed over him and he felt sick. "So, who is Candleswick?" he asked finally, changing the subject.

"Ah, therein lies a tale! He is a daemon of the underworld, let loose when his master gave up all concern for the mortal realm."

Andrew recognised the description instantly. "Cerberus – the three-headed dog of Hades?"

"Indeed. He is the guardian of the dead, set to hunt down those who escape their chains." Gideon smiled. "He is even more your enemy after this."

"It can't be right to imprison people."

"Some people are supposed to die, Andrew. I told you there is a price for power. You learned about the use of murder to empower rituals when Ronald died to get you here. Crimes require punishment: a life for a life. If that life can be given for a purpose, then all the better. Candleswick makes sure people go where they are supposed to go."

"You mean he guarded prisoners who were sentenced to die?"

Gideon nodded. "Yes, he was the gaoler of the condemned; those we would sacrifice to empower our magic."

*

"Okay, let's go."

Jennifer emerged from the shadow of the wall and sprinted to the side of the manor. Ronald followed a pace behind, desperately trying to focus his mind on the task at hand. Ahead of him, the American's chainmail chinked as she ran. When they reached the house, she stopped and inched her way to the corner. She glanced at the guard on the parapet, before peering around and drawing her sword from its scabbard. Ronald wished fleetingly that he'd picked up a weapon to replace his flick-knife, but the chance was long gone.

Jennifer charged, sword in hand, with Ronald close behind. The man whirled in surprise. He was wearing a toughened leather jerkin, stained a rich brown and emblazoned with the symbol of a white stag on green. His hand went to his hip and he struggled to free his own sword. But it was too late; Jennifer barrelled into him, smashing the pommel of her weapon into his forehead, and he crumpled in a heap on the stone steps.

"Move!" she snarled, shoving Ronald forwards. He stumbled on the stairs, then righted himself and peered up. He was immediately under the second-floor balcony. A flicker of movement confirmed the presence of someone above him. He searched around for something to work with.

"Hurry!"

Instinctively, he began to mumble the broken phrases of the incantation Green had taught him. Jennifer took up the chant, adding her voice to his. He needed to find something to draw the runes; he could build a portal from a minimum of five symbols but, without something to mark them onto the stones, it would be no use.

Desperately, he bit into his left palm, tearing open the clotted wound he'd made for the portal in the Valley of Aven. He knelt and began to trace the symbols in his own blood on the whitened stone.

He heard a woman scream.

He glanced up. Time seemed to slow. He saw the balcony rails shatter as the woman tumbled towards him, For the first time, he got a good look at the face of the woman he knew to be Amanda Baines.

Her mouth split open as she fell, blonde hair billowing as if it might cling to the sky and save her. He knew he didn't have time to complete the ritual – he'd drawn the first rune and started the second, but it wouldn't be enough. He sensed the power of the ritual; stirred by the chant, tingling in the back of his mind. He tried to focus, to bring forth a portal by sheer will alone, but something in him refused to accept it was possible. Even as he groped for the magic, it eluded him.

He couldn't prevent her fall.

Solution

The car bounced and bumped over the grass field. Linda kept a steady pace at twenty-five miles an hour, swerving around the stone arches and returning to the same course each time. As they drove through more fields, and avoided more stones, it became harder to remember what direction that was. There was no sense of time passing either. She glanced at the digital clock on the dashboard, but the numbers had gone blank.

"You're doing great," George said.

She glanced at the gauge. The car had less than half a tank left, but that could be a hundred or more miles worth of fuel. "How long will this take?" she asked.

"I've no idea. I guess, as long as it took to come through the other way?"

She bit her lip and kept driving. A mist gathered around them and she switched on the headlights. The full beam picked out the swirling wisps of moisture, reflecting back at her, making the view ahead worse. She dipped the lights and found she could still see well enough to go on, but it was getting more and more difficult to pick out the stones as they appeared ahead. "We'll either hit something or we'll get through," she murmured.

"I love you."

"What?"

"I love you," George repeated. "Whatever happens to me if we get through, I love you. Always have. I … I don't say it enough, I know, but …"

"You silly stick."

"If you're ever going to tell someone, surely now's the time?" George chuckled, put a hand on her shoulder, leaned over and gently kissed her neck. "I probably missed my chance really, but somehow, I got another one."

Linda sighed. "We all regret things. The trick is to forgive yourself, move on and cherish what's important. Forgiving others … well …

You've nothing for me to forgive."

They drove on, mist thickening to fog. The fuel gauge dropped and the stone arches became less frequent. Linda found she was smiling, though she didn't know why.

"We must be getting close," said George.

The bumpy ground became flat and their passage serene. Linda pushed down on the accelerator, taking them to forty, then fifty miles an hour. "I love you too, George," she said.

*

"So why didn't you stop us?" Andrew asked.

"From rescuing those people?" You'd already transported them out by the time you came here," Gideon explained. "By then, it was too late to save them. Remember, this is not an actual place. You killed millions of possible futures with your actions."

"Why help us before if you knew what we might do?"

"A wise man once claimed the only way to understand life is to discover purpose, your place in the grand design. For each of us, the answer is different. I needed to learn yours."

"Functionalism again," Andrew remarked.

"Absolutely. I couldn't prevent you doing anything until I had an idea of your part in the scheme of things."

"For someone who claims to be a god, you hold a great deal of respect for destiny and fate."

"Touché," the old man replied. "Frankly, I had to determine if you would be of use. I also wanted you separated from your friend Ronald."

"Why?"

"You seem to understand things in a different way. Ronald is of little concern; he died the first time you travelled, so his time in this place is finite. Eventually, he will make a trip through a portal and never return. Jennifer Samms is also well known to me. She is dead as well, but her mind hasn't realised this yet; an interesting condition. On some level, she doesn't believe in all this and that's what is actually keeping her alive. She's a bit like a battery, though – sooner or later, she'll run out." Gideon's eyes grew distant as he spoke. Then he blinked and refocussed on Andrew. He licked his lips and smiled. "But you, you see things differently – uniquely, perhaps – or you wouldn't have escaped

Corbenic."

"You lied to us, then. You knew where we would end up."

"It was a test of your newfound gifts. I didn't expect you to escape so dramatically. One day, when we have more time, you must tell me how you did that. To learn what you did, you must have found help."

Andrew thought about Green. He considered telling Gideon about him, but changed his mind. The old man was becoming increasingly untrustworthy the more he talked. "You played with our lives."

"Is that any different from your work on Corbenic?"

Andrew was about to say something when he heard a rustling in the bushes and glanced in the direction of the noise. His injured hand tingled. Standing on the other side of the clearing was a woman he recognised all too well: Ana Arachnovic – The Spider.

Gideon stood up. "At last, Arachne!" he called warmly, and walked over to her. "I was wondering when you would arrive."

Andrew clambered to his feet, startled by Ana's appearance. "What's going on here?"

The old man shrugged. "You needed to be tested. Now I have the answers I need," he said over his shoulder.

"What does that mean?"

"It means I understand you better now. You are an interesting man, Andrew Pryde."

"How did you find out my full name?"

"*She* told me."

*

Ronald froze.

Guards from the wall were shouting and running towards him and Jennifer; yet it was the sight above that held him transfixed. Amanda Baines was falling.

He couldn't stop her fall.

But he might be able to break it.

Realisation got him moving. In the split second before she hit the ground, he ran forwards, arms outstretched. He wasn't strong enough to catch her, but he could cushion her impact.

She crashed onto him, knocking the breath from his body and driving him into the stones beneath her. Something snapped in his chest as they landed in a tangled heap. Hot pain lanced through his left leg. He'd fallen awkwardly, twisting his ankle underneath him. His head banged against the flagstones and his vision clouded as he began to lose consciousness.

He tried to hang on, to remember the last time he'd put himself in harm's way to help someone. Before Andrew and Candleswick, he couldn't recall ever helping anyone without some self-interest. *It was always about me*, he realised. *Maybe now I'm dead, it doesn't need to be.*

He saw booted feet running towards him. The shouting grew louder and a bell rang. Jennifer would never fight them all off and Andrew would be unable to aid them without a portal. With what little strength he had left, Ronald struggled to access the magic again, hoping that the wounds he'd acquired would act as a catalyst to bridge the gap between ritual and power, but it was no use. The quicksilver tingling sensation was still there, but it was weaker than before and he felt another presence siphoning from the potential he had evoked. Then, in a flash, it was gone.

As he lost consciousness, Ronald realised that Candleswick had tapped into his power and created a portal of his own to transport away.

*

Standing on the other side of the pool was the same ageless woman he remembered. She wore the same long silver dress he remembered, but it was her white hair that drew his eyes – a beacon in the sultry gloom of the forest.

"So, you betrayed us to her?"

Gideon looked hurt. "Betrayal would imply some earlier form of loyalty or allegiance. In what way do I owe you that?"

"You know what she did to Ronald."

"You think I should disapprove?"

"Please, Doctor Pryde," Ana interjected, "I do not blame you for your ire, but Ronald Gibbs was my creation; an instrument designed to free me from your world. I regret you were caught up in all of this."

"You intended to kill him all along?" Andrew asked.

"Yes. I will not insult your intelligence by claiming otherwise. I became trapped and needed to find a means of escape."

"Just like you did in Corbenic?"

"Just like I did in Corbenic. I spent a long time carefully training Ronald. The opportunity in Durrington Library was too good to miss and, once he was suitably conditioned, I used his death to power the portal."

Andrew grew angry. He stalked towards her. "You people don't care who you hurt, do you?"

"*Of course* I cared for Ronald." Ana's voice dripped with contrition. "But his sacrifice was necessary."

"To let you continue your safari around reality?"

"Andrew, please," Gideon remonstrated. "We each have a purpose that transcends the needs of individuals. Ronald is but a drop in countless oceans, and the manner of his death was a privilege—"

"A privilege! What the fuck—"

"Ronald spent his entire life trying to find something magical, something special about his existence," Ana urged. "I granted him his wish."

"At the expense of his life?"

"If you asked him what he would sacrifice for the knowledge he gained, how do you believe he would answer?"

"You know he had no idea what it would cost him!"

"Really?" Ana countered. "Are you so sure?"

*

"Put down the sword and step away!"

Jennifer stared grimly at the four guardsmen. They remained at a safe distance, as the unconscious bodies of two of their comrades lay at her feet. Yet one of them held a loaded crossbow aimed right at her heart.

She knew she couldn't take them all. A crossbow bolt would kill her, but she would have time to reach at least two of them before she bled to death. But, with Ronald unconscious or worse, there would be no portal and no escape.

For a moment, she considered it anyway. There had been times since Boston when she'd charged into similar situations, knowing they were suicidal, sometimes hoping it would finally be the end; other times, she had done so under the Gaoler's coercion. But now she had something to lose. Recovery from death would leave her with gaps in her memory and she'd no wish to re-learn who Ronald and Andrew were, or how she'd ended up in this world.

"I said, put down the sword and stand away from the Lady Abbalyn!"

Abbalyn? Where do I remember that name from? Somewhere in a dusty corner of her mind, it resonated with something she couldn't recall.

Slowly, Jennifer opened her hand. Her blade clattered to the stone and she stepped back. "We came here to help," she shouted. "We're not here to fight you!"

Three of the guardsmen charged up the staircase, swords drawn. Two of them forced her back, while the third knelt to examine Lady Abbalyn, who was lying spread-eagled over Ronald. Jennifer could see she was in her twenties, roughly; certainly not a teenager anymore. As the guards pushed Jennifer to her knees, she searched the woman's face for any signs of life. When she let out an audible moan, Jennifer sighed with relief. She almost welcomed the blows that drove her face-first into the ground.

*

"We're wasting time," Gideon said. "He will never accept your reasons."

Ana sighed. "I suppose you are right."

"We must act before this situation becomes more complicated. That's why I agreed to help you."

Andrew stood up. "So, you're going to kill me? I guess another murder makes little difference to you."

"We don't want to kill you," Ana replied. "You transcended the mundane, so to execute you would be a waste."

"Am I supposed to be grateful for that?"

"I wouldn't expect you to understand," Gideon said. "But there is precedent for what must be done to you. Indeed, it's the same ritual that was performed on Arachne."

"I was placed in your world by my peers, after my actions were deemed to be of harm," Ana explained. "My gifts were considered a threat. It took decades for me to find a way out."

"You want to do that to me?"

Gideon walked over to the large tree next to the pool and ran his hands over the bark. "You did a much better job with this than the stone arches. But do you understand how?"

Andrew shrugged. "Not really."

"Somewhere in your mind, you do. In this woodland, there are countless pools overlooked by trees. Each tree is not unique; their roots intertwine and mix with the others. Each blade of grass touches the next; each plant and shrub blends into another. They are all connected. What you do to each one affects them all."

"You talked to me about this before when you lied about Candleswick. Is punishing me your idea of working for some sort of natural order?"

"I didn't lie to you. Candleswick believes there is a natural order and so do I, but we interpret it differently. He decided you were too dangerous to live the first time he met you. I gave you more credit than that."

"So now you've changed your tune?"

"In some ways. The minute you learned to journey through time, you became a threat. You have an uncanny knack of finding places and your gifts make it possible for much of what exists to be unmade." He gestured at the tree. "Time travel in itself is not a problem but, by revisiting events that directly affect your life, you might destroy all of this. Saving Amanda Baines would close off too many possibilities."

Andrew shrugged again. "All right. I'm not stupid. I can see your argument. What if I don't save her?"

Gideon looked at him sadly. "I'm sorry, but we can't take the risk that you'll try."

Andrew felt Ana's cool hands grasp his forehead from behind and the woodland dilated before his eyes. "What—"

"You need to understand that this is necessary," Gideon's words echoed in his mind. "We must protect what we have."

The world spun and Andrew lost his balance. He was falling towards the pool. Desperate to escape, he twisted free of Ana's grip. *I can't let her control me*, he thought. *If I can just reach Ronald and Jennifer, I'll be safe.*

The cold of the water brought everything into sharp focus, like a slap to the face. He popped his head up from beneath the surface and glanced back at Gideon and Ana, but neither moved to pursue him.

"You can't run," Gideon said. "This time, all roads lead to the same place."

*

Mike emerged from the woodland and reached the road. On the other side, he spotted an empty layby. He stared and frowned. Again, the place was vaguely familiar, but the memories wouldn't come back.

It was a cold and misty morning, with no cars on the bypass. He crossed and stood by the parking sign, looking up the road, then pulled out his phone again and checked the time. If Emily had been at the office when he called her, it would take her at least another ten minutes to reach him.

He gazed back at the old forest. It was shrouded in fog, and remained a dark shadow in the distance. He'd wandered for a while before getting his bearings. *It didn't want to give me up.*

He shivered and glanced at the phone; the large audio file was still there. He opened it, pressed play and put the phone to his ear.

As the file started to play, headlights appeared in the distance. *Emily?* Even if it wasn't her, it might be someone he could get a lift with.

He stepped to the edge of the road and stuck out a thumb.

*

Andrew ignored Gideon and tried to concentrate. He took a deep breath, ducked underwater and swam down, before flipping around. The two figures above rippled in the dim light. Ana's white hair shone like a star in the undulating gloom. He concentrated on it, trying to use the image as an anchor to find the magic he knew was still there.

The world above him darkened and the white light divided in two singular points, like stars on a blackened canvas. He was overwhelmed by a sensation of floating; he guessed this was what it was like for astronauts when they were suspended above the Earth. This time he was ready and welcomed it. Gideon, Ana and the woodland slipped away and he gave himself over to the darkness.

The points of light held steady. Much like before, when he'd followed the traces of Candleswick's magic, they acted as beacons in the gloom. *That must be Ronald and Jennifer*, he thought, and hope kindled anew in him. He willed his way towards the lights and they grew large and bright. Then he was falling straight toward them. *They'd better be ready for a change of plan.* He poured every ounce of concentration he could muster into reaching them. The lights grew ever brighter, until they consumed everything, bathing him in their luminescence.

Ronald! he called out desperately, with his mind.

*

"I can see something!" said George.

Linda gripped the steering wheel and leaned forward in her seat. Shadows and shapes were emerging left and right, but straight ahead was clear. She squeezed the accelerator a little harder and their speed crept up to fifty, then sixty. The car vibrated quietly, they were on a road again, the shadows gave way to bushes and trees.

"I think we've made it, George!" she cried, her voice quivering with excitement. "George, I think we've—"

Pain gripped her chest, as if cold fingers had seized hold of her heart. She felt it lurch and throb. Her fingers went numb, then her arms and her legs. She could hear chanting and felt people near her, in water, a woman's voice and a …

A man appeared in the road right in front of the car. She gasped, recognising him, and yanked the wheel to the left.

"George! I—"

The last thing she saw was an empty passenger seat.

*

A moment before impact, Andrew realised he was standing in the middle of a road, staring at two points of light. Then something smashed into him. He hit the ground and vaguely realised he was tumbling along it. The lights swirled and he heard a woman scream into the night.

It was the last thing he remembered before darkness took him.

The Prisoner

"I'm sorry, but you can't go in there."

Detective Sergeant Mike Underhill was standing at reception in the recovery ward of Avebury General Hospital. The man behind the desk was in his late twenties, wearing a male nurse's uniform and an expression of professional disinterest.

"Your people called me and said Pryde had woken up," Mike said. "I came down here with the understanding that he'd be available for questioning."

"Visiting hours are for relatives only," the man intoned.

"Police business makes me a relative of anyone I need to speak to who's well enough to talk," Mike countered, digging out his ID card.

"Oh, right." The nurse's bored look cracked. "I'm sorry, I—"

"Didn't realise? Who the fuck else did you think would want to talk to him?"

"It's just – well, I think you'll want to speak to the registrar."

"And how long will that take?"

"I can page her right now. She'll be with you as soon as she's free."

Mike shook his head. "I'm sorry, but I can't wait. Can she meet me at the ward?"

"I guess so."

"Right then, which ward?"

"D6. Would you like me to—"

"No, I'll find it."

Mike marched away, ignoring the man's hurt stare. He was tired and irritable after a night in the woods and the strange lack of recollection over what he'd been doing before. The audio recording on his mobile phone hadn't helped much, but Emily's briefing in the car had at least made sense. Strange that she had been talking in the recording, but couldn't remember any of it. It felt like there were two versions of events competing with each other, with neither quite making sense.

He walked down a spotless white corridor, pausing only to douse his hands in gel from one of the dispensers, before turning into the correct passageway and pushing through the glass doors. The ward was dimly lit, the curtains still drawn. He saw four beds, with only one occupied. In it lay Andrew Pryde.

Mike was shocked at the man's condition. Less than forty-eight hours ago, he'd seen him at the police station and it was less than twenty-four since the accident, but in that time Pryde appeared to have aged years. His eyes were closed but the skin around them hung loosely in bags. The blankets on the bed had been drawn up to his neck, making him small and vulnerable in the expanse of clean, pressed linen.

"Andrew, can you hear me?"

His eyelids fluttered open, revealing their watery blue occupants. "I'm sorry – I must have dozed off."

"That's all right. Do you remember me?"

"You're the police detective who interviewed me after they found the body in the library," Andrew replied in a weak voice. "How long ago was that?"

"Three days. We spoke the evening after that as well."

"Yes, I remember," Andrew said, but he didn't sound certain.

"You're lucky to be alive."

"I'll take your word for it. I have no idea why or how I got here."

Mike reached into his jacket and pulled out his notebook. "What's your last memory?"

"It's pretty foggy. I remember being on a road."

"I can help with a few gaps: two days ago, you left the station after I questioned you and headed into town. We lost track of you after that. But then, yesterday morning, you appeared in the middle of the bypass near Bedwyn Forest."

"Okay."

"How did you get there?"

"I don't know," Andrew said, frowning slightly. "I mean, I recall leaving the police station ..."

"Where were you going?"

Andrew's frown deepened, then his face relaxed and he shook his head. "I'm not sure."

"We searched Ronald Gibbs' house. We found all sorts of interesting things." Mike edged towards the bed and held Andrew's gaze. "We also took fingerprints from the house and matched them with prints from the girl's body."

Andrew's expression didn't change. "You think he murdered her?"

"We can't be sure until we find him."

"You think I know where he is?"

"I think you knew when you left the station." Mike reached into a pocket and produced a battered business card. "We found this in your jacket. It has Gibbs' address on it. Is that where you were going?"

"To warn him, you mean?"

"Yes, to warn him."

Andrew held his gaze for several seconds, before turning his head to stare at the wall. "I was going to the library," he said softly. "I thought he might be there."

"It was broken into again that night. Books got torn up and someone started a fire. The whole second floor was gutted."

"That's terrible."

"At about the same time, George Frakes – your friend Linda's husband – decided to kill himself, and three children were kidnapped from a family home just down the road from your house."

"Is Linda all right?"

"No. She was driving the car that hit you. She had a heart attack and died."

"I see."

Mike frowned. "You don't seem surprised."

"Detective, I'm numb. Right now, I'm struggling to take in everything you're telling me. It's been a pretty difficult time; please don't take a lack of reaction on my part to mean anything."

Mike stared at him. "I know you didn't kill the girl, Andrew," he said softly. "When I interviewed you, I was suspicious and I still don't think you're telling me everything, but I'm sure you didn't kill Amanda Baines."

Andrew smiled weakly at him. "You've no idea how relieved I am to hear you say that."

"I need you to be open and honest with me about everything you know. No matter how weird or strange."

"I'm not sure you're ready for that yet, Detective."

Mike was not sure what to make of that answer but, as he pondered, the ward door opened behind him and a woman in a white coat entered.

"Morning, Andrew," she said smoothly, before turning to the detective. "I'm the registrar, Doctor Mortimer. You must be Detective

Sergeant Underhill?"

"Yes, Doctor, I am."

"Could I speak to you outside for a moment?"

"Of course."

He followed Mortimer into the corridor. She was a short Indian lady, in her mid-forties, with dark hair and a pinched expression that crinkled her brow and the corners of her brown eyes. "What's the problem?"

"You have every right to be here," she began, "but he really isn't in much of a state to talk to you."

"I'm sorry, but Doctor Saunders and I spoke on the phone. He said I could come and question him."

The woman sighed and gave him a pained look. "Jim Saunders is a consultant. He hasn't been to visit since Andrew woke up. But I can tell you that our boy suffered some head trauma from the accident. I don't think you should rush this; he can be quite incoherent at times."

"In what way?"

"Well, when he was rambling about all sorts, he said that he wasn't supposed to be here and he had to 'reach the portal' – whatever that means. He's only been calm and lucid for the last hour or so, after the morphine kicked in."

"How badly injured is he?"

"Aside from the head injury, he has several broken ribs, a fractured wrist and has lost a lot of blood. By rights, he should be dead. In fact, he *was* dead when he arrived – his heart had stopped."

"So, what do you think is best for him?"

"The important thing is to monitor his recovery over the next day or so, which is why I think you should leave the questions for now."

"I see."

"Please, he's not going anywhere."

"I suppose. How long do you want me to wait?"

"Another twenty-four hours. The test results will be back by then."

Mike nodded. "All right, I think we can manage that."

"Thank you." Mortimer smiled. "After that, I'm sure he'll help you get to the truth."

*

Andrew wasn't a good liar.

He shifted uneasily in the hospital bed, feeling painful twinges all over, despite the painkillers they'd given him. He tired quickly from the effort and his breathing became unhealthy gasps. Eventually, he gave up and lay still. No matter how hard he tried, he couldn't seem to get comfortable. He felt like he didn't belong.

Something was very wrong about this place. He couldn't put his finger on what exactly, but it wouldn't go away.

The reappearance of Detective Sergeant Underhill was at least a little reassuring, but it had restarted the throbbing ache in his hand. He was the first person that Andrew recognised since regaining consciousness. He could still hear Underhill talking with the doctor in low tones outside the ward. He knew he wouldn't be able to hide much from him for long. *I suppose they'll have me committed, if I do tell them*, he thought.

The version of events Underhill had given him didn't fit with what he remembered. He knew he'd reached the library and been there when Ronald completed the ritual. The image of Ana Arachnovic, The Spider, thrusting a knife into Ronald's chest as the books burned all around them, remained etched in his mind. He wondered if he would ever see Ronald again.

Weakly, he flexed his right hand. The arm had a plaster cast on it. He'd been told that his wrist had snapped when he'd been hit by the car. He vaguely recalled hurting it, but had no memory of the accident. He slipped his left arm out from under the covers and examined his throbbing hand. The senation was fading now. The knife wound in his hand had healed over; the puffy scar was all that remained of the cut that had been healed by Gideon. A fresh scab lined the wound on his palm where he'd cut into it to invoke the portal the last time, but it was tiny by comparison. *If none of it was real, those would still be open wounds. There's no way they could heal in three days. So how did I get here?*

The ward doors reopened and Doctor Mortimer returned. Andrew was relieved to see that she was alone. "The detective said he'll be back tomorrow," she said, smiling at him. "How are you doing?"

Andrew sighed. "I'm not sure. Everything's still a bit strange."

"That's not uncommon among patients who suffer your kind of injuries."

"Who brought me in?"

"The ambulance was called out by the detective, actually. Nice of him to follow up and check on you. As I said before, you're lucky to still be with us."

"What about the car?"

"Stolen by a middle-aged woman," the doctor explained. "She was driving alone. They haven't traced the owner yet. It was all over the news. Apparently, she went nuts after her husband committed suicide."

"I wouldn't know."

"No, of course not – I'm sorry. And don't blame yourself."

Andrew didn't reply, but inside he squirmed. *Difficult not to*. Linda had been trying to help him. She didn't deserve …

She didn't deserve any of this.

The doctor walked over to the curtains and pulled them closed. "When these things happen, it can be fatal, particularly at the speed she was driving."

"What did you say?"

"Sorry, what?"

"What you just said. Say it again."

She looked confused. "I said these things can be fatal."

The words chilled him. Gideon's voice echoed through the fog in his head. *Just remember: there's always a price, even if you don't expect it.*

It made sense. Somehow, Gideon and Ana had used magic to transport him to a different place. Had they caused Linda's death to power their spell?

Andrew realised the doctor was still staring at him. "I think I'll get some sleep now," he said.

Doctor Mortimer nodded. "Good idea. Lunch will be in an hour or so. The nurse will wake you up."

"Thanks," Andrew said. He lay back and closed his eyes.

*

"We need to wait."

Half out of his seat, he growled and glared at the man across the table, a detective, wearing thick black glasses. His companion was called Matthew Davies and had the scent of a transgressor, but spent his life betraying his own kind. The others had told him this one had authority and was to be obeyed.

For now.

Slowly, he nodded in response and sat down again. Being in human form was strange after so long as something else. A long time ago, like Davies, he'd had a name of his own, but now he couldn't remember it. Things like that weren't important.

Only the hunt and the prey matters.

They were seated in a café across the road from the hospital. The sky was grey and it was raining. The other detective, called Underhill, had just left the building and was standing by his car, removing a parking ticket. He too was a transgressor now, a criminal in this reality, just like Pryde. Both of them would need to be eliminated.

"We can't attack him in the hospital," Davies said. "We need somewhere less public."

"These matters do not concern me."

"No, but they concern *me*. I'm the one who has to tidy up the loose ends you people leave behind. No more bodies left in libraries. It makes everything complicated."

"We cannot leave you idle."

"I have plenty to do without you making work for me." Davies held out a hand. "Abbalyn had a key on him; did you get it back?"

"We did." He reached into a pocket of his strange clothes and produced the object. Its touch revolted him. He dropped it onto the table.

Davies snatched it up and stowed it away, muttering, "Thank you."

He smiled, displaying as many teeth as possible to intimidate his companion. It worked; Davies looked away, failing to conceal his fear. "You know what fate awaits them," he said.

"I do."

"The same fate will claim you, if you fail to help us."

"Yes, I know."

He leaned over the table, his awkward human fingers digging into wet wood. "Does it give you satisfaction, Davies, sacrificing the ones like you? Is this revenge for what your parents did to you all those years ago?"

Davies shuddered, but didn't meet his eye. "You were one of them, weren't you?" he said. "You were outside the circle."

"Always."

"Did it give you pleasure to torment and torture a young boy?"

"Of course."

Davies turned towards him again. Behind the glasses, he could still see the frightened child in those eyes. "What I do is necessary. I know my place in all this."

"Do you? Are you sure?"

"Yes, I am." Davies stood up. "We need to follow Underhill and see who he talks to. Are you coming?"

"Of course. Good boy, Matty."

Together, they left the café and walked away down the street.

Epilogue

"Get up!"

A bucket of cold water in the face and Jennifer was instantly awake. She shook her head and rubbed her eyes, trying to clear them and recall where she was.

An unshaven man, dressed in leathers, stood over her as she lay on a straw-lined pallet in a stone-walled prison cell. The man carried a lantern – the only source of light in the room.

"You heard me; get up!"

A kick overturned the sewer pot in the corner, sending up a pungent smell of excrement. Jennifer managed to choke her way to her feet, before the man grabbed her shirt and dragged her out of the room. "Don't worry, we'll have you back in there later!" he promised, before hauling her up the tiny stone staircase into the room above. Once there, he threw her onto the cobbled floor. "Here she is, just like you asked," he announced.

Jennifer wretched emptily onto the floor, still overcome by the stink of her own filth. It was all a far cry from Boston and the university dorms. Not for the first time, she wished she had never got curious and ended up on this strange adventure. *The rabbit hole is a shit hole, Alice,* she thought grimly.

She was dimly aware that there were three people in the room; one of them was the man who had freed her.

"I can't see her face," a familiar voice remarked.

A hand gripped hold of her hair and dragged her head up. Jennifer was momentarily blinded by lantern light. "Yeah, that's her," growled the voice. "Beats me how she got back here ahead of us."

"I'll inform Her Ladyship," said a third man coldly.

The familiar voice chuckled bitterly. "You think she's going to believe me over them?"

"She will want to know the truth."

"She won't believe it, especially after they saved her."

"If you weren't telling the truth, why would you come back?"

Jennifer blinked rapidly, trying to adjust to the glare. She guessed she had been in the cell for three or four days since she had arrived in Abbalyn. "Where's Ronald?" she managed to croak.

"Your friend's resting comfortably, but under guard," the cold voice replied from the far end of the room. "You'll see him in a day or two."

"Then why keep me down here?" Jennifer asked.

"We decided it was best, since you were still dangerous," the man who had freed her answered. "And, look how right we were! Vander here says you killed Lord Michael."

"You took something from him," the cold voice added. "Where is the key?"

Jennifer remembered. She had killed Abbalyn in a duel. She'd taken something from the body. It could have been a key, but that was where the memories ran out. "I don't remember," she said.

"Liar!" the one she remembered, who they called Vander, hissed. "You must know!"

"I warn you, we have ways of making sure you confess everything," the cold voice threatened.

"Then you'll be here a long time," Jennifer spat, "because I don't know shit."

She knew the blow was coming before it landed. She wondered dimly what they would choose, before a foot smashed into her chin. She heard something in her neck snap as the force of the blow rolled her onto her back. She cried out as her vision swam.

"That's enough! All of you, get out!"

"My lady, we're just—"

"I said, get out!"

Booted feet echoed and faded away on the stone steps. Jennifer tried to raise her head, but the pain was too much. She was dying. She knew the signs; it was only a matter of ...

"No."

Thin fingers cradled her head. The eyes of a solemn young woman stared into hers. She saw blonde hair and the attractive oval face of a twentysomething who had experienced more pain than she deserved.

"Jennifer, my name is Amanda Baines," said the woman. "You saved my life. Now it's my turn to save yours."

Warmth spread from the woman's slight hands, flowing into Jennifer's body. The pain in her neck vanished along with a hundred other cuts and bruises. Jennifer sat up. "What did you do to me?" she asked.

"I repaid the favour," Amanda replied. "I know you're from another world, like me. We have to help each other some more."

"Doing what?"

Amanda glanced around nervously. "You're going to take me and my children with you when you leave this world."

Thank you for purchasing this book and supporting Luna Press Publishing and our authors.
Please consider leaving a review.

Explore our store at www.lunapresspublishing.com

www.ingramcontent.com/pod-product-compliance
Lightning Source LLC
LaVergne TN
LVHW041624060526
838200LV00040B/1430